A DEADLY NIGHT AT THE THEATRE

Also by Katy Watson

The Three Dahlias
A Very Lively Murder
Seven Lively Suspects
A Lively Midwinter Murder

A DEADLY NIGHT AT THE THEATRE

KATY WATSON

CONSTABLE

CONSTABLE

First published in Great Britain in 2025 by Constable

1 3 5 7 9 10 8 6 4 2

Copyright © Katy Watson, 2025

The moral right of the author has been asserted.

All characters and events in this publication, other than those clearly in the public domain, are fictitious and any resemblance to real persons, living or dead, is purely coincidental.

All rights reserved.
No part of this publication may be reproduced, stored in a retrieval system, or transmitted, in any form, or by any means, without the prior permission in writing of the publisher, nor be otherwise circulated in any form of binding or cover other than that in which it is published and without a similar condition including this condition being imposed on the subsequent purchaser.

A CIP catalogue record for this book
is available from the British Library.

ISBN: 978-1-40872-044-8 (hardcover)
ISBN: 978-1-40872-045-5 (trade paperback)

Typeset in Adobe Garamond by Hewer Text UK Ltd, Edinburgh
Printed and bound in Great Britain by Clays Ltd, Elcograf S.p.A.

Papers used by Constable are from well-managed forests and other responsible sources.

Constable
An imprint of
Little, Brown Book Group
Carmelite House
50 Victoria Embankment
London EC4Y 0DZ

The authorised representative
in the EEA is
Hachette Ireland
8 Castlecourt Centre, Dublin 15,
D15 XTP3, Ireland
(email: info@hbgi.ie)

An Hachette UK Company
www.hachette.co.uk

www.littlebrown.co.uk

To my best theatre buddies,
Emma, Mike and Holly.

What shall we go and see next?

Cast List

Selected members of the *Finding Freddie* Company and Crew at the Prince Regent Theatre
Caro Hooper – as Maggie
Luke Burrows – as Freddie
Darcy Coleman – as Jocelyn
Joshua Griffin – as Damien
Piotr Judd – Director
Amber Reese – Stage manager

Selected members of the *Lights Out* Company and Crew at the Arcadia Theatre
Posy Starling – as Nicki
Taran Brady – as Declan
Keiko – Director
Pollie – Stage manager
Mal – Stage-door keeper

La Vida Tapas Bar and Restaurant
Carlos Moreno – Owner
Gabriella Moreno – Owner's daughter

Other Players
Rosalind King – National Treasure
Martha Burrows – Art gallery owner and Luke's half-sister
Shannon Carpenter – Businesswoman and heiress

Prologue

Dahlia only managed to put one foot inside the room before she saw it, and she recoiled instantly, stepping back into Johnnie's waiting arms.

'What is it?' he asked, urgently. 'What's in there?'

'Death,' she replied.

Dahlia Lively in Look Lively, Dahlia
By Lettice Davenport, 1936

Posy

There was blood on her hands.

Not just specks or spots. It was dripping from her fingernails.

She hadn't meant to . . .

She shouldn't be touching him.

She shouldn't be here at all, even though it was *her* dressing room. She should have listened. Should have gone home instead of sneaking into the theatre after the show was cancelled.

Nobody would believe her when she told them she hadn't done it. That she hadn't meant to touch him. That it was all a misunderstanding, an accident. Why would they?

Another drop of blood dripped from her fingers onto her dressing-room carpet. She needed to wash her hands, but what was the point? It wouldn't change anything, hide anything.

What would Dahlia do?

Posy's mind stayed blank.

Dahlia Lively, the famed, fictional lady detective, wouldn't be in this position in the first place.

Posy stared down at the sightless staring eyes and wondered if she should close them. But she didn't want to touch him again.

So instead, she wiped her hands on her jeans, got to her feet, and did what she should have done much sooner.

She screamed.

Three Days Earlier . . .

Chapter One

'It's hard to believe it isn't real sometimes, isn't it?' Dahlia said, as they both got to their feet to applaud the actors bowing on stage. 'For the length of a play, we're so taken in that everything seems as if it must be true – Romeo and Juliet must be in love, Mercutio must be dead – but then at the end the actors revert to their true selves and just go on about their lives.' She shook her head. 'Such duplicity, really. I'd hate it anywhere but at the theatre.'

Dahlia Lively in *All The World's a Stage*
By Lettice Davenport, 1938

Rosalind

Rosalind King sprang to her feet with the rest of the audience of London's Arcadia Theatre as the final curtain fell and the cast of *Lights Out* took their bows. There, right in the centre, beaming into the stage lights, stood the star of the show, Posy Starling – and Rosalind couldn't be prouder.

Posy was the youngest of 'the three Dahlias', the name the three actresses who had played Dahlia Lively on screen over the past forty-plus years had given themselves. The fictional lady detective had been created by author Lettice Davenport back in the 1930s, but her appeal had proved to be timeless.

Rosalind, of course, had been the first to play her, back in the early 1980s, followed by Caro Hooper, who'd starred in the long-running TV adaptation of Dahlia's adventures twenty-odd years later, until it was cancelled. Now, Posy had taken over the mantle for the new film reboot – and used it to refresh her flagging career as she turned thirty, after flaming out in her late teens following years as a child star.

Posy's role in *Lights Outs* was a complete departure from playing Dahlia, and stage acting a mostly new endeavour for her, but she had absolutely smashed it. The production was a revival of a popular 1980s play set in New York during the blackout of 1977, and Posy's role as a smart-talking, angry young New Yorker had showcased a whole different side of her talents from the elegant – if also smart-talking – amateur sleuth. She'd held the audience in the palm of her hand from start to finish, and she'd done it with charm and pathos. This play was going to be a huge success, Rosalind could tell.

Above them, crystal chandeliers sparkled in the rising lights, and the red velvet of the drapes and the seats couldn't dull the roar of the applause. She turned to her companions, both also standing to applaud beside her in their prime seats at the front of the dress circle. 'Wasn't she amazing?'

Caro nodded sharply, just once. 'It's a good play. I'm sure it will do well for her.'

Not exactly the ringing endorsement Rosalind had been hoping for.

She looked further along the row to Annie, Caro's wife, who gave her a pointed, *I told you so* look, before saying, 'I thought Posy was brilliant. And so were the rest of the cast! Are we going to wait for her at the stage door with flowers like adoring fans?'

Did people still do that? They had, back in the day, when Rosalind was starting out in the theatre. Well, maybe the tradition needed reviving. 'Yes, definitely. Then I think there's an afterparty at a cocktail bar nearby.'

It was the official press night for *Lights Out*, although there had been preview performances for most of the last week, fine-tuning the play until it was as close to perfect as it could be, before they invited the great, the good and the reviewers in for tonight's performance. Now, most people would join the party to continue talking about how great the show was, before the press reviews started to pour in overnight. She knew the producers and PR people for the show would be anxiously checking their phones at the bar, waiting for the first of them to drop. The better the buzz at the party, the more positive the reviews, in Rosalind's experience.

They made their way out of the theatre, and onto the London street outside. The stage door wasn't far from their exit, so Rosalind turned towards it, but Annie spotted a flower cart across the street and dashed over to it between the traffic.

'Are you and Annie going to join me at the afterparty?' Rosalind asked Caro. From what Annie had said when she called she half expected her to say no.

But Caro surprised her. 'Yes, I imagine so. There's actually a few of the *Finding Freddie* company planning on attending – they were in the audience tonight, too.' *Finding Freddie* was *Caro's* new play, opening at the Prince Regent Theatre around the corner for previews the following night. It seemed the stage was the place to be that summer. It made Rosalind nostalgic for her days treading the boards. But she'd had other priorities this year.

Caro looked over Rosalind's shoulder and smiled. 'In fact, here they are now.'

Rosalind turned to see a handsome man in his thirties and a younger woman with black hair cut above her shoulders approaching.

She wore a golden dress that showcased a slim and lithe body, and had her hand tucked through the crook of the man's arm. Behind them followed another woman, probably closer to the man's age – this one in black jeans and a black satin shirt, with wild, red curls around her head.

'Caro!' The man broke away to hug her like he hadn't seen her in days – which, since Rosalind knew the cast of *Finding Freddie* had been rehearsing at the theatre earlier that day, seemed a little excessive. The younger woman air kissed Caro's cheeks, while the older one merely smiled and nodded.

Caro turned to introduce her. 'Everyone, this is my dear friend—'

'Rosalind King!' The man looked scandalised to think Caro wouldn't know they'd all recognise her on sight. The perils of being a National Treasure, she supposed. He stretched out a hand and Rosalind took it, only for him to lean in and kiss her on both cheeks. 'It is an absolute honour to meet you, Rosalind. I'm Luke Burrows, and I'm lucky enough to be playing opposite Caro in our little play this season.' He stepped back, still smiling, to present the others. 'This is Darcy, another of our merry band.' The young woman in the gold dress stepped forward to perform the obligatory air kiss, her lips not getting anywhere close enough to Rosalind's cheeks to mar her lipstick. 'And Amber, our stage manager.' Amber just waved. Rosalind liked her immediately.

'It's lovely to meet you all. I've heard a lot about you from Caro,' Rosalind said.

It wasn't a lie; Caro had been enthusiastic about the company their producer and director had put together for *Finding Freddie*. The play was a new one, transferring to the West End from somewhere up in Yorkshire after rave reviews and success there. Most of the cast had travelled down with it, although Caro and Luke had been brought in for the main roles – a not unusual tactic in Rosalind's experience, as a star name would always draw a bigger audience.

Caro's star had risen considerably over the past few years, since they began solving murders as the three Dahlias and she started chronicling their adventures in her bestselling books. And Luke Burrows . . . well, he was one of those actors who'd apparently been around forever in insignificant roles in major shows or better roles in movies that no one saw, but had finally found his place over the last few years in a popular TV show in the States.

Rosalind hadn't heard of him before he was cast opposite Caro in *Finding Freddie*. But since then she'd already heard more about him than she wanted to – and suspected she was going to hear an awful lot more before very long.

'I found dahlias!' Annie returned with three long-stemmed dahlia flowers wrapped in brown paper in her hands. 'I thought they'd be perfect.'

'They are,' Rosalind assured her, as they waited for the stage door to open and Posy and her fellow cast mates to emerge.

While there were a few other theatregoers still out on the street, most of tonight's invited audience had already made their way over to the cocktail bar, presumably because they knew that they could meet the cast just as easily there, and they could get a drink while they were waiting. Rosalind was glad of it; tonight was Posy's night, and she didn't want her and Caro's presence to take away from that. Usually, if any two of them were together, there'd be someone around snapping a photo.

Which had already proved a problem recently. Rosalind thought of the newspaper article Jack had shown her back in Wales – a photo of Caro and Posy together in a cafe, Caro standing with her hands on her hips while Posy looked mulishly up at her, with the headline IS THE BLOOM OFF THE DAHLIAS?

As soon as they got to that damn cocktail bar, she was going to collar Annie and get the whole story behind that photo.

Finally, the stage door opened, and Posy appeared, her face scrubbed clean of stage make-up, replaced with a minimal look instead, and her costume changed for a short, black silk dress that made her legs look endless. Her blonde hair was caught up in a high ponytail, her cheeks pink and eyes bright with the success of the night.

'Darling, you were wonderful,' Rosalind told her, embracing her warmly. 'This show is a sure-fire hit.'

'That's the hope!' Posy pulled away and Annie darted in to give her the dahlias and a kiss on the cheek.

'Posy, it was brilliant. Best thing I've seen on the stage this year.' Annie lowered her voice to a stage whisper. 'And I can say that because Caro's play hasn't opened yet.'

Everyone laughed at that. Everyone except Caro and Posy.

Amber stepped forward, breaking the awkward moment. 'It really was great, Posy. Sorry, you probably don't remember me – I'm Amber.'

'Pollie's friend, right? We met at that party?' Posy said. Clearly they'd been introduced at some point; theatre circles in London were notoriously incestuous, and Posy had been here working for a couple of months already. 'You're stage manager for *Finding Freddie*? I'm looking forward to seeing it when it opens, if I can find a day I'm not performing.'

Then Luke moved towards them – despite, Rosalind noticed, Darcy clinging onto his arm until the last moment. 'Posy. It's good to see you again. You were incredible up there tonight.'

Posy stared at him for a moment, glanced at the silent Caro, then turned on her heel back to Rosalind and Annie. 'We'd better get to the party before they send someone to look for us.' She linked her arm with Rosalind's. 'Come on.'

Rosalind shared a meaningful look with Annie as they walked.

This was worse than she'd thought.

The cocktail bar that had been booked out for the party was, apparently, styled in the industrial-chic trend, with metal pipes, bare bulbs and a grim, grey sort of aesthetic. Behind the glossy black bar, cocktail waiters were serving up classic seventies cocktails like Blue Hawaiis, Tequila Sunrises and even a Slow Comfortable Screw Against the Wall, if Rosalind overheard the order right.

Posy snagged them a high table by the window, while Rosalind perched as delicately as she could on a backless stool, and let Caro go to the bar for drinks.

Posy managed to wait a full five seconds before asking, 'So . . . did you really like it?'

'I loved it, darling,' Rosalind said, easily. 'Reminded me of my teenage years, apart from anything else. But no, it was smart and funny and biting when it needed to be. And you were *fabulous*. Jack will be so cross he missed it.' Damn it. She hadn't meant to mention Jack – or draw attention to the fact that he hadn't joined her on this jaunt to the city.

Posy beamed. 'Well, you'll just have to bring him down to London and see it again!'

'Perhaps I will,' Rosalind replied, noncommittally.

She waited until Posy was pulled away by someone else wanting to congratulate her, then shifted her stool closer to Annie, glad that Caro was already occupied with her other friends.

'Right. What the blazes has been going on here?'

The three Dahlias might not have got on perfectly to start – fine, they'd all thought the absolute worst of each other when they'd met at a Dahlia Lively fan convention nearly three years ago – but tackling their first murder had brought them together. And regardless of their different generations, pasts and circumstances . . . they'd stayed together. Solving several more cases since had made them first friends, then family.

Until now. *Something* had come between Posy and Caro while Rosalind had been away in Wales with Jack for the past few months. And Rosalind needed to know exactly what it was so she could fix it.

Annie sighed, and reached for her wine glass. 'I don't know everything – at least, I'm assuming I don't. I've mostly heard Caro's side of things. And a flaming row at our house over Sunday dinner about a month ago, where I just took a bottle of wine and hid in the lounge until I heard the door slam, and when I came out, Posy had gone.'

Well. That didn't sound particularly auspicious. The Dahlias had disagreed before, even argued. But for Caro and Posy still to be at odds with each other a whole month later? That was unprecedented.

'You said on the phone it had to do with Luke Burrows?' She glanced over at where the actor was laughing at something Caro had said.

'Yes.' Annie gulped down some wine. 'He and Caro were the two new members of the cast when they started rehearsing, and I think they bonded quickly over that. She said he mentioned that he'd worked with Posy in the past, but more than ten years ago, I think, and it didn't sound like they were still in touch. Posy barely acknowledged the name when Caro mentioned him at Libby's wedding. She definitely didn't say she had a problem with him or anything.'

'But she does.' It wasn't a question; Rosalind could tell that from just thirty seconds in the same place as the pair of them. Luke, however, hadn't seemed to have a problem with *her*.

Annie sighed. 'Apparently so. Caro and Luke got more and more friendly, hanging out together when they weren't rehearsing and such. I've been away such a lot helping my mum since she had that fall, and some weeks it's just easier to stay up in Suffolk than travel to and fro every few days, especially when Caro's working so much and . . . I guess she enjoyed his company.'

'And Posy's been busy too,' Rosalind guessed. 'With the play, of course, and I imagine quite a lot of publicity commitments.'

'Kit was home for a bit last month as well,' Annie added. Posy's film-star boyfriend was away on location currently. 'So, with one thing and another I suppose they hadn't seen each other for a while. And then Caro invited Posy to some event or another – a charity gala, I think – and Luke was there too and, well, I guess it took Posy by surprise.'

'That he was there or how close he and Caro had become?' Rosalind asked.

'Both, I imagine.' Annie eyed Rosalind carefully. 'I don't want you to think I'm blaming you for this, because I'm really not. But you not being here . . . I think they've forgotten how to be the Dahlias without you.'

Rosalind looked away. Nearly six months she'd been hidden away in Wales with Jack, now. The first one or two had been spent watching him anxiously, panicking at every cough or ache, after his brush with death over Christmas. She'd finally relaxed around Easter and accepted that he wasn't going to drop dead on her imminently.

But while she'd been focusing on her relationship, she'd let Caro and Posy's friendship fall apart. They were the *three* Dahlias, not two.

And while they'd never lived in each other's pockets, apparently this time she'd just been gone too long.

She straightened her spine. 'Well, I'm here now. So, what happened at the gala? Or after it?'

'Remember I've only got Caro's side of this,' Annie warned. 'You'll have to get Posy's. But according to Caro, Luke tried to speak with Posy – perfectly politely, in a "good to see you" way – and she cut him off and walked away.'

'Like she did tonight,' Rosalind murmured. Posy's behaviour outside the stage door did add a certain credence to Caro's version of events.

'Anyway, when Caro called her out on it later, Posy said she couldn't understand how Caro could be friends with such a horrible person,' Annie continued. 'I think Caro was quite taken aback, because she said that Luke had always been lovely to her. Posy just stared at her for a moment, and then left.'

Rosalind tapped a nail against the side of her glass, thinking. There was obviously something in Posy's history with Luke that she hadn't shared before making her act this way. Posy wasn't rude by nature. In fact, she tended to go out of her way to be nice to people, probably – Rosalind believed – because she started every interaction from the assumption that people would have heard the worst about the person she'd been in the past, and she wanted to prove them wrong.

Posy's wild-child past was history, but it was one that would always hang over her. Rosalind had already seen a couple of articles about *Lights Out* which, while generally positive, couldn't resist mentioning the partying and drugs that had led to Posy's child-star downfall.

'Okay. Fast forward to Sunday dinner. I assume that was the next time they were together?'

Annie nodded. 'And that's when it all came out. From what I could overhear, the crux of it was that the Luke Posy knew in the past was a liar, cheat and all-round bad egg. Caro asked exactly what he'd done to make her say that, but all Posy would say was that they'd dated and it ended badly. And that she'd expected that Caro would be able to see through his charm and smiles.'

'But she didn't.'

'But she didn't.' Annie grimaced. 'In fact, she and Luke had become friends and *he'd* already told her about his bad-boy past and how hard he'd worked to change over the last five years . . . to become a better man.'

'Oh God, Caro thinks he's another Posy,' Rosalind realised.

'Exactly,' Annie said. 'I knew you'd get it. Anyway, Caro is adamant that Luke has changed – and I have to say, I haven't heard of any problems on their show, and if anyone would know it would be the people working closest with him, wouldn't it?'

'It would.' Rosalind had appeared in enough plays to know that, when you were working so closely with people, day in and day out over an entire run, it became much harder to hide any less desirable tendencies.

'But Posy was adamant that she knew him best, and furious that Caro wouldn't listen to her, wouldn't believe her – even when Caro pointed out that Posy hadn't *told* her any of this before she got to know Luke for herself. She asked Posy for details, to tell her what Luke had done but, beyond establishing that Luke had never *physically* hurt her, she wouldn't say any more. Just that he was a bad person.' Annie gave a heavy sigh. 'I don't know. I don't think either of them are being entirely rational about this. I know Caro's been under a lot of pressure lately – not just with the play, but with edits on the next book, and her work with Ashok, and me being away . . . you know what she's like when she's doing too much. She loses the ability to empathise with *anyone*.'

'Except Luke.' Whatever Posy's past with Luke – and the fact that she called him a cheat and a liar told her a lot – it had happened a long time ago. Back when Posy was another person too. So Rosalind had to allow that Posy wasn't the best-qualified person to say who Luke was now.

But Caro knew *now* that her new friend had hurt Posy, who was family. And she hadn't stepped away from him or acknowledged that, as far as Rosalind could tell from Annie's account.

No wonder they were both so mad at each other.

'Will you stay here a while and fix it?' Annie asked. 'I've got to go back to Suffolk tomorrow but I'll be home again on Thursday evening to watch Caro's play – she doesn't want me there for the first preview tomorrow, says too many things are likely to go wrong, so we compromised on the second preview. She's got tickets for both of us, I think.'

'I'll be there,' Rosalind promised, and tried to pretend that she wasn't secretly glad for a reason to stay away from Wales just a little bit longer.

Chapter Two

Posy Starling fills the stage with an energy and brightness not seen for too long at the Arcadia, which has suffered a run of less-than-stellar productions in recent years. Ably supported by relative unknown Taran Brady, Lights Out *lights up the West End with all the 1970s New York disco vibes you could hope for – but also provides a deeper dive into the chaos of the frenetic, fraught, scary and sweaty moment in time that was the New York Blackout of 1977.*

Review of Lights Out on Behind the Curtain blog

Posy

Posy *loved* the Arcadia Theatre.

She might not have done much theatre work in the past, but she couldn't imagine a theatre with more glamour, more style, more . . . presence, in the whole of London. From the chandeliers hanging in the lounge bar, to the recently replaced ruby-red carpet that swept up the cantilever staircase from the columns at the lobby entrance to the doors that let the audience into the circle seats, it screamed luxury. All that marble and gold, shining and perfect, welcoming the audience to a night out they'd never forget.

Entering through the stage door, however, was an entirely different experience.

The discreet door on the side of the building, away from the posters and the glamour of the main entrance, had only a small sign over it to let guests know it was an entrance at all, rather than an emergency fire exit or something. Posy had seen the Prince Regent Theatre stage door, which Caro and her cast would be using daily, with its Art Deco glass panels and pretty blue-green paint. But the Arcadia just had a nondescript, solid burgundy door that sometimes had a note reading 'back in five minutes' pinned to it when Mal, the stage-door keeper who was in charge of checking people in and out, had to dash off and do something else.

Today, the twenty-something Mal was ensconced in his usual position behind the counter at the stage door, ignoring something flashing away on his computer screen while he glared at his phone.

'Hi, Mal,' Posy said, as she slipped through the ajar door. Mal never bothered to close it completely at the busy times of day when people would be coming and going, especially when it was as warm outside as it was currently.

'Hi, Posy.' He didn't even look up. Her first day he'd been genuinely starstruck and stumbled through an awkward hello. Now, she was old hat. Posy supposed that was how it went.

With a small wave, she left it to him to register her presence in the theatre on his system, and headed towards her small – but blissfully private – dressing room. She was halfway there when she heard him swear behind her; presumably he'd just spotted whatever had been flashing red on his screen. Hopefully nothing important.

It seemed that she was the first one there today – not an uncommon occurrence. The whole theatre seemed quiet, almost waiting, breath bated, although Posy wasn't sure what for. Another stellar performance? Maybe even a standing ovation? She was sure that the crew would be in place already, setting up for the night ahead, and

Mal was just by the stage door, but still she felt strangely, scarily alone. A light flickered overhead as she made her way towards her dressing room, and then another one, and she swallowed, willing her heart to beat more quietly.

The corridor didn't echo with her tread on the thin carpet tiles, seeming strangely muffled in its silence, and she ran a hand along the wall as she walked as a sort of reassurance she hadn't slipped from one world to the other.

Finally, she reached her dressing room, but frowned when she realised the door was ajar, and she could feel a breeze from an open window within, bringing with it the sounds of the city.

Had someone been in her dressing room? Who? And why?

What if they were still there?

A shiver danced across her shoulders as she heard a small sound within. Like someone leafing through the pages of a book.

Through the crack of the door she could see the room was in darkness. Because of the room's position and the high buildings on the other side of the narrow street, it barely got any natural light at this time of day, and blinds blocked most of the light it *did* get. If anyone from the theatre or the show had been there to see her, they'd have turned a light on while they waited.

She hesitated a moment. She could go back and get Mal, ask him to come in with her, but he shouldn't leave the stage door unattended. She could seek out one of the crew, or even their company stage manager, Pollie.

Except if the room was empty by the time they got back, she was going to look like a total idiot. And she'd lose any chance of finding out who was in there.

Posy straightened her shoulders, pushed open the door, and reached for the light switch, flipping it quickly.

Nothing happened.

The room stayed dark, and she couldn't make out any shadows that looked like a person. Maybe she'd been wrong. Maybe whoever had been there was long gone, and the bulb had merely blown.

She crossed to the dressing table, planning to switch on the lights that surrounded the mirror, but then she heard that same noise again, followed this time by footsteps. There was a flash of something in the mirror and—

Posy acted on instinct, grabbing the book that sat on her dressing table and hurling it in the direction of the footsteps, just as the silhouette of a man, backlit by the brighter lights of the corridor, came into view.

Her aim was good. She could tell by the swearing.

The man clutched his head. 'Jesus Christ, Posy.'

And somehow, the noise sounded again, although this time he obviously wasn't making it. And it sounded more like . . . flapping, now.

She fumbled in her bag for her phone and switched on the torch.

Luke Burrows put a hand up to his eyes as she shone it on him. 'I guess I should have knocked?'

'I'm . . .' She couldn't bring herself to apologise. 'I thought I heard someone in here. An intruder.'

They both stilled as the flapping sounded again. Posy turned her torch towards the noise, and saw a pigeon trapped between the window and the blind. It must have been open enough for it to get in, then dropped mostly closed behind it.

The cleaners. The cleaners must have opened the window, and accidentally left my door ajar.

She hurriedly pushed the window open and set the bird free, before turning back to Luke, who still stood awkwardly in her doorway. Bleeding.

'You should, uh, sit down.' She waved a hand towards the small sofa at the side of the room, then reached for the hand towel from beside the sink by the dressing table and tossed it to him. He caught it and pressed it against the side of his temple.

'What did you throw at me, anyway?' he asked, as if it were a curiosity rather than assault.

He could press charges, she realised suddenly. Call the police and have her arrested.

The Luke she used to know probably would have done. This one still might – unless he had an ulterior motive for being there in the first place.

She bent down to pick up the book. 'Um, Lettice Davenport's autobiography. Signed first edition.' It had been a gift from Kit, and happened to be not just valuable but also a heavy hardback with wickedly sharp corners, it seemed. 'I thought you were . . .' What had she thought? That someone was coming to get her? 'I was startled. That was all.'

Posy sank down onto the stool by the dressing table, finally switching on the mirror lights, and looked away when Luke shifted the towel from his head and she saw the blood soaking into it.

God, she'd been so on edge the last few weeks. Was it knowing that Luke was in town, or that Caro had decided he was her new best friend? Or was it the stories she kept seeing, online and in the papers, dredging up parts of her life she thought she'd never revisit? She'd been trying not to read them, trying to stay away from the memories.

Of course, the living embodiment of those stories was now bleeding on her sofa, so obviously she hadn't been very successful.

'Why *are* you here, anyway?' She knew she sounded belligerent, more than she should given that she'd just brained the guy. But really, what possible reason could he have for surprising her in her dressing room?

Luke held out a brown envelope she hadn't noticed before, and she eyed it with suspicion. 'What is it?'

'Just a present.' He shrugged, then winced as the movement seemed to jostle the towel he was still holding against his head with his other hand. 'I was going to leave it for you at the stage door, but the guy there – Mal, I think? – he was dealing with some sort of crisis and said that you were here anyway so just to . . . bring it down to you myself.'

That tracked, she supposed. Mal's screen had been flashing red. But it didn't explain the most important part. 'Why are you bringing me a present at all?'

His smile was part sad, part hopeful – and utterly unfamiliar. 'Call it a peace offering. Caro . . . I know it's hurting her that you two are on the outs, and I hate that I'm the cause of that. So, I wanted to bring you something to say . . . if you want me to stay out of your way, I will. But please don't freeze Caro out because of me.'

Posy let his words hang there as she worked through them in her mind. 'A peace offering.'

The last thing Luke had ever wanted was peace, in her experience. He thrived on chaos. On manipulating situations to his own advantage. He spouted lies and half-truths until she didn't believe her own memory. Until she didn't know whether she truly wanted to do something for herself, or because she thought *he* wanted it. Whether she was really being unreasonable, or unfair, or unfaithful, or if he was twisting her reality to make her believe it.

Not everyone had seen it, though. When they'd met in LA, Luke had seemed to have friends in every corner. He'd prided himself on not just knowing everyone, but also knowing their needs and desires. In some ways, he'd been a fixer first and actor second – more famous for getting anyone anything they wanted or needed, even if they shouldn't have it in the first place.

Did he really expect her to believe he'd changed so much?

Caro believes it. Maybe she should have told Caro all about her history with Luke the first moment she mentioned his name. But that had been at Libby's wedding, and she hadn't wanted to ruin the day with the memories. And after that . . . it was just easier not to think about it.

You mean you were too ashamed to admit to everything that happened in LA.

Fine, yes, there was some of that too. Shame, it turned out, was a powerful motivator. But mostly . . . she'd worked so hard to earn her place in the three Dahlias, to become a woman she was proud to be. She hadn't wanted Caro and Rosalind to see her differently when faced with the girl she *had* been, with Luke.

It was stupid. But by the time she'd plucked up the courage to tell them the whole sorry tale, it was too late. Caro was already firmly on Team Luke, and wouldn't hear a word against him. So what was the point of getting into the gory details?

Especially when Posy wasn't confident Caro would pick her over Luke anyway.

She's definitely not going to take my side now I've caused him actual bodily harm, is she?

She still hadn't taken the envelope from Luke, and eventually he placed it beside him on the sofa, then struggled to his feet, keeping the towel in place. It was more red than white, now.

Head wounds bled a lot, didn't they? It didn't mean he was *dying* or anything.

'Should I call for an ambulance?' She nodded towards his head. 'Or find our first-aid person, at least?'

'Nah.' He gave her another one of those not-quite-smiles. 'I need to get back to the theatre. Amber will patch me up well enough to go on stage tonight. I swear she has half a hospital in her stage manager's kit anyway.'

'Right. You've got . . . previews.' Their first performance, and Luke was going on with a bleeding head wound. 'You didn't lose consciousness at all when I . . . you know. Did you?'

If she'd given Luke concussion on opening night Caro really wasn't ever going to speak to her again.

Luke started to shake his head, then winced. It didn't make her feel any better.

She trailed behind him as he made his way back down to the stage door. With perfectly horrible timing, the rest of the cast were just starting to arrive, and all greeted him first warmly, and then with concern as they spotted the blood-soaked towel.

'Just a misunderstanding between me and Lettice Davenport, the book,' he joked. 'Could have happened to anyone. Mostly I blame the pigeon.'

Mal looked at her with concern from behind the stage-door counter. 'Are we sure he doesn't have concussion? There's probably an incident form to fill in . . .'

'You really should go to A & E,' Posy told Luke. 'There's . . . quite a lot of blood.'

'Nah. Curtain will be going up soon. I'll be fine.' He shrugged and smiled at the rest of the crowd like it was nothing, but she knew his game.

Luke was obviously relishing being the martyred hero, with the rest of her cast looking on with admiration for his adherence to the old 'the show must go on' maxim. He'd probably burst into a Broadway number on the subject any moment now.

He exchanged goodbyes with the gathered cast – including a complicated handshake with Taran, and a wink for Mal, who'd come out from behind his counter for once. Posy finally exhaled as Luke walked out of the stage door and staggered off in the direction of the Prince Regent Theatre. God, she hoped he was able to make it through tonight's performance, or Caro was going to murder her.

The rest of the cast started to disperse, with only Taran pausing to give her a half-hug from the side and ask in a whisper if she was okay. Of all the cast of *Lights Out*, Taran was the one she was closest to. They'd bonded over their terrible parents, even if their teenage years had been very different.

Posy nodded, assuring him she was fine, even though she wasn't.

'I thought she was involved with Kit Lewis,' she heard one of the ensemble actresses murmur to another, obviously not realising that Posy could still hear them. 'Is Luke Burrows an upgrade or a step down?'

Definitely a step down, Posy thought, tuning out the ensuing debate as the two actresses climbed the stairs in the direction of their shared dressing room.

Back behind his little counter, Mal was looking guilty. Obviously he knew he shouldn't have let Luke through without checking with her, but she was too exhausted by the events of the evening to berate him for it, and they still had a play to perform.

'Mal, if Luke Burrows comes here looking for me again, don't let him in, okay?' She raised an eyebrow at him, and waited for his nod.

'Yeah, next time she might do him some *real* damage,' Taran joked. He slung an arm around her shoulder, and led her towards their adjoining dressing rooms. 'Come on, slugger. Curtain up in less than an hour.'

Posy managed to shrug Taran off when she reached her door. She winced at the sight of a small bloodstain on the sofa, but without the overhead lights working she could mostly ignore it. The lamps and the bulbs around her mirror were enough for tonight, anyway. She could deal with everything else tomorrow. Right now, she had to get ready for the show.

Then she spotted the envelope still lying beside the bloodstain. Her present. Right.

Her hands shook, just a little, as she opened the envelope. It made her think of another place and time – Aldermere, three years ago, the China Room, and photos slipping from an envelope not unlike this one. Photos of her – blackmail material.

Was that what Luke thought he had on her? If so, he was very wrong. Her past relationship with Luke might be humiliating, but if it came down to blackmail she'd tell him to publish and be damned.

She wasn't the sort of woman who could be blackmailed, any more.

But what slid out of the envelope this time wasn't photographs. It was a script.

The yellowing edges gave away its age, as did the slightly faded print on the cover. The signatures scrawled over the front page told her, even before she focused in on the title, that this wasn't a new script for her consideration.

This was Luke's gift.

The Switch Up

And those signatures.

Posy Starling

Luke Burrows

Shannon Sharp
Patrick Dunbar
Maisy Meadows

The list went on. People from another lifetime. Friends she'd almost forgotten over the years.

She knew without reading more than the title that it was the story of two teenaged girls who swapped places for the summer. The only film she and Luke had ever appeared in together. She'd been nineteen at the time.

Why had he given it to her, really? A reminder of the supposed good old days, perhaps?

Then why did it feel like a warning?

Chapter Three

'So, what do we do now?' Johnnie sank despondently into the nearest chair. 'How are we going to solve this one if we can't even get all our suspects in the same room?'

'Simple,' Dahlia said with a smile. 'We shall organise a tea party. Nobody can resist tea and cake. Not even a murderer.'

Dahlia Lively in *Alibis and Afternoon Tea*
by Lettice Davenport, 1950

Caro

Caro really didn't have time for afternoon tea, but Rosalind hadn't left any room for argument in her 'invitation' to join her and Posy at the Ritz on Thursday.

It wasn't as if Caro were against the concept of scones and little sandwiches – quite the contrary. It was just that she had so many other things she should be doing. Like the revisions on *Seven Lively Suspects* that her editor had sent over, including a few changes she thought would increase the tension of the story – even if it went against actual documented reality – along with a slew of comments on pacing and repeated words. Even characterisation! As if the people she was writing about weren't already actual real people she knew and understood.

At least, she'd *thought* she knew and understood them all, until recently.

The point was, between the book and the play, she was busy. She'd even had to beg off any of the private investigation work she usually undertook at the detective agency she ran with Ashok. It didn't help that Annie was away looking after her mother so much, either. Not that she'd begrudge her mother-in-law the support, it was just that the woman made even the usually implacable Annie tetchy, which meant they were *both* running low on patience and empathy and that never boded well.

Caro was run ragged *before* Rosalind showed up with her obvious plan to play mother and make the children get along again. As if the only reason that she and Posy had fallen out in the first place was because their resident National Treasure wasn't there to keep them in line. Rosalind might be the eldest of them by twenty years, but that didn't mean Caro was a child. She was forty-three for heaven's sake, and even Posy was in her early thirties now. It was just so damn patronising.

Caro paused halfway up Piccadilly, leaned against the nearest wall, and rubbed a hand against her forehead. She was getting herself all worked up, and that wasn't a good way to start this afternoon tea.

She was just so damn *frustrated*. With Posy, mostly, and the stupid argument that she didn't know how to fix even if she had the energy, which she didn't.

That was another problem. The not sleeping. She never slept well alone in the bed, and she'd been alone too often recently, resulting in lying awake running through problems over and over and over in her head. At least she'd have Annie back tonight for their second preview performance.

And at least they'd survived the first one, even if Luke had needed butterfly stitches across his temple for it, courtesy of Posy.

If Rosalind thought she wasn't going to mention *that* at tea, she was sorely mistaken.

Caro pushed away from the wall – realising she was just outside the famous Waterstones Piccadilly, with its 1930s handrails and endless floors of books to choose from. She checked the window displays, smiling to herself when she saw *A Very Lively Murder* in prime position.

That was something. She might be exhausted, and Posy might not be speaking to her, but professionally? She was doing better than ever.

She had a new soon-to-be hit show on the West End stage, and a bestselling book in the window of Europe's biggest bookstore.

Caro Hooper was back on top and it felt bloody marvellous.

She wasn't about to let a little disagreement take that away from her.

Pepped up again, she headed along Piccadilly towards the Ritz with a new spring in her step. She smiled at the doorman as she hopped up the steps and through the revolving door under the famous blue canopy and lights.

Normally, she knew, getting a reservation at the Ritz required booking well in advance, but she suspected there was some leeway for that rule when Rosalind King rang asking for a table. Caro made her way through the lobby, letting the luxurious surroundings relax her a little, and checking her lipstick in one of the many panelled mirrors. There were bound to be cameras, after all.

She found Rosalind sitting at a prime table in the Palm Court, surrounded by tall pillars, gold detailing and chandeliers dripping with crystals. Keeping a fixed smile on her face, she made her way towards her, aware of the murmurs and the odd camera flash as she passed. Rosalind got to her feet and pressed kisses to her cheeks, murmuring the obligatory 'Caro, darling,' just loud enough for anyone who hadn't recognised her on sight to know who she was meeting for tea.

The Ritz was one of a declining number of places in London that still set a dress code for afternoon tea. Rosalind, of course, cleared it easily with her stylish pussy-bow silk blouse and pale skirt, and Caro felt suitably attired in her own wide, olive trousers and linen top. Around them, the men were all in suits and the women in various degrees of summer formalwear. Caro wasn't sure if it was the people or the surroundings that gave her the strong feeling of déjà vu, as if she might have just stepped back onto the set of *The Dahlia Lively Mysteries*, ready to take tea with a suspect. Had they ever filmed at the Ritz? Yes, surely they must have done.

'No Posy yet?' Caro asked as she took her seat. Soft piano music filled the air, hopefully keeping their conversation private, especially beneath the sounds of clinking teacups and cutlery. Being seen was one thing. Being heard was another entirely.

'I'm sure she's on her way,' Rosalind replied, serenely.

Caro wasn't. 'Did she actually tell you she was coming? Because she hasn't been the most . . . reliable lately.' She'd tried to meet up with her multiple times since their argument at Sunday dinner, but Posy had always flaked out at the last minute, citing rehearsals or interviews. Which might well be true, but Caro had managed to make the time, and it wasn't like she had any less to do.

'She'll be here,' Rosalind said, in a tone that made Caro wonder what she'd threatened Posy with. 'But before she arrives, I want to hear your side of this ridiculous spat between the two of you. Really, Caro, you couldn't just nod and agree with her when she complained about this man? He's her ex, I suppose?'

'As far as I can tell. And no, Rosalind, I *couldn't* just nod and agree, because I have to work with Luke for the rest of the summer and, besides, she didn't even tell me she had a problem with him until I'd got to know him and we'd already become friends.' If she had – if Posy had told her, right when she first mentioned Luke at Libby's wedding, that she had history with this guy and didn't want him in her life, Caro would have respected that and kept a professional but distant relationship with him.

The fact that she didn't raise the issue until *after* she knew that Caro and Luke had become friends smacked of just a little bit of jealousy to Caro. Whether of Caro having other friends or Luke wanting to be *her* friend, she wasn't sure. Either way, she had neither the time nor the patience for it.

'I'm not asking her to spend time with him – well, not now I know about their history, and apart from the party the other night which, really, he was invited anyway, so that's not my fault. But I don't see how she can be mad at me for spending time with a man I am contractually obligated to get along with.' Caro sat back, picked up her menu, and listened for Rosalind's inevitable sigh. She wasn't disappointed.

'What has she told you about him?' Rosalind asked, after a moment.

'Just that they worked together on some movie in LA thirteen years ago,' Caro replied. 'I got the impression that they dated, or at least had *some* sort of romance, because she also told me he was a liar and a cheat and she wouldn't trust him as far as she could throw him.'

'Not a great start.'

'No. But that was thirteen years ago, Rosalind. Posy must have been, what? Nineteen? Luke couldn't have been much older. And we both know that Posy at nineteen wasn't exactly a peach either.' If Rosalind needed any reminders of Posy's wild-child past, she could just pick up a paper or google the gossip blogs. Posy's re-emergence into the celeb circuit with the Dahlia films and now the play had put them all into overdrive, going back over her history. Caro wondered if maybe *that* was why she was so touchy about Luke – too many reminders of the past.

'She was obviously badly hurt by this man—' Rosalind started, but Caro cut her off.

'I know! And as a good friend, I want to respect that, I do. But I have to work with him, Rosalind! I can't jeopardise our working relationship – and the whole show – because Posy's boyfriend cheated on her over a decade ago. I'm trying to be professional.'

Rosalind gave her a look. The pianist nearby was playing a little louder now, maybe to cover her outburst. Caro sank into her chair and resolved to keep her voice down.

'Can't you be a friend as well?' Rosalind asked, plaintively.

Because of course this was all on her – just like everything else in her life right now. Fine. Caro would keep her voice down, but she was keeping her boundaries firmly in place.

'Rosalind, I will be as sweet as pie to Posy, as long as she has a really good explanation for why she gave my co-star a bleeding head wound and possible concussion right before he was due to go on stage for our first preview performance last night.'

'What?' Rosalind sat up, eyes wide and startled. 'What happened?'

But before Caro could fill her in, a new buzz started by the entrance, a sudden rise in chatter and camera-phone clicks that had nothing to do with her and Rosalind.

She didn't bother turning in her chair. She didn't need to. She could tell by the way Rosalind's posture relaxed, just an iota, and the murmurs of the crowd continued to grow.

Posy's here.

Posy

Posy knew the moment the first person in the Palm Court recognised her, despite the sunglasses she wore, and the cap on her head that didn't really go with the red linen dress she'd donned for the occasion. First there was the intake of breath, then the muttering, then the phones angled suspiciously at something just beyond where she walked. The further she made it into the Palm Court, the louder the hum of speculation and gossip became.

Posy forced her face into a neutral expression and tried to ignore it, focusing instead on the table where Rosalind and Caro were sitting. If she could just make it there . . . well. Then at least it would only be her friends talking about her and accusing her of stuff.

Somehow that didn't make her feel much better.

She slid into the last empty seat at the round table before Rosalind could get up to greet her – and before Caro obviously didn't.

'Hi.' She tucked her hat and sunglasses into her bag and tried to smile as she reached for her menu. Before she could even look, a waiter took it from her, informing her that Madam had already ordered tea for the table. She assumed 'Madam' was Rosalind.

Another waiter brought them two glasses of champagne and what was apparently non-alcoholic sparkling tea for her. Posy sipped at it cautiously as she waited to see who would speak first.

After several weighty glances between the other two, she realised they were waiting for her.

Okay, then.

'How did the first preview go last night, Caro?' If they could pretend that everything was all champagne and afternoon tea and *fine*, so could she.

'As well as can be expected when one of the stars is bleeding from the head.' Caro reached for her glass, before turning to Rosalind. 'Apparently he had an unfortunate run-in with a Lettice Davenport autobiography in Posy's dressing room.'

Posy could feel the heat rising in her cheeks as Rosalind turned to look at her, eyebrows raised. 'You threw an actual book at him?'

'He startled me. It was an accident.'

'Right.' Caro didn't look convinced.

Fortunately, at that moment their tea arrived in its silver pot, followed shortly by three tiers of sandwiches, scones and cakes. Maybe if she kept her mouth full for the rest of the meal, she wouldn't have to answer any more questions about Luke Burrows – or anything else.

She didn't want to cause a scene. Not here. Not anywhere, really. There was enough gossip about her at the moment that anything she did could only make things worse. All she wanted was to get through afternoon tea and head to the theatre in time for tonight's performance. Was that so much to ask?

Apparently so. 'Right. Now we're all here, can we just get down to it? Some of us do have other places to be this afternoon, you know.' Caro sat back in her chair, arms folded across her chest, the perfect image of disgruntled for anyone with a camera. Which was everyone. 'Rosalind, we know you're obviously here to play mother and put an end to this disagreement between me and Posy, so let's just get on with it.'

Rosalind set the silver tea strainer above the first of the white cups with gold trims before reaching for the silver teapot.

'Since you're both adults,' Rosalind said, pouring tea into Caro's cup, 'I shouldn't think you'd need anyone to play mother.'

Except there she was, pouring tea for them all like they were having a nursery supper in a Dahlia Lively book. Posy dipped her head to try and hide her amusement at the contradiction, but she clearly wasn't successful.

'Yes, obviously it's *hilarious* that you maimed my co-star before our first performance, Posy,' Caro said. 'So glad we can all laugh about your attempts to ruin my stage career before it even begins.'

Posy's eyes widened in surprise. 'That's not . . . I told you it was an accident! He shouldn't have been lurking around *my* theatre bringing me unwanted presents.'

'He was there to bring you a gift and you assumed he was out to get you?' Caro snorted. 'Sounds about right.'

Oh, she was done playing nice for mother now, especially since Caro wasn't even going to *try*. 'What's that supposed to mean?'

'That you haven't given Luke a chance, even when he's been going out of his way to make things up to you!' Caro shot back.

'I think if we could both just calm down for a moment, maybe we'd be able to enjoy our tea and cake before we get thrown out of here for causing a fracas,' Rosalind said mildly, raising her teacup to her lips. But Posy could see the tension in the lines between her eyebrows, the ones at the corners of her eyes.

She was worried about this. About them.

Maybe she was right to be.

'If you could have just trusted my judgement in the first place and kept your distance from him, maybe he wouldn't still be sneaking up on me at my place of work,' Posy shot back.

Caro gave a theatrical gasp. If she'd had pearls she'd have clutched them. God, she was probably *enjoying* this, putting on a show for all the punters. That was what really mattered to her, wasn't it?

Making a hideous display of their private lives, and not caring what parts of Posy's history she exposed while she did it, as long as it earned her column inches.

'Trust *your* judgement?' Caro taunted. 'Because yours is so superior to mine, right? Why is that again? Because you're the bigger star, you got the biggest theatre? Or because you're Dahlia now, not us? Is that why?'

'No. Because I *know* Luke,' Posy said, low and dark, trying to bring the volume of the conversation down a few notches. 'I know what he's like.'

'No, you *knew* him,' Caro replied. 'And even then, you didn't even *tell* me—'

'I think,' Rosalind interrupted, perfectly calm despite the rising tension at the table, 'that we need to treat this like any Dahlia case. We don't *J'accuse* until we have all the facts. Posy, it has been a long time since you knew Luke—'

'That doesn't matter. I still know him.' Men like Luke didn't change. Why wouldn't they believe her about that?

Caro shook her head. 'That's the thing I don't understand. You want everyone to believe that *you've* changed, but you won't admit for a moment that he might have too, will you?'

Posy stared at her friend over her cooling tea and the cakes and sandwiches they hadn't even touched. And finally she understood exactly what Caro had been really saying all along.

You don't believe people can change? Maybe that means you haven't, either.

Her hands were shaking too much to pick up a teacup. Her eyes stung – must be the pollen from the floral displays. She felt suddenly, inexplicably cold.

And silenced.

Like Caro had taken away her voice with her words.

Taken away the woman she'd become.

She reached down for her bag and stood, turning away from the table and walking straight for the lobby, the door, the world outside

– ignoring the sound of Rosalind calling her name, Caro trying to justify herself, the gossip and the chatter and the noise of a hundred camera clicks.

She couldn't stay a moment longer. Not with them, the Dahlias. Not when she wasn't sure she was one any more.

Chapter Four

Fires in theatres have been frighteningly common over the years. The Royal Opera House, for instance, is the third such structure to be built on the same site, after the first two were destroyed by fire! Perhaps this is why it's said to be bad luck to have three lit candles on stage at the same time. Although, really, perhaps in this day and age we should go for the battery-powered ones . . .

                Wendell Malcolm, 'A Theatreland Audio Tour' script

Caro

Some days, Caro enjoyed surveillance work.

It *could* be fun. Sneaking around London on the trail of an unsuspecting target, ducking in and out of doorways to avoid being spotted, and taking sneaky photographs when appropriate. Dark glasses and a headscarf, when she needed not to be recognised. It was a challenge, being invisible as a public figure, but that just made it more of a game.

But some days – like this one – surveillance made her feel just a little bit dirty.

Here's what you're going to do, Rosalind had instructed her in a tight voice, after Posy stormed out of afternoon tea at the Ritz. *You believe this man has changed, and Posy doesn't – so we're going to find out which one of you is right. Investigate him, just like any other suspect. Talk to people who know him. Follow him to see where he goes, who he talks to. You're the PI, so it's up to you to track down the truth. Then maybe we can put this whole mess behind us.*

As if she didn't already have enough to do.

Following Luke – her friend – around London, looking for any evidence that he wasn't who he'd told her he was . . . that felt wrong.

But she'd promised Rosalind, so she was doing it anyway.

Even though she knew that proving a negative was almost impossible. Unless she saw something to prove Posy right – which she didn't expect to – this was a complete waste of time. Luke could be blamelessly feeding orphans or raising funds for a donkey sanctuary or whatever, and Posy would still believe it was all an act.

She didn't have any better ideas, though. So here she was, waiting around outside a cafe in a part of London she rarely visited, her coffee long gone cold on the table in front of her, waiting. She'd dressed in her most un-Caro-like clothes – nondescript leggings and trainers paired with a band T-shirt of Annie's and a hat that hid the dark curls she'd tucked up under it. She'd even foregone her usual bright red lipstick. With her sunglasses in place she was confident she looked enough unlike herself to pass unnoticed by anyone who wasn't actively looking for her.

And nobody had any reason to expect her to be here.

Piotr, their director, had called for an extra rehearsal, before the third preview that night, so both Caro and Luke were due at the Regent Theatre that afternoon. But the night before she'd heard Luke breaking plans with Darcy to grab brunch with her friends beforehand, because he needed to visit his sick father. Darcy hadn't sounded completely convinced by his excuse, which had given Caro pause.

It had seemed like too good an opportunity to miss. Photograph him visiting his elderly dad in his spare time, and hope it was just the first in a long line of evidence to try and convince Posy she was wrong. Or, if he was lying, find out what he was really doing – and if Darcy was right to be suspicious.

Luke's father was famed director Gregory Burrows. Caro had a feeling they'd been estranged in Luke's youth, but they seemed to have made up now, as she'd seen them appear in at least one Sunday supplement article and photoshoot together recently. Finding out where Gregory lived had been simple enough – she'd asked Ashok to get her the information and not questioned him about his methods.

Gregory Burrows, it seemed, lived in an exclusive block of serviced apartments, right across from the cafe where she now sat.

A waiter was hovering, waiting to see if she was going to vacate her table or order anything else, so Caro took a pointed sip of her cooling coffee – and looked up to see Luke Burrows approaching on the other side of the road.

He seemed mostly unaware of his surroundings, no furtive glances around or hurrying along to avoid being seen. Which made sense; he was exactly where he was supposed to be, doing exactly what he'd said he'd be doing.

Caro raised her phone as if checking her reflection in the forward-facing camera, tucking a stray curl under her hat as she snapped a few photos of Luke entering his father's building.

Then she waited again, wondering whether to order another coffee. Maybe a croissant. He'd probably be a while . . .

A couple of minutes passed before another person approached the building from the opposite direction. A dark-haired woman, Caro noted absently, cataloguing her linen blazer and matching skirt, the high heels that clacked on the pavement and the designer bag on her arm. She input the key code at the gate, the same way Luke had done, and pushed it to enter. Probably nothing to do with Luke, but she caught her image on her phone just in case. It was habit, rather than suspicion.

Caro picked up the menu and was about to cast a hopeful glance at the waiter when more movement at the gate caught her attention. It swung open and Luke stepped out onto the pavement again, glowering, hands in his pockets.

She checked her watch. He'd only been in there five minutes, ten at the most. Hardly the extensive familial visit she'd expected. Caro tossed a ten-pound note on the table to cover her coffee and a tip for the very patient waiter, and made to follow him.

It was still too early for him to be heading to the theatre, but maybe Darcy had persuaded him to make brunch after all. That was probably it. But she'd promised Rosalind she'd undertake this assignment with an open mind, so she'd check. It was easier to follow him without being seen when he was walking away from her, anyway. As long as she kept enough people between them, he was unlikely to spot her, especially with her hat and sunglasses on.

Luke took a meandering route through side streets and back passageways, clearly confident in where he was going as he bypassed tourists and locals alike. After fifteen minutes or so, the small alley he'd last ducked down, the one Caro had *almost* missed, opened up into a square lined with tall, pale-stone townhouses. A flower stall of the old-fashioned barrow type sat in the centre, near a bronze statue of some dignitary or another, with a pop-up coffee and crêpe stand on the other side.

Caro hung back in the alleyway to see what Luke did next. As he studied the flowers and talked to the stall owner, Caro took a few photos of the square. Most of the houses now appeared to be occupied by businesses, if the bronze plaques and labelled door buzzers were any indication. She assumed that property in this area of London was far too lucrative to be used for housing any more.

Luke purchased a few blooms, wrapped in brown paper, then stepped away – but didn't leave the square. He was waiting for something – or, more likely, someone. Someone he planned to give flowers to?

For the first time, Caro felt the tingle of suspicion that maybe there *was* more to Luke than she knew.

Staying hidden, she watched as a woman approached him from the far side of the small square, and Luke smiled at her in greeting. It was hard to tell the woman's age, because she had the kind of timeless elegance that very few except the extremely rich could carry off. She was dressed in camel and ivory tones, with oversized sunglasses and a wide-brimmed straw hat perched on top of silky-smooth highlighted hair that flowed past her shoulders.

She greeted Luke with a kiss on both cheeks, which he returned, with a quick touch of his hand at her waist but nothing more. And he kept hold of the flowers. Caro snapped a few photos, then leaned back into the shadows to watch.

Their conversation didn't last long, a few moments at most, before she led him to a townhouse with a dark green door, not far from the alley where Caro was hiding. She couldn't see a plaque beside *that* door, but once it had shut behind them she risked stepping out into the square for a moment or two, lingering near the railings outside. When she zoomed in with the camera on her phone she could just make out a reception desk and computer behind the front window.

How long would he be inside this time, she wondered? Were the flowers for someone inside that house?

She couldn't risk sneaking out again to get a coffee from the stall, unfortunately. With a sigh, she leaned back against the alley wall, one eye on that green door, and waited.

In the end, it took about twenty-five minutes before Luke exited, alone this time, but still holding those flowers, now wrapped in newspaper. He strode straight towards the edge of the square, in the open. Caro waited a moment or two, then followed again, hoping she wouldn't lose him once he hit the busy high street.

They walked for some time before it became clear where he was going. They were heading back to the theatre.

'Could have taken the tube. Or a taxi,' Caro grumbled. A whole morning of trailing after Luke, and for what?

All she'd learned was that Luke had visited his father, as he'd promised, and had a mysterious appointment at some expensive townhouse business Caro fully intended to google later. For all she knew, the woman could have been his theatrical agent and it could have been a business meeting. Probably was, one way or another.

But Luke had one more stop before he made it to the Prince Regent Theatre. He slipped in through the stage door of the Arcadia first. Caro ducked behind the corner, so she couldn't see exactly what he was doing there, but whatever it was it didn't take long – he was back on his way, whistling, hands in pockets, moments later.

The flowers. He'd left the flowers.

Rosalind

Rosalind liked to think she knew most of London's Theatreland secrets. After all, she'd appeared on stages across the district for decades, in between her TV and film work. From Juliet to Lady Macbeth, Antigone to Medea, even Lady Bracknell, most recently. She'd played them all over the years.

Still, when an old friend from her own theatre days asked her to test run the audio walking tour he'd just recorded for some company or another, she could hardly say no. Especially since it gave her the opportunity to do a little bit of investigating of her own, while Caro was off tailing Luke.

Rosalind had attended the second preview night of *Finding Freddie* with Annie the night before and enjoyed it immensely. Caro's return to the stage was a light-hearted pastiche of classic suspense pieces, up until the unexpected happy ending. It centred on a lonely middle-aged woman (Caro), in the 1950s, who was faced with the unexpected return of a man claiming to be the younger brother of her dead fiancé. As various people came out of the woodwork to support or deny his claim, Caro's character, Maggie, found herself with a houseful of new friends until it almost didn't matter when Darcy's character, Jocelyn, made the fatal phone call in the middle of the second half proving that Freddie couldn't possibly be who he said he was.

By that point in the play he was family, and the audience was rooting for him. So Maggie and her new friends forged the necessary evidence to prove it and they all lived happily ever after.

It was all wildly improbable, of course, but Rosalind had found herself drawn in, laughing and crying at all the right moments despite herself. Sure, it was still a little rough in places, but that was what previews were for – smoothing out those rough patches. As it was, the fifties costumes were delightful, the background music catchy, and the set and vibe of the piece pitch perfect. It was going to be a hit, she was almost certain, and Caro deserved every moment of its success.

Rosalind dressed so as not to be disturbed – usually, when out and about in London, she could expect to be stopped more than a few times for selfies or autographs. Although she'd found that, as she aged, fewer people tended to recognise her in public. She assumed this was because people's mental image of her as a person was a decade or two out of date. Or maybe she really did look so different after an hour or more in hair and make-up.

Either way, she hadn't taken any chances today. With her hair covered by a straw fedora and oversized sunglasses on, she could be anybody. Today, she was just a tourist in a city where she'd spent most of her life. A strange feeling, she had to admit – when had London stopped being home? She wasn't sure. But it had.

Standing, as instructed, with her back to the statue of William Shakespeare in the centre of Leicester Square, Rosalind popped her headphones into her ears and pressed play on the app with the audio tour. She smiled to herself as her old friend Wendell's voice filled her ears, opening with a self-deprecating joke as she'd aways expect from him. Then, when instructed, she started to walk.

It took a little getting used to, following instructions from a disembodied voice in her ears. Her phone stayed mostly in her pocket, only getting pulled out when she realised she'd taken a wrong turn somewhere and needed to get back on track. Mostly, though, she walked, and she listened.

It was blissful, the way she didn't have to think at all – about which route to take, where to cross the road, what to pay attention to. The tour told her everything she needed to do – and explained all the interesting things she was seeing on the way. She'd *thought* she knew this area better than anyone, but the secrets and stories it held surprised even her.

From backstage feuds – and on-stage fights – to falling scenery and famous names, she drank all the stories in as she walked from Leicester Square past Seven Dials, through the theatre district, down to the Strand, and back up towards Covent Garden. There'd been so many fires, not all of them as long ago as she'd expected. Mind you, she remembered when she started on the stage, and sometimes she couldn't make out the audience over the haze of smoke, before smoking was banned indoors.

Rosalind smiled to herself as her tour brought her to the Arcadia Theatre, with its curved entrance on the corner and its name in stained glass above posters of Posy and co in *Lights Out*. With the decorative architraves and rounded turret, it was a quintessential traditional London theatre. She learned about a tragic on-stage accident in a production of *Romeo and Juliet*, long before her time, where Mercutio really had been run through with a non-prop sword before the interval. There was talk, of course, that it hadn't been an accident at all, but nothing had ever been proven . . .

She just hoped that Posy's run there would be less eventful.

The tour took her around the corner, past the stage door with its small red and gold sign, and she noticed it was propped open, probably in deference to the warm weather. Perfect.

It was far too early in the day for any of the cast to be arriving for that evening's performance, but the stage door would be manned from first thing for deliveries and such. As she expected, the stage-door keeper was in situ behind his counter just inside the door. Rosalind slipped off her hat and sunglasses so as to be more recognisable – a move that paid off when the young man jumped to attention the moment she stepped through the door.

'Ms King! Um, welcome to the Arcadia. It's . . . it's an honour. How can I help you?' He had to be in his early twenties, but if anything he looked younger, with his mousy curls flopping over his forehead and his brown eyes wide underneath.

Rosalind smiled. 'Hello. Mal, isn't it? Posy's told me all about you.' Actually, all Posy had told her was that he was in some very dramatic on-again, off-again relationship with his boyfriend that the entire company seemed to have opinions on, despite none of them having actually met him.

'Oh, well, Posy . . . Ms Starling, I mean, is very kind.' Mal's cheeks were pink, and his throat bobbed as he swallowed. 'How can I help you today?'

'I just wanted to stop by and introduce myself,' Rosalind replied, easily. 'I'm in town for a few weeks, so I imagine I'll be popping in often to visit Posy, and it's always helpful to be on good terms with the person who guards the door.'

'Right, yes, of course.' He sounded baffled at the concept. Probably, she supposed, because she rarely needed any actual introduction.

'And I understand that stopping by Posy's dressing room unannounced can be somewhat dangerous these days.' She allowed herself a small smile under her raised eyebrows to show that she was joking, but Mal still turned a little pale. Clearly he knew exactly what she was referring to.

'I . . . I shouldn't have let Luke down there without letting Posy know he was coming. It was all my fault.' Mal sounded so remorseful, standing there with his puppy-dog eyes, that Rosalind almost felt guilty for bringing it up.

'You weren't to know,' she said. 'And I understand that Luke can be very charming – especially when he wants something, I imagine. How do you find him?'

'Oh, Luke's great!' Mal said, with obvious and unfeigned enthusiasm. 'I've met him a few times at this tapas bar casts and crew working at the Arcadia sometimes go to after a show – the company from the Regent have been going there too, recently. Their rehearsal space was only around the corner from here, you see, and by the time they moved into the Prince Regent, La Vida Tapas was already the unofficial cast hangout. It's been nice, actually, having another cast to spend time with, too.'

'Does Posy often join you there?' Rosalind asked.

'She has, but only once or twice.' Mal frowned. 'And not when the *Finding Freddie* cast were there, I don't think. She's not so big on socialising.'

'Unlike Luke.'

Mal nodded enthusiastically. 'Exactly! He's always got time to chat, and he's not showbizzy at all, if you know what I mean.' Mal leaned over the counter and lowered his voice. 'Some of the actors we get in here think they're better than all that, you know? Chauffeured cars everywhere, not wanting to be stopped in the street, that kind of thing?'

'I know the sort you mean,' Rosalind said, with a carefully maintained straight face.

'But Luke's not like that at all. He's always looking for how he can help you out – even though he must have people asking him for favours all the time. He's great.'

Well, at least it was clear why Mal had let Luke down to Posy's dressing room the other night – a plain and simple case of hero worship.

'That's always good to hear,' she said. 'I know he and Caro have grown close too. Anyway, I must be on my way, but it was so good to meet you. I'm sure I'll see you again soon – maybe in that tapas bar you mentioned. Where exactly was it, by the way?'

With the name and address of the tapas bar in hand, Rosalind restarted her tour and followed it the long way round, via a couple of other notable sights, until it reached the Prince Regent Theatre. There'd been a theatre on that spot for almost forever, although not *this* theatre, of course, which had been rebuilt after – what else? – a fire in the early 1920s.

The Regent, as it was known, was only half the size and of a very different style to the Arcadia, with its white and blue-green frontage and Art Deco windows with diamond glass. Inside, the cool classic colours continued, with a huge round window above the entrance hall and stairs that flooded the place with light.

She listened, fascinated, as the narrator talked about the sailors who would arrive in London and then, since they weren't paid when they were in dock, head to the theatres for work – often through tunnels that led up from the Thames directly into the backstage area, tunnels that had mostly been blocked up these days but still existed – including the ones under the Regent. She'd known that a lot of maritime language was used backstage – stagehands instead of deckhands, for instance – but she'd never really questioned why before.

Rosalind was just making her way around the side of the theatre, learning about the sailors' whistles, when she realised that the woman approaching the theatre from the opposite direction was Amber, the stage manager. She paused the tour and called out a greeting.

Amber looked startled to see her. 'Ms King. Are you looking for Caro?'

'No.' Rosalind tapped the earbud still in place in her left ear. 'Believe it or not, I'm taking a Theatreland audio tour. Long story.'

'Sounds . . . fun,' Amber said. 'Is it good?'

'It's fascinating,' Rosalind admitted. 'I thought I knew everything about this area, but apparently not!'

Amber smiled. 'I'll have to try it. Sounds like the sort of thing my son would love. He's seven, and absolutely *fascinated* by the theatre.'

'I'll leave the details with Caro later for you,' Rosalind promised. 'Actually, while I have you, there was something I wanted to speak with you about . . .'

'Oh?' Amber shifted where she stood. 'How can I help?'

Rosalind considered how best to phrase her query. She didn't want word to get back to Luke that she was quizzing his friends about him, but at the same time . . . that's exactly what she was doing.

'I was just wondering, how is the new cast gelling? I know one or two of the roles were recast when the show moved down to London. I assume you joined then too?'

Amber nodded. 'Yeah, the backstage crew is all new for the London production. And yes, Caro and Luke came on board for this run, but honestly, everyone has really settled in incredibly well. I think it helps that Caro and Luke are both so personable. It's hard not to get on with either of them, isn't it?'

Rosalind's answering smile was somewhat forced. 'Of course.' Although Posy seemed to have managed it. With both of them.

Amber keyed in the code to open the stage door and held it for Rosalind. 'Are you coming in?'

'No, thanks. I've got my tour to finish. And the name of an excellent tapas bar to try for a late lunch.'

'Ooh, Carlos's place? La Vida Tapas?' Amber asked. When Rosalind nodded she went on, 'It's wonderful. If Carlos's daughter Gabriella is serving, tell her I sent you and she'll make sure you're well cared for. I think we've kept that place in profit since we started rehearsing!'

'I will do that.' All this walking and talking had made her rather hungry. Plus, if Posy was right about Luke, he might have kept his guard up around fellow professionals, but let it slip in front of people he considered less important – like a young waitress. There could be useful intel there – as well as food.

She let Amber go, but no sooner had the door swung shut behind her than she saw Luke Burrows himself approaching – and, about three people behind him, Caro, dressed in some rather unflattering leggings and one of Annie's T-shirts.

Deciding it wasn't the right time to confront Luke himself – she wanted a little more information before that – Rosalind stepped back towards the corner and the front of the theatre – and almost crashed into Piotr Judd, the director, coming the other way.

'Rosalind! Well, this is a nice surprise. Were you looking for me? I'd been hoping we'd have a chance to catch up while you were in town. Ideally over a gin and tonic or two?' Piotr was an old, old friend . . . or at least a friendly acquaintance of Rosalind's from her theatre days. And he, of anyone, surely would know the truth about Luke's reported conversion from sinner to saint.

'That would be lovely!' And a perfect opportunity to quiz him on Luke's behaviour. 'Perhaps later today? I'm just in the middle of something, as it happens. An audio tour . . .'

But she'd lost him. She trailed off as she realised he was already looking over her shoulder at someone else.

'Later sounds great.' He gave her a tight smile. 'If you'll excuse me a moment, I just need to talk to Luke.'

Piotr moved past her, calling, 'Luke! Before you go in . . .'

Obviously, this conversation was not meant for her ears. Which meant that naturally she intended to hear all of it.

Rosalind ducked around the corner, headphones in place, as if about to continue her tour. Then she turned and listened, glad that Piotr and Luke had moved away from the stage door and towards her hiding place. She wondered where Caro had hidden herself, although at least she had a better reason to be heading towards the stage door. Rehearsal must be starting soon.

'I just wanted to let you know that I had a word with Amber last night, and everything should be sorted,' Piotr said.

Luke let out a heavy breath. 'Oh, good. Thank you for that. I didn't want to get anybody into trouble but . . . I felt I had to raise it. She wasn't upset?'

Well. That explained why Piotr had wanted to have this conversation *outside* the theatre. If the conversation was about Amber, he wouldn't want to have it in front of her.

'Amber's a professional,' Piotr replied. 'She understood. We all want this show to be a success, don't we?'

'Absolutely.' Rosalind could hear the relief in Luke's voice. 'Speaking of, I'd better get inside and get ready for rehearsal!'

Interesting. Amber had seemed very positive about Luke's place in the cast. And if anything, Luke had sounded apologetic about raising whatever his problem with her was.

Rosalind wasn't sure what this said about either of them, but she had to admit it made her curious.

Chapter Five

'What can you see?' Dahlia pressed into Johnnie's side, trying to get a good view out of the same window. 'Can you see them yet?'

'Not with you pushing me out of the way like that,' Johnnie grumbled. 'Which one of us is the professional at work here?'

'Well, that depends entirely on which one of us spots something that will solve this case first, I'd say,' Dahlia replied, pertly. 'Wouldn't you?'

Dahlia Lively in Death Comes to Hazelwood
By Lettice Davenport, 1944

Caro

Rehearsals during previews weren't unprecedented, but the fact Piotr had called one for today suggested he wasn't entirely happy with the few wobbles in the performance they'd given the night before. Caro changed quickly out of her surveillance outfit before joining the others on the stage. Although she was determined to focus on the rehearsal, not Rosalind's extra-curricular assignment, she did make a point of hovering nearby as Darcy greeted Luke with a warm kiss, and asked him how his dad was.

'He's okay. Well, as okay as he ever is these days.' Luke gave Darcy a sad smile. 'I couldn't stay long; he was pretty tired.'

'You should have come and joined us for brunch after all, then!'

Darcy pouted a little that he hadn't, and Caro resisted the urge to roll her eyes.

'I would have, but I got a text from an old friend who's in town for a little while, so I swung by to catch up with them on my way here instead.' Luke didn't mention that the old friend was a beautiful woman, assuming that was the meeting she'd witnessed. And he didn't explain why they were both visiting that townhouse together. But neither of those things were hangable offences, and probably perfectly reasonable if Caro could ask for those reasons without admitting she'd been betraying his trust by following him in the first place.

The afternoon's rehearsal went well – or well enough for Piotr to still be smiling when he called them to an end at five to allow them all time to take a break and get something to eat before having to be back at the theatre to prepare for the evening performance.

'I heard we needed this extra rehearsal because some of the early reviews on the blogs aren't as good as they hoped.' Darcy leaned against the back of the high wingback chair that served to denote the inside of the cottage on stage. That and a small telephone table beside it were enough to tell the audience when the characters were inside. 'Piotr's saying it's to let the understudies get more rehearsal time in, just in case. What do you think?'

Reviews weren't really supposed to be printed until the official opening night, but a few of the smaller blogs liked to post them early so they didn't get lost in the noise of the bigger publications reviewing at the same time. It wasn't really fair to judge a play on the previews, in Caro's opinion, but there also wasn't anything much they could do about it.

'Well, it was definitely useful to run through your phone-call scene in Act Two a few more times,' Caro pointed out. 'It wasn't exactly smooth last night. And I know that wasn't entirely your fault,' she added quickly, when Darcy turned to glare at her.

'That whole set-up is a nightmare,' Darcy grumbled. 'Why on earth they thought that putting the phone box up on that scaffolding was a good idea is beyond me. It worked perfectly well at the Mill with just a cut-out we pushed on stage when we needed it.'

Caro didn't point out that the Yorkshire theatre the play had transferred from was even smaller – and certainly less well equipped – than the Prince Regent. She was more distracted by the sight of Luke and Joshua laughing together, and the reminder that, while he now played several smaller roles in the production as well as serving as Luke's understudy, in the Yorkshire production Joshua had played the titular character of Freddie.

The woman who'd played Caro's role in the original production had stepped back from the play altogether when Caro was brought in to play Maggie in the West End. But Joshua had been offered the chance to join the cast in another capacity and had chosen to take it.

Luke had effectively stolen Joshua's job – and best shot at fame. If *he* still thought Luke was a good guy, surely that had to carry some weight with Posy?

Caro leaned back on her hands. 'What do you think those two are finding so hilarious?'

'No idea,' Darcy said, her eyes narrowing, before she headed towards them, obviously determined to find out.

Caro watched her go. Before she reached them, though, Luke clapped Joshua on the back and turned to head out, Darcy following. Caro took the opportunity to swoop in and have a quick word with Joshua before he left the building, too.

'It's good to see you two getting on so well,' she said, falling into step beside him as he headed for the wings and the dressing rooms. 'How are you finding understudying?'

'It's a different dynamic, for sure,' Joshua replied. 'Especially when I have my other roles to think about too – and my own understudy for them! It's bonkers, really.'

'But Luke's been okay with you? I know I'm lucky not to have my predecessor watching my every move, reminding people how she would have played the part differently . . .'

Joshua laughed. 'No, Luke has been ace about it. He took me aside right back when we started rehearsals, actually, and we spent a lot of time talking about the character and stuff. Made me feel really involved.' He shrugged. 'I'm not saying it was easy to take that step back, but Luke made it about as good as it could be. And Piotr's assured me I'll definitely get some performances as Freddie during the run to put on my résumé, so it really could be worse.'

She let him disappear into his dressing room and was about to follow when she spotted Luke talking to Amber, who looked a little pale and uncertain. Darcy was nowhere to be seen. Caro edged closer to listen.

'Your mum's feeling better now, then?' Luke asked.

'Much, thank you.' Amber nodded fiercely. 'You don't need to worry about that.'

Caro frowned, trying to imagine why he'd be *worried* about it – before she remembered the previous weekend, when Amber's son, who usually spent the time she was working at weekends with his grandmother, had been at the theatre while they rehearsed instead.

'I-I know it was disruptive last weekend, having Milo here,' Amber went on, stuttering slightly over the words.

'No! It was fun to have him around,' Caro burst in, without thinking. Amber and Luke both looked up at her in surprise.

Probably no point pretending she wasn't eavesdropping now, was there?

'Milo seemed very interested in the theatre, and how everything worked,' Caro finished, lamely. 'It was nice to see his enthusiasm.'

'It was,' Luke agreed, with a smile. 'But all the same, I'm glad your mum's feeling brighter. It must be hard worrying about childcare as well as your job.' He patted Amber on the shoulder, and headed towards the stage door, rather than his own dressing room.

Somewhere behind her, a ringtone rang out – one she recognised instantly as the theme tune to *The Dahlia Lively Mysteries* TV show. She'd programmed it in for Rosalind and Posy's phones too, but unless one of them had shown up unexpectedly, that was probably hers. She'd been sure she'd silenced it before rehearsals. Oh well.

But where had she left it? She usually left it in her dressing room, but it didn't sound like it was coming from there. She'd spoken to Ashok just before she went onto the stage for the rehearsal, so . . .

She headed for the wings, and quickly located the ringing phone on a small ledge, where she'd obviously abandoned it when Piotr had called them all to the stage. The phone stopped ringing as she reached it, of course, but started again a moment later, Ashok's name flashing across the screen as the TV theme tune blared out.

'Ashok? What have you got for me?' She'd asked him to do a little looking into Luke too, in the hope of speeding things up.

'Not a lot. I'm emailing what I have over to you now but the top line is, it looks like you're right. Luke Burrows has been a changed man these past few years, ever since he reconciled with his father.'

Caro smiled at his words. Of *course* she was right. 'Thanks, Ashok. That's a great help.'

He sighed. 'Try not to be too smug when you tell Posy about it, yeah? And remember, she has a right to still hate him for whatever it is he did, even if he *has* changed.'

'I know. I'll try,' she told him, before hanging up. But really, it wasn't easy being right *all* the time.

Rosalind

After a leisurely lunch at the tapas bar, Rosalind had to admit she didn't pay *quite* as much attention to the rest of the tour as she had the first part. Not that she'd learned anything particularly useful at La Vida Tapas, beyond confirmation of the fact that the casts from both Posy and Caro's plays tended to congregate there of an evening, given the convenient location right between the two theatres, and that the staff loved having them there.

Luke, in particular, was a favourite it seemed – especially with Carlos, the owner. A generous tipper and a respectful patron was the verdict – he'd even helped Carlos persuade a particularly rowdy and difficult group to leave the restaurant peaceably a few weeks earlier. Rosalind had managed a private chat with Gabriella, Carlos's nineteen-year-old daughter, but she'd only echoed his sentiments. Apparently Luke had been helping her with her application for drama school next year.

Perhaps Luke was overcorrecting for so many years of bad behaviour, she mused, as the tour ended and she wended her way back towards the Prince Regent to see what Caro had discovered. Her rehearsal should be over by now, but they still had time before the evening performance.

Before she could find Caro, however, she remembered Piotr's promise of a drink, and headed in through the front door to see if someone could find him for her.

The Prince Regent was known as one of the West End's most intimate theatres – which a lot of people took to mean small, since it only had a capacity of around six hundred. But having sat in the deep green seats of the auditorium the previous evening, she knew that really it meant that the set-up in there somehow drew you in to the action on the stage, until you could almost forget that you were surrounded by other theatregoers. The audience were part of the action, and you could see everything from every seat in the house.

It did mean, however, that like so many of the older London theatres, there was a lot of theatre crammed into a rather small space – the queues for the bathrooms at the preview performance she'd attended had snaked halfway down the stairs, and the wait at the bar had been even worse. As she'd overheard one woman lament to a friend while queuing, West End theatres were '*a very British mixture of glamour and inadequate plumbing*'.

But now, with no performance in progress, she had the front of house almost to herself, and it looked like a different place without the crowds. While she waited for Piotr to join her, she took a moment to stand in the centre of the well-designed foyer, just before the spiralling stairs that led to the circle seats, and look up through the massive circular window above the doors, framed in black ironwork that matched the Art Deco theme, and enjoy the summer sun pouring in. Despite its smaller auditorium, nobody could argue that it wasn't an impressive theatre.

'It's beautiful, isn't it?' Piotr appeared beside her, hands in the pockets of his dark trousers as he joined her in looking up. 'I do always think there is something just a little bit more special about this theatre than the grander ones, like the Arcadia, don't you?'

The twinkle in his eye when he glanced over told her that the director knew full well what he was doing, comparing the two theatres where two Dahlias were appearing that season.

She returned his smile, but added a raised eyebrow. 'I think every theatre has its own particular charm, personally. It's what you do with it that counts. One of the reasons I wanted to catch up with you this afternoon, and tell you what a wonderful job you've done with *Finding Freddie.*'

Piotr beamed. 'You are too kind. Now please, come join me in the bar, so we can sit comfortably while you flatter my ego for a while! The Regent Bar really is one of my favourites . . .'

'Well, if you're sure you're not too busy,' Rosalind said.

'What could be more important than listening to important people saying lovely things about me?' Piotr laughed, as if it were a joke, even though Rosalind was 90 per cent certain it really wasn't.

The bar at the Prince Regent Theatre really was stunning, despite its compact size. The elegant colour scheme of the foyer – pale blue-green, cream and gold – continued onto the walls and velvet chairs of the bar. Lined with arch-topped mirrors with decorative black leaded detailing, it felt much larger than it really was, thanks to all the reflections. It became hard to tell where the real bar ended and the mirror bar began. But maybe that was just because she'd never seen it empty before – only in the inevitable scrum for an interval drink.

Piotr ordered their drinks from a bored-looking bartender, and they took them to a window table, looking out over the street at the side of the theatre.

'So, everything is going well with the play?' Rosalind asked, after a sip of her gin and tonic. 'Annie and I adored it last night. Just such a delightful piece of theatre.'

Piotr beamed. 'Yes, there's plenty of buzz already. I think the whole aesthetic is doing well with a certain subset online – all the classic fifties stuff, but with a twist, you know?'

'Absolutely,' Rosalind said with a nod. 'And the cast is gelling well? You recast some of the roles, didn't you? From the original cast up in Yorkshire, I mean?'

'Standard practice,' Piotr replied. 'You know what it takes to get a new play on in London these days. And Caro was just so perfect for the role.'

'But it wasn't just Caro you brought in, was it? Luke was a new addition too, I think?' She knew. But let him believe he was educating her, if that's what it took.

'Yes, that's right.' Piotr reached for his drink. 'The producers really wanted a name, for the publicity, you know. Something to draw people in to start with, until word gets around about how good the show is. And Luke, well, he's definitely an up-and-coming name, isn't he?'

Rosalind raised an eyebrow. 'Caro's name wasn't enough on its own, then?'

'Luke, ah, appeals to a different demographic than Caro, was the reasoning.'

'I can see that,' Rosalind admitted. Luke's good looks could carry him far. 'I have to admit, though, I'd heard stories . . . how are you finding him?'

'Oh, he's an absolute dream,' Piotr said, without missing a beat. 'I'm sure there are always tales of youthful hijinks – even for a National Treasure like yourself! And I know your Posy knew him when he was younger. But on this production he's been the consummate professional.'

'That's good to hear.' She paused for a moment, wondering how far to push him. This wasn't a real investigation, after all. But at the same time . . . 'I have to admit, I overheard the two of you talking after we bumped into each other earlier. Is there a . . . well, problem with your stage manager?'

'No, no! Absolutely not.' Piotr shook his head violently for emphasis. 'There was the *tiniest* issue with the deputy stage manager who was calling the show from the wings the other night not being quite as experienced as we might like, and it caused a slight problem with the telephone box scene in the second act – she didn't allow enough time for Darcy to get up the scaffolding and into place, essentially. Amber is sorting it, though, so I'm sure it won't happen again.'

'I see.' Rosalind wasn't entirely sure why the star name would need to raise such an issue with the director for him to bring it up with the company stage manager. In her experience it would have come up naturally in notes after the show or the next day.

But Piotr was already distracted, frowning at something outside the window as he drained the last of his drink. He slammed the glass down and jumped to his feet, flashing her a brief smile.

'Sorry to have to run.' Piotr was already halfway to the door. 'But you know what preview week is like. So much to do!' Then he was gone.

The moment he was out of sight, Rosalind moved swiftly to the window to see if she could spot what had drawn his attention, but the London street seemed perfectly normal to her.

Strange. Maybe it was time to go and find Caro.

Getting backstage was easy enough; while security in theatres was far more stringent than when she'd been starting out, she was a recognisable enough face to find someone to let her through, especially since she'd already been there before with Caro that week.

She paused outside Caro's open dressing-room door, and saw her friend frowning at her phone. The window behind her was open, and the familiar sound of London's streets – sirens and horns and car alarms – floated in on the summer breeze.

'Do you know why I have two missed calls from Posy?' Caro asked. 'She must have called while I was speaking to Ashok.'

'No idea.'

Before Rosalind could begin to speculate on why Posy might have been ringing Caro, the sirens outside the window grew louder, and echoed like there were many of them layered on top of each other.

And then she smelled the smoke on the breeze, and heard one alarm ringing louder and louder under it all.

Caro

By the time they made it out of the stage door and around to where the sirens were coming from, there was already quite a crowd gathering outside the Arcadia Theatre – mostly held at bay by the uniformed police officers forming a cordon outside the theatre while the fire crew worked. Shiny red fire engines blocked the nearby roads, and one had a hose running from it, although Caro couldn't get close enough to see where it was going or if it had been used.

There was smoke, though. She could smell it. *Something* was on fire.

She just hoped it was still early enough for the theatre to be empty – or at least easily evacuated.

Stretching up on her tiptoes, she thought she spotted Posy further forward in the crowd – she saw a blonde ponytail bobbing under a familiar-looking baseball cap, anyway. She called out to her, but either it wasn't Posy or she didn't hear. Or she was ignoring her completely.

Actually, Caro thought she might have been more surprised if she *had* turned around and acknowledged her.

'Can you see anything?' Rosalind asked from just behind her. 'Is the theatre on fire? Where's Posy?'

Unable to answer any of those questions accurately, Caro looked around for someone who could – landing on Posy's co-star, Taran, who was smiling charmingly at a police officer as he gestured towards the theatre. Other cast members from the Arcadia gathered nearby in a huddle, obviously held back on their way into the theatre. Posy wasn't with them, she noted. But was that Darcy Coleman, lurking in the shadows a little further over? Even the staff and patrons of the tapas bar had stopped serving and come out to see what was going on – she spotted Gabriella standing with her arms folded and her back to her father as they watched the firemen converge around the side of the building.

When Taran shook the police officer's hand and stepped away, towards his cast mates, Caro managed to squeeze through and follow.

'Looks like a cigarette stub flicked into the bins down the side alley,' Taran was telling them. 'Nothing serious, just annoying, and it's out now. The theatre itself is fine, but the smoke got in through the open windows and set off the alarms. Should be sorted in no time.'

'Lot of fuss over nothing, then,' somebody said. 'Some careless teenager, probably, not putting their cigarette out properly.'

'I thought teenagers didn't smoke these days,' Caro commented. 'They vape instead, don't they?'

'God knows. The point is, we should be able to get inside again soon,' Taran said.

'Are we still on for tonight's show?' somebody else asked.

Taran shrugged. 'Not looking likely now – too late. But I'll check with Pollie. She'll know.'

Caro grabbed him before he could leave. 'Have you seen Posy?'

'Not to speak to,' Taran replied. 'But I think I saw her over there – round by the stage door. Excuse me, I need to check in with our stage manager.'

She let him go. Rosalind caught up to her as she turned the corner to the side of the theatre where the stage door was.

'What's happening? Where's Posy?'

'That's what I'm trying to find out.' Caro quickly filled her in on the little intelligence she'd gleaned so far, all the while scanning the crowds for Posy.

She wasn't in any danger; the fire was out and it had never been within the theatre to start with. But all the same, there was a creeping, unsettling feeling in Caro's stomach that told her they needed to find Posy.

Now.

But there was no sign of that blonde ponytail or familiar cap.

Just when it seemed that the show was over – the firemen were posing for photos with the tourists, and Posy's company stage manager had gathered the cast together to inform them that they had an unexpected evening off, while someone from the box office made an announcement about refunds and rebooking – something changed.

Caro didn't know exactly when or why it happened. Probably a crackle on someone's radio, easily missed in all the chaos. Or, no. Maybe it was when she looked up to see the boy from the Arcadia stage door standing white-faced and wide-eyed at the entrance.

But she knew it for sure when Posy appeared on the single step outside the stage door with blood on her hands.

All over her hands.

'He's dead.' Caro shouldn't have been able to hear Posy's wavering voice, but the crowd had fallen deathly silent. 'I need . . . I need the police. In my dressing room.'

A moment of complete stillness.

Then the camera-phone clicks and flashes started, and the nearest police officer ran for the door and all hell started to break loose again.

Chapter Six

Finding a body is never a pleasant experience. Having done it more than once now, all I can recommend – if you ever find yourself in that unfortunate position – is that you keep your cool and, for the love of everything holy, don't touch the body!

Seven Lively Suspects
By Caro Hooper

Caro

'We need to get in there.' Rosalind was already pushing her way through the surging crowd, despite the assembled police officers' best efforts to keep people back.

Caro followed. 'They're never going to let us just walk into a crime scene.' If that's what this was. *He's dead*, Posy had said. But who? And how?

Something bloody, if her hands were anything to judge by.

Not anything natural, going on past experience.

Rosalind shot her a censorious look. 'I don't want to get to the crime scene. We need to get to *Posy*.'

Right, of course. She should have thought of that first.

Except . . . would they let them talk to Posy, either? She'd had blood all over her hands . . .

In my dressing room. Her voice had been shaky, but the words had been clear.

And it wasn't like this was the first time someone had been bleeding in Posy's dressing room. It wasn't even the first time this week.

Luke. What if it was him? If so, Posy was going to have questions to answer.

A lot of questions.

But no. What would Luke be doing at the Arcadia anyway? It could be anybody. She couldn't panic about this yet. Posy wouldn't kill anybody. Not in cold blood.

She *couldn't.*

Posy had found a body. That was all. It wasn't the first time, and it probably wouldn't be the last given the three Dahlias' penchant for murder investigations. They just needed to talk to Posy, find out what had happened, and then they could solve the case, together. Murder was bigger than any petty disagreements between them, anyway. Perhaps a really juicy mystery was exactly what they needed.

Maybe it wasn't even murder! Although the blood on Posy's hands and jeans didn't exactly scream natural causes.

Why did she touch the body? She knows better than that.

There would be an explanation, Caro was sure. There had to be.

Rosalind had reached the front of the crowd, and seemed to be arguing with a police officer who was looking around anxiously for reinforcements. From the sound of the approaching sirens, those reinforcements were coming. They'd already ushered Posy back inside the building, away from the gathering crowds.

They were never going to let them talk to her. Not before the police had asked her everything *they* wanted to know.

Maybe not even then.

As more police officers streamed onto the scene, and tape went up to keep everyone else back, Rosalind stamped her foot and rejoined Caro.

'We need to regroup and come up with a plan.' Rosalind glanced back at the Arcadia Theatre. 'And I need to phone my lawyer and get her down here. Fast.'

Caro stared at the stage door and finally admitted to herself that this was more than just another potential investigation.

Posy was in trouble.

In Caro's experience, secrets never lasted long in theatre circles. Knowledge was power, it was leverage. It got you in places, through doors that might have otherwise been closed. It wasn't everything – knowing *people* still often worked better than knowing *things* – but it was definitely something.

And right now, Caro felt like she knew nothing at all.

They headed back to the Prince Regent Theatre when the police had cleared the crowd. Where else were they supposed to go? After all, they had a show to put on that evening.

Except it quickly became clear that *Finding Freddie* would not be performed that night.

Piotr made the announcement to the whole cast from the stage at the Regent. Caro sat with the others in the plush, green seats of the audience, wishing that what she was hearing, watching on the stage, was just another fiction. A play.

But the police officer standing with Piotr wasn't wearing a costume. And his solemn expression wasn't an act.

Luke was dead.

'The police will want to speak with you all in the coming days,' Piotr went on, but Caro had stopped listening.

Luke, her friend, her co-star, was gone. The man who made her laugh when she thought she was too tired to smile, and who brought her oat-milk lattes to her dressing room most days. Who'd told her, in a small, sad voice, all about the man he'd used to be – before showing her, day after day, how much he'd changed.

But it hadn't mattered. Because now he was dead, in what she had to assume was a horrible, bloody way.

In Posy's dressing room. The thought thundered around Caro's head.

Posy. Her friend, her fellow Dahlia. She'd watched her grow and blossom from an insecure, troubled ex-child star to the accomplished, confident woman taking on London theatre – and the mantle of Dahlia Lively. She'd solved murders with her, confessed fears and past horrors, spent high days and holidays with her.

Before this summer, if anyone had asked, Caro would have told them that Posy was the closest thing she had to a little sister.

Now . . . now Posy believed she'd chosen a man she hated over their friendship, even though that wasn't what Caro had meant to do at all.

None of that seemed to matter any more.

Because Luke was dead, and Posy . . . Posy was in trouble.

'We've cancelled tonight's performance out of respect,' Piotr said, as Caro tuned back into reality again. In the row in front of her, Joshua, who'd been understudying the role of Freddie, looked down at his hands, but Caro couldn't make out his expression from this angle.

The fact that she'd instantly looked for him to see how he'd taken the news told her more than she'd like, though.

She was looking for a murderer, again.

Anyone other than Posy.

Caro took in the rest of the cast and crew as they were dismissed from the auditorium. Piotr must have had the sensitivity to break the news to Darcy privately, because Luke's girlfriend was nowhere to be seen. The rest of the cast, however, clung together like orphans in a storm, trying to process what had happened.

Naturally, they decided to do that in the bar.

Caro tried to ignore the whispers as the cast and crew gathered in small clusters around the room, but the bar was so small it was hard not to hear every insinuation, every murmur of accusation.

'I heard the two of them had history,' someone said, and Caro watched the mirrors to try and figure out who had spoken. 'Posy *hated* him. That's what she and Caro were arguing about in that photo that went viral.'

God, she hated it when gossip was right.

'Do you really think she did it, then? Killed him, I mean?' This time, Caro knew exactly who'd spoken – one of the girls from the wardrobe department – and she jumped to her feet before the girl had even finished speaking.

'Posy Starling is *not* a murderer.' Caro's voice reverberated around the tiny bar area, all other conversations ceasing. 'Whatever any of you think you know, you don't, okay? Posy would never—'

Her voice cracked, just as Rosalind came up beside her and slid a gin and tonic into her hand.

'Come on,' Rosalind murmured. 'Let's . . . just sit for a moment.'

She led her to a different seat, one tucked away in the corner, and Caro tried to stop her hands shaking so hard that the ice rattled in her glass. 'I just . . . they don't know what they're talking about.'

'No, they don't. Of course, neither do we, yet. What *do* we know?' Rosalind slipped into the seat beside her, all while eyeing the people around them with suspicion.

They were all watching them the same way, Caro realised. If they'd all already decided that Posy was guilty, then she and Rosalind were tarred by association.

What did they know? 'Not enough.' Caro wished more than anything that Posy was there with her notebook and pen, scribbling down her thoughts as she spoke them. 'We know that Luke is dead. We know that it was bloody, and that Posy found his body, in her dressing room. How it got there and who killed him . . . ?' She took another swig of her gin. 'No bloody idea.'

In the Dahlia Lively mysteries, the person who found the body was often a prime suspect themselves. Under the circumstances – the circumstances being that Posy had been taken straight to the police station for questioning, with Rosalind's lawyer, Samantha, hopefully following very closely behind – that seemed to be the case in the real world, too.

'You've been investigating him. Who might want Luke dead?' Rosalind prompted. Caro gave her a look. '*Other* than Posy. Obviously.'

'I don't know. Nobody I spoke to.' Nothing she'd found out about him or his relationships added up to murder, did it?

Rosalind leaned closer, her voice low and hard. 'Then you missed something. Or I did. We need to speak to them all again. Because there are going to be photos all over social media by now of Posy getting into a police car with blood on her hands. And even when my lawyer gets her out of there and the police realise that she couldn't have had anything to do with it, those photos will *still* be out there. We need to find the real killer and get them behind bars if we're going to clear Posy's name. And we need to do it fast.'

Caro looked down into the depths of her glass. She didn't want to say it. Didn't want to let the thought out of her head and into the world. Especially not after her sudden outburst to the rest of the bar.

But one of them had to, and it obviously wasn't going to be Rosalind. She wasn't thinking straight.

Posy wasn't a murderer – Caro would stake her life on that fact. But if Caro had been wrong about Luke . . . if Posy had been right all along . . . if he'd cornered her in her dressing room, or threatened her . . . if it had been self-defence . . . or an accident even, like with the book.

She hated even thinking it. But the truth was, they *had* to consider Posy a suspect – not because she was the only person they knew who hated Luke, but because the *police* thought she was a suspect. And so did the rest of the world, it seemed.

Where had Posy been when the theatre was evacuated? Was it her that Caro had seen in the crowd, or had she been in her dressing room all along? Had Luke surprised her there? Those flowers . . . had he left them for her? Had he gone back to see her after their rehearsal?

What if there was more between them recently than Posy had led them to believe? What if she hadn't told them everything?

What if . . .

'What if she *did* kill him?' The words were barely a whisper. But Rosalind recoiled as if she'd yelled them in her ear.

'You cannot believe that. This is *Posy*, Caro. Our Posy. She's a *Dahlia*.'

Caro jerked her head up to stare at her friend. 'Is that what you're really worried about, then? The Dahlia name being besmirched? Because if this were any other case you know we'd be asking the question. The police sure as hell will – and so will everyone else. She found the body, alone. She was covered in his blood. They had history – bad history, from what I could tell. For God's sake, Rosalind, she brained him with a book last week in the same dressing room where he was killed! We *have* to ask the question, or we're no Dahlias at all.' She kept her voice low, so no one else could hear her treacherous words. It was bad enough Rosalind looking at her like she didn't recognise her.

Of course she didn't want to believe Posy was a murderer – even if only by accident or in self-defence. But if she wasn't . . . then they'd missed something about Luke. A reason for someone else to hate him as much as Posy did.

But what?

Rosalind

She couldn't look at Caro, couldn't watch the worry in her eyes. Couldn't hear her suggest that their Posy might be a killer, after everything they'd been through together.

I thought we were stronger than this.

She'd thought *Caro* was better than this.

What had Luke Burrows told her that could make her believe Posy might kill him? What wasn't Caro telling her?

There were too many secrets between them. Too many things unsaid. And maybe it was too late to say them, now.

Awkward conversations had started up again around the bar after Caro's outburst, people trying to make sense of the incomprehensible events of the day. Memories about Luke, all rose-tinted, she was sure, but she listened in anyway in case there was a clue hiding in them.

And then the phone calls began.

Kit, first, which wasn't a surprise. Posy's boyfriend was away filming overseas again, but this news was already everywhere. He'd obviously known to call her rather than Caro, though, which was interesting. Maybe Posy had told him more about this business with her and Luke and Caro than Rosalind had been able to wangle out of her.

'I just saw the breaking news banner and Posy's name on it.' Kit's voice was tight, controlled, and Rosalind could hear the familiar sounds of a film set behind him. 'Before I get sucked into the social media speculation, you need to tell me what's really going on. Now.'

Kit had been caught up in murder investigations with them before – in fact, that was how he and Posy had met, back at Aldermere House. He also played Detective Inspector Johnnie Swain to Posy's Dahlia Lively in the latest movies – becoming a murder suspect himself when they were filming the first one. Of everyone, Kit would know exactly what Posy was going through. He had to be losing his mind not being there to support her.

Rosalind stepped outside the bar onto the spiral staircase to tell him what little they knew, listening to his worried breathing and watching the lights of the chandelier sparkle around the abandoned theatre foyer.

Kit let out a long breath. 'Should I get on a plane?'

'No,' Rosalind said. 'We're handling it. And you flying back to Britain right now . . . it would only add fuel to the story.'

'Right.' Kit didn't sound happy about the idea of staying away, but he didn't argue at least. 'How bad is it?'

'Don't check social media,' Rosalind replied. She had, back in the bar while waiting for their drinks, and none of it was good. The story was everywhere, and until the media had a better story to tell than 'reformed disgraced child star murders fellow actor' she couldn't see it going anywhere, either. And they'd thought the recurrence of press about stories from Posy's youth had been bad before.

'Your lawyer is there with her?' Kit asked. 'She's good?'

'Samantha is the best. If I can't be there with her, she's the next best thing. And if things go . . . further . . .'

'If they charge her with murder, you mean,' he said, bluntly.

'Samantha will know who to hire to get her off.' Rosalind swallowed. She sounded like Caro. 'To prove her innocence, I mean.'

On the other end of the phone, she heard someone calling for Kit. 'I think I preferred it when *I* was the police's prime suspect for a murder.' He sighed. 'You'll keep me up to date?'

'I will,' she promised, and let him go.

She didn't even make it back into the bar before her phone rang again, though; Jack this time. She stumbled through the same answers with him, including telling him not to come to London.

'I need to focus on Posy right now,' she explained, not adding that she couldn't cope with the idea of managing his emotions as well as her own, Caro's and Posy's right now.

'I can be there in three hours. Four at the most,' he said. 'If you need me. Just call.'

'I will,' she lied.

It was another hour – and another drink – before the phone call she was really waiting for came through. Rosalind fumbled to answer it, pacing back out of the bar towards the stairs as she listened to the confident, calm voice on the other end.

'So, I've persuaded them to let her go home for the night.' Samantha had been Rosalind's lawyer for over a decade now, dealing with everything from copyright infringement to libel. This was the first time she'd had to bring her in for a murder, though. 'She's pretty shaken up, poor kid.'

'Finding a body will do that to a person.' Rosalind leaned her head against the pale blue and gold wall behind her, wishing it would stop thumping.

'Normally I'd agree. But it's hardly her first time, is it? You'd think she'd know better than to touch the body.' Samantha sounded disbelieving, but Samantha didn't know Posy yet. She could forgive it in her.

'I'd imagine she hoped he was still alive and she could save him,' Rosalind said.

'That's her story,' Samantha confirmed.

'And do you believe it?'

'That's not my job here.' Was she hedging? Or just being a lawyer? Rosalind couldn't tell. 'But I think it's only the fact that she didn't have the murder weapon on her – and as far as I can establish the police haven't found it yet – that stopped them keeping her for the full twenty-four hours. That and the fact she only had blood on her hands and knees. If she'd been the one to cut his throat she'd have been covered in it. The stage-door kid helped her out too – Posy told them he'd followed her in when she went to her dressing room, and he confirmed it – although it seems he waited outside until she screamed.'

'But she couldn't have killed him. There wasn't time.' Rosalind felt her shoulders drop, even though of course she already knew that.

'A cut throat bleeds out fast,' Samantha said, bluntly. 'But the stage-door kid is on her side, he says there wasn't. Not when she supposedly found the body, anyway. But I haven't heard a time of death yet. If it was earlier in the day . . .'

She didn't need to finish the sentence for Rosalind to know that Posy was still very much in danger.

'And you're going to need someone more specialised than me to defend her, if the police dig up enough evidence to charge her formally,' Samantha went on. 'I'll email you over some names and CVs, and you can choose who you want. I don't think Posy has the space to even think about it right now.'

'Does she need me to pick her up?' Rosalind didn't have a car in town, but she could order one easily enough.

'I've put her in a cab home,' Samantha replied. 'You might want to go over there, though. I'm not sure that she should be alone tonight.'

'Agreed.'

After a few more logistical arrangements, Rosalind hung up, and glanced back into the bar. Caro was still sitting where she'd left her, but looked up the moment Rosalind walked back in.

'That was the lawyer?' Caro guessed.

Rosalind nodded. 'She got them to let Posy go home for the night. I'm going to go over there and . . . check on her. You should stay here.'

'Because she won't want to see me. Right.' Caro sounded mildly offended. Rosalind only just resisted the urge to remind her that she was the one who thought Posy was capable of murder.

There were more important things to do now than argue.

'You need to stick with the suspects,' she said, softly. 'If Luke was murdered after he left your rehearsal this afternoon, chances are it was by someone in your company who followed him, or somebody already at the Arcadia. So start by figuring out where everybody was, and when, okay? Then we'll regroup.'

Caro straightened up and nodded, and Rosalind grabbed her jacket and left.

Posy needed her.

Chapter Seven

It's a delight to see Caro Hooper take to the stage (for what I think might be the first time) in this joyous, life-affirming period piece. Despite being written only recently, it perfectly brings to life that homespun post-war feeling of the fifties in rural England – and gave this theatregoer the same vibe as a really good Sunday evening TV drama. Heart-warming!

Review of *Finding Freddie* on *Theatreland Today* blog

Caro

Caro didn't like being left behind, but under these particular circumstances she had to admit Rosalind was right – she was more useful where she was. Even if she didn't like how she'd left things between them.

It wasn't like Caro really thought Posy was a *murderer*. But Rosalind had to recognise that it was a possibility that, somehow, Posy had caused Luke's death. And they both had to face the fact that other people *would* believe it. Posy's past was chequered enough to be an actual chessboard, and once someone leaked the story of her causing him a head injury in the same dressing room just two days ago, along with all the photos doing the rounds of her standing on the step outside the stage door with blood on her hands, well. That was game over, wasn't it?

Pretending that wasn't true didn't help anyone. Caro wasn't being disloyal, just a realist.

But right now her job was finding alternative suspects.

Figuring out who from the *Finding Freddie* cast and crew had left the Prince Regent Theatre after rehearsals ended but before the police and fire brigade stopped anyone entering the Arcadia should be easy. Caro had been there, for a start. She'd double check with the stage-door log but, from memory, only Joshua, Darcy and Amber had not been around when she and Rosalind heard the sirens and headed out with the crowds to find out what was happening. Oh, and Piotr; Rosalind mentioned that he'd left the bar before her, and he'd not been with everyone else when they reached the Arcadia.

So, four suspects. And three of them were in the bar with her right now. That was a start, right?

What next?

What would Dahlia do?

She'd watch, Caro realised. People always thought Dahlia was constantly in motion, darting from one suspect to the next, asking questions, searching for clues, talking a mile a minute and saving the day. And she *was*, a lot of the time. It was when Caro felt most like her, doing all that.

But right now, she needed to utilise that other skill of Dahlia's, the one that she'd used with Luke.

She needed to watch. Observe. Take note, and piece it all together, so that later she could ask the right questions of the right people.

And she was in the perfect place to do that.

Caro didn't move from her seat, and she kept her glass clutched in her hand, but no one came to join her now she was alone. She was tainted by association, it seemed. Actors were a suspicious and a superstitious bunch. She'd been close to Luke, and he was killed. She was close to Posy, and she might have killed him.

That certainly seemed to be the consensus from the chatter she could overhear.

The buzz of conversation was low, but Caro had always had excellent hearing, and was halfway decent at lip reading after working on distance surveillance with Ashok, which helped.

Nearest her, standing at the bar itself, were their director and stage manager, Piotr and Amber, deep in conversation about what happened next. While Caro was sure they *were* both personally affected by the death of a friend, nobody would be able to tell it by looking at them. Right now, finding a way to ensure the show went on, after a respectful pause to acknowledge the death of its star, seemed to be their main priority.

'Joshua can step up to start with,' Piotr was saying. 'But he's not a name.'

'That was what we had Luke for.' Amber swilled the contents of her glass around thoughtfully, before adding, 'And Caro, I suppose.' Nice to know her own name recognition was still remembered, even if only as an afterthought.

'Is that enough, though? It's only a short run, after all – three months. But if sales plummet, it could get even shorter, and fast.' The line between Piotr's eyebrows deepened at the idea of the play being cancelled, after opening to such fanfare.

'That won't happen,' Amber reassured him. 'Think about it. We're now the play that got Luke Burrows murdered. That's a selling point in its own right – ghoulish as it sounds. The last role he ever played. That might get the punters in, don't you think?'

'Maybe if he'd been killed here . . .' Piotr worried at his right thumbnail with his teeth. 'But he died at the Arcadia, so they'll probably get most of the morbid trade, I'd have thought. What was he even doing over there?'

'No idea.' Amber sighed. 'One moment he was chatting with everyone after you called the break, the next he was heading out the stage door. I didn't think to ask him where he was going – I guessed he just wanted a smoke, or some air, or a break from everyone. I wish I had, now.'

Was there anyone in either theatre who knew *why* Luke was visiting Posy's dressing room? Someone must have let him in, mustn't they – presumably the stage-door keeper. Someone else to add to her list of people to talk to.

A member of front-of-house staff stopped by to murmur in Piotr's ear, before hurrying off again.

Piotr sighed. 'Right. Well, we need to do something about this lot. Get their attention, will you?'

Amber grabbed a spoon from behind the bar and clinked it against her glass, like they were at a wedding, not a wake. The bar fell silent, all the same.

'Friends, we have suffered a great loss today,' Piotr said, his sonorous voice projecting marvellously. Maybe it was the acoustics. 'I think it is natural that we should want to stay together and share our grief. But apparently the bar is closing, so I suggest that we move our solemn wake to the tapas bar, and supplement some of this alcohol with food. Agreed?'

Everyone did agree, and it didn't take long to get them all out of the theatre and round the corner to Carlos's restaurant. Caro hoped that some of Carlos's best wine might loosen some tongues.

La Vida Tapas Bar and Restaurant was unexpectedly busy when they entered. Apparently the cast of *Lights Out*, having been turfed out of their own theatre while the Arcadia was being examined as a murder scene, had all had the same idea as the *Finding Freddie* cast, and now there were twice as many thespians sobbing into their sangria over the loss of Luke Burrows.

Or twice as many suspects, depending on how you looked at it. Caro was leaning towards suspects.

She'd already figured out who from the Regent could have followed Luke to Posy's dressing room, and now she had the chance to narrow down the suspects from the Arcadia. It had been early; if she was lucky, not many of the cast or crew would have arrived at the theatre before the fire alarm sounded and the place was evacuated.

There was no sign of Mal, the stage-door keeper at the Arcadia, so Caro did the next best thing and made her way around the various *Lights Out* cast and crew, accepting and offering condolences as necessary, and casually asking if they'd been at the theatre when it happened, or if they'd seen Luke before his death.

'I just don't understand what he was doing over at the Arcadia in the first place,' she said, with a mystified air, and waited for the theories to flood in.

By the time the food was mostly gone, she'd spoken to almost everyone in the restaurant, playing the 'show mum' role in a way she'd never really wanted to before, offering hugs and platitudes to all and sundry.

And she'd learned a few things, at least. None of the cast she'd spoken to had been at the theatre – and all of them had reasonable alibis. She'd check that with Mal when he arrived, of course, but she trusted that the police would do a much better job of following up on who was where than she could. Although maybe she could get Ashok to talk to his police contact and double check.

The only people from the company who'd been at the theatre at the time were the director, the company stage manager and her stage management team, and they'd all been in a meeting together, in another part of the theatre. Unless the four of them were in it together, which Caro didn't find likely, talking to them, then they were out too.

Which left only the stage-door keeper and two missing actors to speak with. Mal, Posy and Taran.

Where *was* Taran? She was sure she'd seen him earlier, but now he seemed to have disappeared.

A movement outside the restaurant window caught her attention; even this late, there were still plenty of people passing by the busy streets, but the man she saw outside *wasn't* passing, he was lingering. Pacing, even.

Caro slipped outside, her Dahlia intuition tingling.

'Taran?'

Posy's co-star leaned against the wall beside the restaurant window, one hand cradled against his chest. In the streetlights, Caro could see blood on his knuckles. Had he hit the wall?

No. She scanned the area and saw, immediately, what had borne the brunt of Taran's anger or frustration. A poster, one of a run of three in plastic frames along an expanse of wall, advertising *Finding Freddie*. The plastic had splintered over images of her and Luke's faces.

Taran's shoulders slumped against the brickwork. 'I'm sorry. I just . . . today has been a lot.'

'You were close with Luke?' Caro moved to lean against the wall beside him, keeping a little space between them.

'I was friends with both of them.' Taran shook his head, staring down at his feet. 'I knew Posy was uncomfortable with Luke coming by the theatre, but I never thought—'

'Uncomfortable how?' Caro interrupted. She didn't want to hear the end of that sentence. *Was that how Rosalind felt with me?*

'Luke was trying to apologise. Make amends. Some twelve-step rubbish probably. Like he hoped they really could be friends again.' He glanced up at Caro. 'She didn't tell you?'

'No.' Posy hadn't told her much of anything recently. But Luke hadn't mentioned it, either. When she'd asked, he'd said he was giving her space. Especially after the book incident.

But she *had* said something about him bringing her a gift the night she threw the book at him. And then he'd delivered flowers to the Arcadia that afternoon. Had they been for Posy? If she'd been allowed into the scene of the crime, maybe she could have found out.

'Were you at the theatre when the fire alarm went off?' Caro asked him, casually, but Taran ignored her, almost as if he hadn't heard at all.

'You know, I was at drama school with Luke, and I'd worked with him a couple of times over the years.' Taran stared up at the summer sky as he spoke, at the full, solstice moon overhead and the sprinkle of stars visible through the light pollution. 'Back then, I'd have told her to keep her distance – not that she needed me to. She knew Luke better than I ever did, I guess. But this summer . . . he really did seem to have changed, you know? Cleaned up his act. He . . . he came to see me, too, and we had a good conversation. He was even helping me out with some career moves – mentioned my name to the right people to get me a TV audition next week. I think . . . I think if Posy had given him a chance, she might have even liked him. I didn't expect that.'

He fell silent and, after a moment or two, Caro took him inside to present him to Amber and her ever-present first-aid kit, so she could clean him up.

Amber, who'd been talking with Gabriella, the daughter of the restaurant owner, threw her hands up and sighed. 'Come on. Let's fix you up.'

'Is he all right?' Caro turned to find Gabriella eyeing Taran with concern. Her eyes were red and swollen. Apparently Luke's death was affecting everybody.

'He'll be fine. It's just been a difficult day.' Caro tried for a reassuring smile.

'Of course. Luke . . .' Gabriella broke off. 'We got to know him a bit here, you know? We got to know all of them.'

'Did you ever notice any . . . tension between Luke and Taran?' Caro asked. Taran's explanation about how Luke had changed was one thing, but punching out a poster of him? That felt like something else. Something unresolved.

'Luke and Taran?' Gabriella's eyebrows jumped in surprise at the question. 'No, they seemed friendly. Everybody liked Luke.'

She gave Caro another sad smile before moving away to clear plates and glasses.

'Everybody liked Luke,' Caro muttered, under her breath. 'That's the problem.'

Rosalind

Posy kept telling them that the area in which she'd bought her flat was up-and-coming, but Rosalind had yet to see any evidence of it beyond the vegan deli on the corner. When Posy didn't answer her buzz on the door plate with the numbered buttons, Rosalind pulled out her phone and called her while pressing the button at the same time.

Her phone was off. That made sense; she had to be getting a million calls from journalists and gossip websites – not to mention all those well-meaning friends she hadn't heard from in years who'd suddenly come out of the woodwork now there was a scandal to get the gossip on.

Rosalind knew only too well how that went.

She could sense that she was being watched; a couple of paparazzi must have tracked Posy down already. Maybe even followed her home from the police station, now the news was breaking. It wouldn't be long before this road was packed and Posy couldn't step outside her front door without dealing with reporters.

Rosalind pressed the buzzer again. She was about to start pressing all the buzzers for every other flat in the building when a delivery driver swung off his bike and pressed for the floor below Posy's. When the door opened, she slipped in behind him as if she'd been invited, and hurried away to Posy's front door before anyone could ask any questions.

Hammering on the flat door didn't get her very far, either, until she gave up and yelled, 'Posy! It's me – let me in before someone calls the police. Again.'

There was a shuffle of movement inside the flat, and finally the sound of locks being undone.

Posy looked terrible. Rosalind wasn't sure that she'd ever seen the youngest Dahlia looking anything except perky and beautiful and fresh and young. But today terrible was the only word for it. Her hair hung limply around her pale face, the bags under her eyes dark and hollow. She'd changed out of the clothes she'd been in at the theatre – the police had probably taken them, Rosalind assumed – and she'd washed away the blood from her hands. Or mostly; on closer inspection, Rosalind spotted dried blood around the nail beds.

'I don't think I can take any more police today,' she said, flatly. 'Otherwise I might not have answered the door.'

Rosalind made a decision. She'd never been the mothering sort, but neither had Posy's own mother, by all accounts. And she and Caro couldn't always leave the coddling to Annie or Kit.

She was what Posy had right now, so she would do her best. Murder investigations would have to wait until Posy was at least closer to being herself again.

'Right. Here's what's going to happen now,' she said. 'You're going to get in the shower, then put on some of those godawful sweatpants you love, and meanwhile I'm going to order us some food and put the kettle on. Okay?'

Rosalind wasn't entirely sure, but she thought she might see a hint of relief in Posy's eyes. Sometimes, a person needed someone else to tell them what to do, when even making a simple decision like what to eat for dinner was too much.

'Okay,' Posy said, softly, before padding away towards the bathroom.

Rosalind took a deep breath, held it, then let it out again.

Then she grabbed the stack of takeaway menus off the kitchen counter and began the internal debate of which global cuisine best said 'I'm sorry you're a murder suspect.'

Posy didn't look all that much better after her shower, but at least she'd pulled her damp hair back into a clip and smelled more fragrant. *Hand cream*, Rosalind realised, as she watched Posy rub her fingers over the backs of her hands, over and over. *She's trying to get rid of the blood.*

If Posy was going full Lady Macbeth they were in trouble.

What had Posy been thinking? Rosalind had been over and over it in her head on the drive to the flat, and she still had no idea. Posy knew better than to touch a body or disturb a crime scene. She'd certainly seen enough of them before. But perhaps when it had been

Luke there in her dressing room – someone who she'd once known so well – she'd simply acted on instinct. It was the only explanation that made sense to her.

'I've ordered Chinese,' Rosalind said, as Posy stopped hovering by her bedroom door and re-entered the living area. 'I thought something classic and simple was probably best. There are spring rolls. I know they're your favourite.'

Posy's smile was forced as she dropped into her armchair and watched Rosalind fluttering around the lounge, tidying up magazines and papers that didn't need tidying, before turning to straighten the cushions on the sofa.

Rosalind *never* fluttered. Jack wouldn't know what to make of her if he saw her.

But she needed to do *something*.

'I'm sorry we couldn't come to the police station,' Rosalind said. 'The police wouldn't let us near you and I thought, well, Samantha would be more use than we were.'

'Thank you for sending her.' Posy's voice was dry, hoarse. Like she'd been talking for hours. Or crying in the shower. Or both. 'She was very . . . efficient.'

'She is that.' Rosalind cast around for something else to say, but Posy beat her to it.

'You're here now, anyway. But . . . you came alone?'

Of course she'd noticed that Caro wasn't here. And of course she'd infer certain things from that.

Things Rosalind absolutely wasn't going to confirm, like the fact that Caro might actually suspect Posy of the murder.

'I left Caro in the bar at the Regent, keeping an eye on the suspects.' Rosalind gave up on her tidying and sat on the edge of the sofa cushions instead.

'Suspects?' Posy barked a harsh laugh. 'As far as I can tell, there's only one. Me.'

'Except you didn't kill Luke Burrows.' There was no question mark at the end of Rosalind's statement, no hint of doubt, and she held Posy's gaze the whole time, daring her to try and deny it.

Whatever Caro said about entertaining possibilities and what the police believed, what Posy needed from them right now was blind faith. And Rosalind was the only one who seemed able to give it to her.

In return, hopefully Posy would give Rosalind her full version of events.

Finally, the buzzer rang – the Chinese, of course – and Posy flinched away as Rosalind went to answer it.

She waited until all the food was laid out on the coffee table before she spoke again.

'Posy, you know I want to help you. I want to find who really did this so we can prove your innocence.' Posy didn't reply, just watched her steadily over her spring rolls, so Rosalind took a breath and continued. 'I need to know, what happened today? And what did you tell the police?'

'I told them what happened,' Posy replied, softly. 'Everything that happened today.'

'And will you tell me?'

It took a moment before Posy nodded. Then she started to speak.

'I was at the theatre a little early, before the alarm went off. I planned to do some reading – I'd left a script in my dressing room that my agent was waiting for me to feed back on. So I was probably the only one at the theatre then – you'd have to check with Mal. I signed in with him on the door and then . . . I went towards my dressing room, but the alarm went off before I reached it. So I turned around and headed out again.'

'Caro said she thought she saw you in the crowd.' That was good, that she'd been with witnesses then. Less good was the part where she was alone in the dressing-room corridors – and they only had her word for it that she'd never made it to her room, and potentially Luke. 'Mal didn't mention Luke coming by the theatre to see you?' Posy shook her head. Did that mean that he hadn't come in through the stage door? Or that he sneaked in after Posy had left? That seemed less likely, given the police presence. Hopefully Caro would clarify with the stage-door keeper who was at the theatre when. In the meantime . . . 'Go on.'

'Once we got the all-clear about the fire, and we knew the performance was cancelled for tonight, I was going to head straight home. But then I remembered about that damn script.' Posy swallowed, looking down at the cartons of untouched Chinese food. 'I asked Mal if I could sneak in and get it, and he said okay. But he came with me, all the way to my dressing-room door. He waited outside and I pushed the door open and reached for the script on my dressing table and then . . .'

'You saw Luke?' Rosalind prompted, when her voice faded away.

Posy nodded. 'In the mirror. I don't think . . . I wouldn't have seen him otherwise. He was right in the corner, almost behind the chair, like he'd been pushed there. But I saw his reflection in the mirror. The blood . . . I panicked – I thought he must have hurt himself – so I ran over to check he was okay. It was only after I turned his head I realised how much blood there was. It was dark, you see – the bulb has gone in there and I still haven't replaced it. He had no pulse, and when I pulled my hands away they were covered in blood. I think . . .'

She wrung her hands so tightly her fingers were white. 'I think he must have been stabbed in the neck, or had an artery cut, or something.'

'That would certainly mean a lot of blood.' Rosalind's mind was already whirring with possibilities. 'What happened next?'

Posy dropped her chopsticks into the spring-roll carton. 'Mal, our stage-door keeper, came in behind me. I think I screamed. He came running in and started saying, "Oh God, oh God," so I got up and he backed away from me. Like he thought I'd done it.'

'He wasn't with you when you found the body?' Rosalind pressed.

Posy shook her head. 'No. He'd waited outside. Anyway, that was when I ran back to the stage door to call for help.'

And the whole world had seen her, pale and panicked, with blood on her hands. Rosalind hadn't been back on social media since she left the bar, but the photos had already been everywhere.

Posy looked guilty in them. That was going to be their first and biggest problem.

But everything she'd told her tallied with what Samantha had said, so at least her story was consistent. If Mal was backing her up the way Samantha had intimated he was, that might be enough. The police wouldn't want to risk getting this one wrong. Accusing an innocent celebrity of murder wouldn't go down well – even if the public believed it. They'd need evidence – forensics and such. And that would take time.

Time they could use to find the *actual* murderer.

'What did the police say to you? Did they give you any information about what they thought happened, or when?'

Posy gave Rosalind a dry smile. 'Rosalind, they think I killed him.'

They weren't the only ones, unfortunately. 'Okay, so we know that they're idiots. Anything else? Did you see a weapon there?' Samantha had said she didn't think the police had found it yet, but she wanted to hear it from Posy. Especially if there was any chance that Posy *had* found it and had done something even more stupid than touching the body, like hidden a bloody knife that now had her fingerprints on it and was just waiting to be discovered.

Posy paused, eyebrows furrowed, and Rosalind knew she'd be running back over the scene in the dressing room in her mind – as horrific as it was. 'He was on his side, and I pulled him up to feel for his pulse. There was blood seeping from the wound, but it wasn't gushing any more, and I don't remember seeing anything that could have caused that kind of wound, I don't think.'

'You don't think?'

Posy screwed her eyes tight. 'It was dark. But . . . no. There was nothing there.'

Rosalind relaxed, just a touch. 'Well, that's a start, then. What happened to the murder weapon? You can be sure the police will be asking that question. And now, we have a timeline of events, so that's good too.' She hadn't made notes, and neither had Posy, but she'd be sure to type the major events into the notes app of her phone before she spoke to Caro.

'Posy, do you know why Luke was at the Arcadia today in the first place? You hadn't . . . arranged to meet him or anything?'

Posy stared at her, wide-eyed. 'No. Of course not. He . . . he's shown up a couple of times. With presents. Probably it was just that again.'

'Presents?' She'd mentioned a gift before, hadn't she? 'What sort of presents?'

'The guilt-tripping sort.' Posy jumped to her feet, collecting containers of barely touched food and moving them to the kitchen counter. 'Things to remind me that we used to be . . . together. A signed script from an old movie we were both in. That kind of thing. Presents that would make me feel bad about not wanting to forgive him.'

'Did you tell the police about them?' What would the detectives in charge of the case make of that, she wondered? Would there be a conversation about stalking? Self-defence? A plea bargain even?

She was getting ahead of herself. Worse, she was thinking like Caro.

'Of course I did,' Posy said. 'I'm not an idiot.'

'No, of course not. I didn't mean to imply . . .' Rosalind trailed off, knowing that her next question was only going to annoy her friend more. But Caro had been right about one thing – they had to ask the difficult questions in this case. It was the only way to solve it. 'Posy, I just need you to confirm one thing. You definitely didn't go into your dressing room, or see Luke at all, the first time you arrived at the theatre?'

Posy turned from the kitchen counter to stare at her. 'Don't you believe me?'

'Of course I do,' Rosalind said, calmly. 'But I can't help you if I don't have all the facts.'

And she couldn't shake the feeling that there was *something* Posy still wasn't telling them.

Posy's lips twisted into an ironic smile. 'You know, Rosalind, I appreciate your efforts, but you might be the only person interested in actual facts in this whole case. For everyone else, gossip and theories are going to be more than enough to convict me – in the court of public opinion if not a legal one.' She left the food on the counter and stalked towards her bedroom door, shutting it firmly behind her.

Rosalind stared after her for a long moment. Then she put the food away in the fridge and let herself out of the building, still thinking hard about everything she'd learned that night, and what the hell they were going to do next.

Chapter Eight

'Would you like me to call Inspector Johnnie, Miss?' Bess asked, anxiously.

Dahlia shook her head. 'No thank you, Bess. He's made it clear that he can manage without me. So I shall manage perfectly well without him, too.'

Dahlia Lively in *Love Her to Death*
By Lettice Davenport, 1961

Caro

Caro was sure that the tapas bar would normally have closed by now, but Carlos seemed happy to stay open for the assorted casts and crew that had gathered there for Luke's informal wake.

Drinks were still flowing when the door opened once more and Mal, the stage-door keeper at the Arcadia, entered, looking tired and about ten years older than the last time Caro had seen him. Since he usually looked about twelve, even looking his real age he was still clearly the youngest in the room, except for Gabriella.

Silence fell over the restaurant as the door swung shut behind him, and for a moment everything froze. Then Taran stepped forward to guide him to a chair, motioning to Gabriella for another glass, and everyone huddled closer to hear what he had to say.

'Thanks, guys. I . . . I just got done at the police station and I wanted to update everyone. And I guess I . . . well, I didn't want to be alone.' Mal took a large gulp of the red wine Gabriella handed him.

'How were things?' Caro managed to ease herself into the chair beside him, as the others gathered up a plate of the remaining food for him. 'What did they want to know?'

'Everything.' Mal huffed a small laugh. 'Several times. I think they let Posy go home before I did.'

That would be thanks to Rosalind's sharp-talking lawyer, Caro assumed. 'You told them everything that happened?'

Mal nodded, then took another gulp of wine. The others had grown distracted again, probably due to the fresh round of drinks Gabriella was serving, which meant that Caro could ask all the questions she wanted, too. Except . . . Mal looked exhausted, and probably questioned out. Which meant she had to ask only the questions that really mattered, to get the most important answers before he flaked out on her.

She wanted to ask everything. But she forced herself to be strategic about it. Rosalind was with Posy; she'd get the basic timeline of her movements from her. Caro needed to ask Mal the things Posy *wouldn't* know.

'Mal, I know you must be done with answering questions by now. But for Posy's sake . . . can you answer just one or two of mine?'

He gave her a weary look, and reached for his fork. 'I'll do my best. But honestly . . . I don't know what you think you can ask or find out that the police haven't already.'

'I know. I'm sure they've been very thorough. But sometimes . . . solving a case like this takes a new perspective.'

Mal sat up just a little bit straighter. 'You don't think Posy did it either.'

'I'm hoping to prove she didn't.' That much was true, at least. 'Can you tell me, who else was in the backstage area of the theatre when Luke arrived? And what time was that?'

'Nobody, except me,' Mal said. 'There was a meeting going on somewhere front of house, but it was quiet backstage. Still early. Luke came in at . . . the police have the logs, so I can't check, but I think just around five thirty, maybe five forty at the latest.'

That tracked with when Luke had left the Prince Regent. He must have gone straight over to the Arcadia, and any of her suspects so far could have followed him.

'And Posy? When did she arrive?'

Mal reached for his wine, staring down into his glass at the mention of her name. 'After Luke but before the alarm. I'd have to check the logs for the exact time. And before you ask, she was the only person to come in through the stage door during that time.'

'You're sure?'

He gave a hollow laugh. 'Very.'

The alarm had gone off around six, maybe five past, she was pretty certain. So that didn't leave a lot of time for a murder.

'Okay, so what happened after the alarm went off? Were you in charge of checking everyone was out of the building?' Caro asked.

Mal shook his head. 'Above my pay grade. Technically the stage manager is responsible for the cast and crew in case of a fire, and the front-of-house staff deal with the audience. But there was hardly anyone in the theatre. I handed the stage-door log to our stage manager, Pollie, when she and the others appeared together from their meeting, but I think we knew it wasn't serious before she even got to checking it. They still should have checked all the rooms, but

Luke's body . . . I can see how they might have missed it. It was dark in that room and he was kind of hidden. They'd probably just have called out for anyone there to get out and if he was already dead . . .'

'Yeah. I can see that.' Caro had once got locked in a bathroom during a fire drill and nobody had noticed until she'd phoned to tell them. Once they knew the fire wasn't actually in the theatre, everyone would have relaxed. And then Posy had arrived with blood on her hands, so it had been a moot point.

'None of this matters anyway.' Mal drained the rest of his wine. 'The police have access to the stage-door logs *and* the theatre CCTV. They'll be checking it, and they'll know exactly who went in and out. I did my best, only answering what they asked me, like they say to in the cop shows, but I'm not about to start lying to the police, not even for Posy.'

'Where are the cameras?' Caro asked, trying to get him back on track. Mal was obviously indulging in some sort of TV stardom daydream, making himself the hero, saving Posy from herself. But the cameras might be useful. Maybe Ashok could get her access to the footage – or Mal might show her once the police let them back into the Arcadia again.

'We don't have them everywhere,' Mal said. 'But there's one above the stage-door counter and others showing areas around the stage and auditorium.'

He got to his feet. 'Now, if we're done, I need to get to bed. I think tomorrow's going to be another long day, especially once the police get a proper look at that CCTV.'

'Why?' Caro felt a slight pang of unease at his words. What if Mal wasn't just making himself the hero after all?

'Because they're going to see that Posy arrived at the theatre twice before the alarm went off, but she only left once.'

Rosalind

Rosalind knew from experience that the worst thing to do with disagreements and fallings out was to let them fester. Obviously, that didn't mean she always faced things head-on in her *own* life, but when it came to Caro and Posy, she had no intention of letting a potential rift develop for any longer than necessary. Which meant getting them all together, working on finding a murder suspect who *wasn't* Posy, as soon as possible.

Posy didn't want to go out in public, understandably, and the Arcadia Theatre was still a crime scene, so they met the next afternoon at the Prince Regent in Caro's dressing room instead. Not exactly the neutral territory Rosalind had been hoping for, but probably better than Posy's flat – which was now being staked out by paparazzi they had to dodge to get into the car Rosalind had ordered.

Besides, Caro needed to be on stage that night. The afternoon's matinee had been cancelled, but the producers didn't want to lose any more money, so . . .

'Apparently the respectful mourning period is over and the show must go on,' she said, as she waved them both inside.

The smallness of the room made the tension between them all loom even larger. They each settled into their own seats – Caro on the stool by her dressing table and mirror, Rosalind in a comfortable armchair that took up a large corner of the room, and Posy perched on an old steamer trunk opposite, looking down at her hands in her lap.

Then, silence.

Finally, Rosalind cleared her throat. Obviously this was all going to be up to her. As usual.

'Right. So, first things first. It seems we have another investigation on our hands.'

'Are you sure we shouldn't leave this one to the police?' Posy's voice was dull, and so unlike her it made Rosalind's chest ache. 'I was thinking about it last night, and the only way anyone is ever going to believe I'm innocent is if the *police* decide I am.'

Judging by the bags under her eyes, Posy had been dwelling on this *all* night. Which might explain her erroneous conclusions. She had to know by now that they were more motivated and more likely to find the real killer than the police, surely?

'The only way people are going to believe you didn't do it is if we find someone else who *did*,' Caro said, bluntly.

Posy's head jerked up to stare at her. Rosalind decided it was probably time to intervene. Already.

'But proving your innocence can't hurt, either. Let's start with what we already know.'

Posy was silent, so Rosalind started by filling Caro in on everything Posy had told her the night before about her movements at the theatre.

'That tallies with what Mal told me,' Caro confirmed. 'Except for one thing. He said . . . he said you arrived at the theatre twice. But only left once?'

That got Posy's attention. She blinked up at Caro. 'No, I didn't.'

'According to the CCTV you did,' Caro said. 'So the police believe you did – or they will once they've seen it.'

Posy jumped to her feet. 'I . . . why would I . . .'

Rosalind took her hand to try and calm her down. 'Look, why don't you talk us through the rest of your movements yesterday? Before you arrived at the theatre, I mean.'

'You're trying to find me an alibi,' Posy said, dropping back down to her seat. 'Of course, I'd have one already if *someone* hadn't stood me up.' She glared at Caro, who looked to Rosalind in confusion.

'What's she talking about?'

'*She* is talking about the message you sent me!' Posy pulled out her phone and shoved it towards them. 'See? You asked me to meet you for coffee and then you never showed up. That's the only reason I went to the theatre early at all, because you stood me up, and I figured I might as well use the time to read that damn script.'

Caro took the phone from her, frowning at the screen. 'But I . . . I didn't send this message.'

'Looks like it's from you, though,' Rosalind said, peering over her shoulder.

'But I didn't send it,' Caro insisted. 'I was rehearsing all afternoon. We only broke for the day an hour before the fire alarm went off over at the Arcadia, and we all went out to see what was going on.'

Caro stared at the phone in confusion for another moment, then pulled out her own phone and scrolled through to her last chat with Posy.

'No message on mine,' she said. 'Did you respond?'

'Just gave it a thumbs up, I think,' Posy said.

'Then it's been deleted,' Rosalind surmised. 'If Caro didn't send it, someone else must have, then deleted it from her phone while leaving it on yours.' Jack hadn't quite got the hang of editing WhatsApp messages yet, and often deleted messages when he'd misspelled or misphrased something, then sent them again. But just as often he only deleted them from his phone, rather than for everyone, and she ended up with a raft of grammatically challenged messages as well as the correct ones.

'I lost my phone,' Caro said, suddenly. 'Well, not really. I thought I'd left it in my dressing room, but it turned out I'd put it down somewhere in the wings. Someone must have used it then, without me knowing.'

'Don't you have Face ID on it?' Posy asked.

Caro pulled a face Rosalind was sure her phone wouldn't recognise. 'I did. But it kept not working. Every time I put my sunglasses on, or my reading glasses. Or first thing in the morning when I'd just woken up, for that matter. It was getting insulting. I mean, it's my face! So I just switched to the passcode instead.'

Which Rosalind – and Posy – knew from past experience was Caro and Annie's wedding anniversary date, to make sure Caro didn't ever forget it again. It was also something that anyone in the theatre could have seen her putting in at any time, and remembered, if they planned to use it. That didn't narrow things down at all. If they'd picked up the phone quickly enough after Caro set it down, it might not even have been locked to begin with.

'The big question isn't *how* someone got hold of Caro's phone and sent that message,' Rosalind said, dragging them back on track. Finally, they had a clue and they were not going to waste it arguing about how Caro could better use her iPhone. 'The most important question is *why would they send it in the first place?*'

The other two fell silent. But not for very long. Rosalind could hear the cogs whirring now.

'The coffee shop the text said to meet at was miles away from the theatre,' Posy said. 'I remember being annoyed because it was so out of the way, and I couldn't understand why you wanted to go so far away from the theatres unless . . . well. I kind of assumed you wanted to talk to me about Luke, somewhere no one from either of our casts would see us.'

Caro nodded. 'That makes sense. Someone wanted you away from the Arcadia. Why?'

'To frame me?' Posy suggested. 'If I arrived at the theatre twice, I mean . . .'

'The first Posy was someone disguised as you, you think?' Rosalind guessed. 'And they sent that message to keep you out of the way – they probably expected you to wait longer for Caro, or at least not rush back to the theatre.'

'I wouldn't have done if it wasn't for the script,' Posy admitted. 'I probably wouldn't have been there that early otherwise, but I am usually the first there. Maybe they didn't want to take any chances.'

'We need to tell the police about this.' Rosalind reached for her phone, but Posy stopped her.

'Let's talk through the rest of it first,' she said. 'I don't want to be calling them every five minutes if we figure out anything else.'

That made sense, she supposed. Posy had already spent enough time being questioned. She'd want to get it all over with in one go.

'Fine. Let's go over the timeline, then,' she suggested, waiting for Posy to pull out her usual notebook.

Except, she didn't. Finally, Rosalind pulled up the notes app on her phone and went through what they had so far and added in anything extra from Caro, including her suspect rundown.

It didn't take long to fill out what they already knew.

Early that afternoon, Posy had received the text message from Caro's phone, and headed off to the relevant coffee shop an hour later, reaching there at 4.30 p.m. as requested. She returned to the Arcadia, having been stood up, just before 6.00 p.m.

'But you didn't make it to your dressing room?' Rosalind asked.

Posy shook her head. 'The fire alarm went off before I got there.'

That got noted down, too.

Rosalind turned to Caro. 'What time did Luke leave rehearsals?'

'Five thirty, or so, I think. It can't have been more than half an hour before the alarm. We were all over at the Arcadia to find out what was going on by just after six.'

'And then we were kept outside for a while – until after seven, I think,' Posy said. 'Because we had to cancel the performance that should have started at seven thirty.'

'And that's when you went back into the theatre to find your script – and found Luke's body instead.' Rosalind sat back in her armchair.

Well. That gave them the timeline – and a very narrow window of opportunity for the murder. Somewhere between five thirty and six, someone had lured Luke into Posy's dressing room, knowing she wouldn't be there, and killed him, then escaped.

'Is the fire linked, do we think?' Posy asked, staring down at her empty hands.

'I don't know,' Rosalind admitted. 'It could be, if the murderer hoped that burning down the theatre would hide the evidence of the murder and destroy Luke's body. But if that was the case, you'd hope they'd do a better job of setting the fire, wouldn't you?'

'And why bother trying to frame Posy if they were going to burn the place down anyway?' Caro shrugged. 'Feels like overkill, don't you think?'

'A coincidence, then?' Posy said the 'c' word with obvious distaste. Rosalind knew how she felt. She always hated it when things just *happened*, and had nothing to do with their case other than muddying the waters.

'It looks like. Taran told me the firemen said it looked like a cigarette stub flicked into the bins around the side of the theatre,' Caro said. 'If they were trying to burn the place down, I doubt that is how they'd go about it.'

'But it might have been enough to hide the murder for a while longer, and muddy the waters,' Rosalind mused. 'If Posy hadn't gone inside to fetch that script, it might have been tomorrow before the body was found.'

'So it's either a very convenient coincidence or meticulously planned.' Posy sighed. 'Great.'

Despite Posy's frustration, it finally felt like they were working together as the three Dahlias again. Yes, things were still tense and unsettled, but the old rhythms were falling into place, like muscle memory.

At least until Caro said, 'Now she's given us her account of events, I think Posy should sit the rest of this investigation out.'

Posy was on her feet objecting before Rosalind could even groan at Caro's insensitivity.

'No, hear me out,' Caro insisted. 'It's your life and reputation on the line here. The more you're involved the less people will believe whatever plausible answers we come up with. You *can't* meddle in this one.'

'Meddle?' Posy scoffed. 'It's precisely *because* it's my reputation on the line that I *have* to be involved! What else am I supposed to do? Trust that you really do have my best interests at heart? You already chose Luke over me once. How am I supposed to believe that you won't do it again?'

Caro looked taken aback. 'I didn't—'

'Yes, you did. And don't try to pretend you're not treating me as a suspect.' Posy pointed a finger at her. 'You know, one of the first things Rosalind said when she came to my flat last night was "you didn't kill Luke Burrows". But you haven't said anything like that, have you? It's all "we have to pin this on someone else", or "whatever plausible answers we come up with". Because you . . . you really think I did it, don't you? You think that I killed Luke.'

'I never said that.' Caro folded her arms and tried to stare Posy down.

It was, Rosalind noted with a twinge in her chest, not a denial. However stridently she'd defended Posy to the rest of the cast in the bar the night before, Caro *did* have doubts.

'You didn't have to,' Posy said, softly. 'Don't bother telling the police about that text message. I'll do it myself when they drag me back in for questioning again.'

Then she grabbed her bag and walked out.

Rosalind looked at Caro. 'Well. That went well.'

Chapter Nine

Dahlia stared flatly through the bars of the small cell at Johnnie, who was looking far more amused than she felt was really appropriate in the circumstances. 'Are you going to straighten all this out and get me out of here or not?'

'Oh absolutely,' Johnnie replied. 'Just give me a moment to enjoy it first, eh?'

Dahlia Lively in *The Other Foot*
By Lettice Davenport, 1939

Caro

Caro stood in the doorway and watched as Posy pushed her way out of the Prince Regent theatre, leaving Darcy pressed against the wall as she went.

'Of course I don't think she killed him,' Caro muttered, well aware that she hadn't actually been quite so definitive when Posy was in the room. But she *didn't*, not really. She just knew they had to accept it was a possibility if they were going to investigate properly – and letting Posy investigate *herself* was a recipe for disaster.

Assume nothing. Believe nothing. Check everything. Those were the ABCs of investigation, and Caro intended to follow them. Even if it meant Posy hating her for a little while.

She'd forgive her once Caro solved the case and proved her innocence. Wouldn't she?

Rosalind sighed, and gave Caro her disappointed look. Caro let it roll over her. It wasn't exactly the first time.

'I suppose we'll just have to see how far we can get with this investigation on our own, then,' Rosalind said.

Caro shut the dressing-room door. 'Are you worried that she didn't want us to tell the police about that message I didn't send?' Was there something Posy wasn't telling them?

Rosalind's eyebrows jerked upwards. 'She said she would tell them. If she's being framed, what reason would she have not to?'

'I don't know.' Caro worried at her lower lip with her teeth. It didn't make any sense, but then, what about this case did?

She hurried back to her dressing table and picked up her handbag. She didn't have a notebook in there – she mostly just left herself voice notes on her phone when she needed to remember something – but Caro managed to find a couple of pages of something she could write on the back of, and a pen somewhere in the depths of her bag.

Clearly notes on a phone weren't working for them, and writing things down had always worked for Posy, so maybe it was time to give it a go.

'First off, we need to look into who had a motive to kill Luke.' She wrote MOTIVE on the top of the first page.

'Except we already did that, didn't we?' Rosalind's voice was dry. 'Aren't you the one who gleefully told me yesterday that even Ashok agreed Luke had changed his ways? That everyone loved him now?'

Well, yes, she had done that, while they were loitering outside the Arcadia after the fire alarm. 'Then we must have missed something. Because someone hated him enough to kill him, right? And if it wasn't Posy . . .'

'Then it could be anyone in London,' Rosalind finished, despondently.

No, that was no good either. They needed firm suspects. A closed circle, like in the Dahlia books. 'Not if they used my phone to send a message to Posy, or pretended to be Posy to get into the Arcadia. It has to be someone with access to both theatres, and history with Luke – so somebody here at the Regent – and I've already narrowed that list down to four people – or someone at the Arcadia – which I've got narrowed down to two. Maybe three.' She hadn't included Mal last night, but he was the one who'd been in charge of the stage door. They had to count him too, right?

'Give me the names.' Rosalind grabbed another sheet of paper – possibly the back of a royalty statement from her publisher now Caro looked at it. She probably needed that for her taxes.

Rosalind wrote SUSPECTS across the top and Caro dutifully recited the names of the possible culprits she'd come up with the night before. 'Piotr, Joshua, Darcy or Amber here at the Regent, Mal and Taran at the Arcadia. And, well, Posy.'

Taran never had answered the question about where he'd been at the time of the murder. And while Mal was adamant that nobody had come in through the stage door, getting into a theatre wasn't like breaking into Fort Knox. There were passages between the front of house and backstage, and no stage-door keeper could be infallible at tracking everyone who entered. There was security, yes, but it wasn't impossible to breach.

And if Posy hadn't done it, someone else must have got in too. If it was her double at the stage door, they'd still managed to *leave* without being seen.

'You're right.' Rosalind stared at the list. 'If Posy is being set up, it has to be by someone who knows her, too – and that she had history with Luke. That would include all these people, I'm guessing.'

'We need to see the CCTV,' Caro said. 'If our killer pretended to be Posy to get in, odds are good it was a woman if they convinced Mal. That could cut our list down to two.' They could have this solved by dinnertime if they were really focused.

But Rosalind shook her head. 'Unless she wasn't working alone. If the killer didn't come in through the stage door, they'd need to go through the pass door in the auditorium to get backstage – and they might need an accomplice for that. And for framing Posy.'

Speculation, of course. But she had a point. They couldn't rule it out.

The Arcadia was a bigger theatre than the Regent. Mal said it had been quiet backstage at the time of the murder, but there were still bars and even the occasional theatre tour there. Not to mention the front-of-house staff. It might not have been busy, but it wouldn't have been empty either.

'Should have known it wouldn't have been as easy as narrowing our list down to two women from the off,' Caro grumbled. 'Well, I guess we start with the cast here at the Regent, right? We're the people Luke had been spending the most time with lately. Who do we talk to first?'

'Significant other?' Rosalind suggested. 'He was dating Darcy from the cast, yes?'

'Yes. Actually, that's a point!' Caro beamed. 'She might be our strongest lead. Remember how I followed Luke yesterday morning? He only stayed a couple of minutes at his father's, where he told Darcy he'd be, then went to meet another woman at some business or another. I don't know what it was about, but he told Darcy he'd met up with an old friend. She was watching him quite carefully when he was talking to Joshua yesterday afternoon, like maybe she was a little suspicious about something? Might be nothing, but it could also be a start . . .'

'If Darcy suspected Luke was lying to her or cheating on her, she might have followed him to the Arcadia,' Rosalind agreed. 'Did it look like he was?'

Caro pulled a face. 'Not really. But we should try and track down this other woman, all the same. I'll get Ashok to check out the address I saw them at, and maybe see if he can do anything with the photos I took. Facial recognition and what have you.' She wasn't sure how likely it was to work, but it had to be worth a shot.

Darcy had disappeared around the time Luke left the theatre and had then been lurking around the Arcadia when Caro and Rosalind got there after the alarm went off. That gave her opportunity, and a possible motive. She had to be first on their list to talk to.

Something in Caro's chest loosened a little now they had a firm plan of action. Talk to Darcy. Find a killer. Make up with Posy.

Easy. She hoped.

Rosalind

The only problem with Rosalind and Caro's carefully crafted plan to question Darcy was that Darcy was nowhere to be found.

'She was here,' Eddie, the Regent's stage-door keeper confirmed. 'But she had to pop back out for something. She didn't say what. She'll be back, though.'

'Who *is* here right now?' Caro asked, leaning over the desk to look at the log. 'How about Joshua?'

'Should be in his dressing room.'

'Perfect.' She dragged Rosalind away, back towards the dressing rooms. 'He was one of the last people to talk to Luke before he left the theatre – him and then Amber. I was there for Luke's conversation with Amber, but I'd really like to know what he and Joshua were chatting about that had Darcy watching them so carefully.'

'Then we'll start with Joshua,' Rosalind agreed. They were on Caro's turf here, after all. She had to let her take the lead at least a little. It made sense – she knew Joshua well after rehearsing with him for the last couple of months. Knowledge, familiarity and trust were a definite advantage here. But Rosalind had her own advantage, too: that of an outside eye.

They found Joshua in the dressing room he still shared with another minor cast member. Despite stepping up into the main role now Luke was gone, Joshua hadn't moved into the larger, star dressing room Luke had occupied before his death. Rosalind couldn't blame him. Dead man's shoes on stage were one thing – preparing to do the role while surrounded by the dead man's belongings was another.

'I'm not really sure what you're asking.' Joshua looked between them with confusion as they both took seats on the narrow and uncomfortable bench underneath an empty row of hooks. 'I already spoke to the police, of course. I think almost everyone has by now, or will do tomorrow. What else do you expect to find out that they haven't?'

'Maybe nothing,' Caro admitted, cheerfully. 'But in our experience, people closer to a situation see different things in it than outsiders coming in to investigate.'

'And of course, it is our friend's reputation at risk here,' Rosalind added. 'We owe it to Posy to do everything we can to help resolve this situation quickly and prove her innocence.'

'Right.' Joshua looked less than convinced about this happening. Rosalind kept her smile fixed in place all the same. 'Well, what do you want to know?'

Caro jumped in with their first question. 'Yesterday, you were laughing with Luke about something after Piotr called the break. Then he clapped you on the back and said something before he headed for the stage door. What did he say? Did he tell you that he was going over to the Arcadia?'

Joshua looked slightly taken aback at Caro's detailed recollection of the scene. People always underestimated Caro, in Rosalind's experience – they expected her to be scatty, or over-exuberant and extroverted enough to miss the nuance and detail. And sometimes they were right. But Ashok hadn't hired her as a partner in his detective agency for nothing.

She was a Dahlia, underneath it all.

'Oh, well . . . I can't remember what we were laughing about. Probably nothing, you know – just a stupid joke or something. But I remember him saying he had to go over to the Arcadia to "see a man about a dog, as my grandfather would say".' He shrugged. 'It was a weird thing to say, which is why I remembered it. And, well, I just assumed he was actually going to see Posy, if he was going to the Arcadia.'

'Why?' Rosalind asked, quickly. 'Why assume it was to see Posy?'

'Because . . .' Joshua trailed off, glancing at Caro awkwardly. 'Everyone kind of knew that Posy had a problem with Luke and that you two had fallen out over it. I think Luke was trying to, well, put things right for you? Obviously not quite how it worked out, though.'

'Do you know what their history together actually was?' Rosalind didn't want to admit that *they* didn't already know the full story, but if Posy wasn't going to tell them, maybe someone else could.

Of course, if there were always two sides to every story, she had a feeling that Posy's recollection of events would be rather different to Luke's, anyway.

'Just that they dated a long time ago, and he screwed her over.' Joshua shrugged. 'He'd never go into details. Said he'd learned that lesson, at least.'

'It sounds like you knew him well,' Rosalind observed. 'Were you friends before this production?'

Joshua gave a half-smile and waggled his hand from side to side. 'I wouldn't say friends – not before this run, anyway. But yeah, we knew each other before. He, uh, dated my sister – a few years ago now. I hadn't seen him much since.' From his tone, she assumed that Joshua's sister's experience hadn't been any better than Posy's.

'Let me guess. It ended badly?' Caro's expression was grim. Rosalind wondered if she was starting to see a side of her friend that explained why Posy might have wanted to keep her distance from him – even if not why he ended up dead in her dressing room.

'I don't think Luke knew any other way to end a relationship back then,' Joshua joked. 'But like I said, it was quite a few years ago now. Water under the bridge and all that. Meeting him this time around . . . it's like he's a different person. He actually came and *apologised* to me our first night here.'

'You got on okay during rehearsals for *Finding Freddie*, then?' Rosalind surmised. 'Even though Luke took on the role you'd been playing in Yorkshire?'

'Had to,' he replied. 'I mean, when you're performing together . . . you've all got to pull the same way, right? No room for petty disagreements. And the show needed a star to succeed here in London. At least, that's what Piotr and Amber keep telling us.'

'So you didn't resent him at all?' It seemed unlikely to Rosalind that there wouldn't be *any* ill feeling about the change in casting.

'I wanted to, sure. Planned to, even, when I got the news,' Joshua admitted. 'But the Luke I met here . . . he made it pretty damn hard to hate him, didn't he? He was a charming bastard, apart from anything else. And like I told Caro yesterday, he came and apologised, talked to me about the role as I saw it, involved me . . . and made sure I got my chances to perform too. He was a good bloke.'

'How did the rest of the cast get on with him?' Caro asked. 'I mean, from my point of view everything was hunky-dory, but I'd be interested in your view, too.'

'Honestly, I think it was fine. It helped that he addressed his reputation early on, told everyone how much he'd changed . . . I think the worst he got up to on this show was a few overenthusiastic PDAs with Darcy in the wings, and that might well have been her not him.'

'I didn't see any of that,' Caro admitted, when Rosalind looked at her for confirmation.

Joshua looked a little awkward. 'I just know Amber had to have words with them a few times. I heard her and Luke really getting into it last week. That's all.'

Rosalind wondered if *that* was the real problem between Luke and Amber she'd heard Piotr addressing with him outside the theatre. If so, why was Piotr lying about it?

'Did you talk to Darcy at all yesterday, after rehearsals?' Caro asked, moving them on. 'Did she ask where Luke was going, for instance?'

'Uh, yeah, actually, just briefly, after I spoke to you. She wanted to know what Luke and I had been talking about. If I knew who the old friend he'd spent the morning with was.'

'And did you?' Rosalind pressed.

'Not a clue,' Joshua admitted, easily. 'But I think she thought it might have been Posy. Especially when I told her he was going over to the Arcadia.'

Rosalind and Caro exchanged a glace. Looked like their theory was stacking up.

'Do you think she might have followed Luke when she left the theatre?' Rosalind asked.

'Maybe. I don't know. I went out to get some air – you know how claustrophobic it gets when you haven't left the theatre all day. I didn't see her again. But then I heard the sirens and . . . well. You know what happened next.'

But that was the problem: Rosalind wasn't sure that they did. They knew what they were supposed to know. But there was something missing. Something or someone who'd make sense of it all – and put Posy in the clear.

It wasn't going to be Joshua, though.

The call went out for the half a moment later, warning all the performers that they needed to prepare to go on stage in thirty minutes. Rosalind and Caro made their excuses, closing the dressing-room door tightly behind them.

'I've got to go and get ready. But I'll talk to Darcy next? After the show tonight?' Caro asked, and Rosalind nodded.

'Darcy next.' Hopefully she'd have the answers they needed.

And in the meantime, maybe there was something else that Rosalind could do while Caro was performing.

One of the advantages of being a media-proclaimed National Treasure, Rosalind had discovered, was that people very rarely had the nerve to ask her what she was doing or whether she was supposed to be doing it. As long as she moved with enough confidence and a smile on her face, other people basically let her go wherever the hell she wanted.

Even backstage at the Prince Regent Theatre, after a performance had started.

She'd headed out to the bar area after the half – the thirty-minute warning for the cast and crew – was called and Caro needed to get ready to go on stage. At that time, the backstage area was a buzz of activity and noise, and she could only be in the way. Once they were on stage, however, and the performance was under way, everyone's focus would be on the stage and the wings for a time. Which gave her the space she needed to do just a little bit of snooping.

In a theatre as small as the Regent, the space between backstage and front of house was little more than a poorly watched pass door from the edge of the auditorium into the wings. It didn't even have a keypad lock or anything.

She waited until just before the curtain rose to head backstage again. She could have gone back out and round to the stage door, she supposed, but it felt like an unnecessary walk under the circumstances. So instead, she smiled charmingly at the usher selling last-minute programmes in the aisle, and ignored the way his mouth opened as if to ask her where she was going, and then shut again when it was clear she was going there anyway. She slipped through the pass door, taking care to stay out of the way of the cast and crew in the wings, and out into the passageway that led to the dressing rooms.

They still didn't know enough about who Luke Burrows really was, that much had become painfully obvious. And while it was possible to get a good feel for him from talking to everyone who'd known him recently and taking an average . . . Rosalind thought there might be a quicker way.

Searching the spaces he'd inhabited last.

It had occurred to her that if Joshua was still in his old dressing room, Luke's must still be as he'd left it. And she wanted to see what that looked like.

Luke's dressing room was next to Caro's, his name still affixed to the door. Rosalind half expected it to be locked, but when she tried the handle it opened easily. As she stepped inside it became clear why.

It was empty. No sign of the man who had occupied it until so recently. No clothes hanging on the rail, no personal effects on the shelf, no half-read book left abandoned on the arm of a chair, nothing.

The room had been cleared out, that much was obvious. But who by? The police? The theatre? Or someone else? And when? The poor man had only been dead a day.

She took a moment to walk around the room, looking for anything that had been mistakenly left behind, any hint of the man Luke Burrows had been that lingered there. At first, it seemed a fairly hopeless task, until she took a seat at the dressing table and checked around the edge of the mirror. Whenever she was in a theatre dressing room for a long period of time, she'd always keep photos and memorabilia tucked into the edges of her mirror, to remind her of the world outside the show – and all the people who were rooting for her.

Luke's dressing table was a smidgen too high for the mirror attached to the wall – perhaps it had been a later addition; he'd been a tall man, maybe he needed the legroom.

Rosalind reached down behind the dressing-table back, and found one small photo trapped between the mirror and the wall, as if it had been knocked down and then missed by whoever had collected the others. She pulled it out and studied it carefully.

It seemed to be a fairly recent photo, printed out at one of those booths that turned phone photos into old-fashioned prints. She recognised Luke in it immediately, but the older man in the wheelchair looked familiar, too. The woman on his other side, dark-haired, scowling, only a little bit older than Luke if she had to guess, was a stranger. Were they family? Caro had mentioned Luke going to visit his father . . . but Rosalind knew Greg Burrows, and he didn't look like that back when she worked with him. But then, that had been a long time ago now.

She peered at it a little closer, searching for anything familiar in the eyes, the nose, the jawline. Yes . . . there it was. Hiding behind the image of a frail, old man was the powerhouse director she'd once known. So, who was the woman, then? The latest in a long line of Greg's wives, perhaps? His marriages never did seem to last very long, and Rosalind had stopped trying to keep track of them years ago.

She tucked the photo away in her bag, and headed out, shutting the door quietly behind her. Looking up, she found Amber watching her from the end of the corridor, just by the wings. At Rosalind's nod, she moved towards her.

'Everything okay?' Amber's gaze darted to the door Rosalind had just exited, clearly noting that it wasn't Caro's. 'Are you waiting for Caro?'

She shook her head. 'No. I'm just on my way out. How are things going? I heard from Piotr there'd been a problem with your DSM?' The deputy stage manager would spend the show in the wings of the stage, attached to her headset, calling the performance – the cues, the lights, everything, to make sure it all went to plan. 'And Joshua told me you had to have words with Luke. What was the problem exactly . . . ?'

'Oh! No, no problem really. Just . . . you know how it gets when people are amped up on adrenaline. The backstage pranks and behaviour were getting a bit out of hand and, well, getting to my DSM.

But everything's sorted, now,' Amber said. 'I'm just . . . staying close, keeping an eye, same as usual.' As company stage manager, Amber's role was more supervisory, in Rosalind's experience. She had to keep everything running smoothly, even when it felt like things might fall apart.

She didn't envy her the task, especially now.

Rosalind considered for a moment, then pulled the photo she'd found out of her bag. 'I stopped by Luke's dressing room. I wanted to . . . I don't know. Pay my respects, I suppose.'

Amber gave her a sceptical look, her arms folded over her chest. 'Do you honestly expect me to believe you weren't looking for clues?'

There didn't seem much point in arguing with that. 'Fine, yes, I was. But it had already been cleared out. Did the police do that?'

'No, I don't think so.' Amber frowned. 'I know they came and searched it, but since he didn't die there, once they were done they gave us permission to let the family come and take his things. Honestly, I'm not sure Luke spent much time in there in the first place, so there probably wasn't much to clear.'

'Were you here when the family picked up his belongings?'

'Probably.' Amber shrugged. 'Seems like I'm rarely anywhere else these days. But I didn't see them, if that's what you're asking. I think Eddie on the stage door said it was Martha, his half-sister, who came, earlier today.' Damn. If she hadn't been so busy trying to persuade Posy to leave her flat and meet with Caro, Rosalind might have got in there first.

Martha. Wait. She *did* know the woman in the photo, she realised suddenly. Not another wife, but the daughter, of course. How had she forgotten Greg's only other child?

Rosalind held up the photo for confirmation. 'This is his family?'

'Yes.' Amber took the photo and squinted at it. 'Not a great shot of Martha, but that's her, and his father – you know Gregory Burrows, don't you?'

'I used to,' Rosalind admitted. 'I didn't realise he'd become so . . . ill.'

Amber's smile was sympathetic, like she knew Rosalind had been about to say 'old' instead of 'ill'. If Greg was as ancient and decrepit as that photo suggested, what did that make her? Surely she wasn't anywhere near the wheelchair and tartan blanket stage. Was she?

'I understand he's been very unwell for a few years now,' Amber said, delicately. 'I imagine that's what prompted the grand reconciliation between him and Luke.'

'I met his sister Martha, too,' Rosalind admitted, looking down at the photo again. 'Although she can only have been about eight, then. She was hanging around the theatre on the show I was rehearsing with Greg at the time. I remember she was adamant that one day she'd be designing costumes and sets for our plays.'

'Just like my son, Milo,' Amber said, with a smile. 'And she did for a while. That's how I met her, actually, a few years ago now. But she left the theatre to run an art gallery in north London.' She handed the photo back.

'So Martha rushed over here to clear out Luke's dressing room, then?' She hadn't wasted any time, that was for sure. 'Were she and Luke close, do you know?'

Amber pulled a face. 'I don't know how much you know about Luke's family, but he and Martha were . . . the opposite of close. Luke had been estranged from their father for years, and the timing of his return to the fold was, well, convenient.'

'You mean he showed up wanting to be part of the family when Greg got sick,' Rosalind guessed. 'Just in time to get written into the will, I suppose.'

'That's Martha's theory.' Amber shrugged. 'She thinks he was faking his big wake-up call and rehabilitation from his wicked ways just to get back into their dad's good graces.'

'What do *you* think?' Rosalind asked. Of everyone involved in the show, Amber was the only one she knew to have had professional disagreements with Luke.

She sighed. 'I don't know. Martha's a friend, but . . . she's biased about this one. And Luke genuinely did seem to have changed his ways. Impending death – or loss – can clarify a lot of things, I guess. I think his father wrote to him, and maybe Luke realised this was his last chance to have a relationship with him.'

Which one was the truth? Was Luke's reconciliation with his father a cynical ploy to inherit, or a wake-up call that changed his whole personality? And how were they supposed to figure it out now he was dead?

'She runs an art gallery, you said?' Rosalind asked, thoughtfully.

'The Silver Goose Gallery, in Islington.' Amber glanced behind her, back towards the wings of the stage. 'I need to get back and check on things . . . was there anything else?'

'No, thank you. You go.'

Amber had already given her a whole new angle to look into in this case – and the details of one person who might be able to help her figure out once and for all who Luke Burrows really was.

Chapter Ten

The acting profession and those who undertake it are, by necessity, rather dramatic. And sometimes the drama on the stage can spill into the wings – and sometimes it happens the other way around. One of the most famous on-stage murders happened at the Arcadia Theatre in London, during a 1948 performance of Romeo and Juliet, *when the actor playing Mercutio was run through with a real sword – accidentally, by all accounts, although friends did note that he had allegedly stolen the real-life wife of the actor playing Romeo . . .*
        Wendell Malcolm, 'A Theatreland Audio Tour' script

Caro

The first performance with Joshua playing Freddie in place of Luke went . . . well, it went, anyway. Joshua knew the play inside out, of course, but there had been so many changes in staging and blocking since he'd played the part in Yorkshire, and everyone else in the cast had got used to playing opposite *Luke's* Freddie – especially Caro, who had never actually performed with Joshua in the lead before tonight. They'd rehearsed, of course, but it was always different once the curtain opened and the audience was watching.

And there was certainly a good audience. Caro didn't know if it was the scandal factor or what, but they had a full house. So that was something.

Still, small things kept going wrong, as if none of them were quite on their game. Which, she supposed, was only natural after the trauma of a murdered co-star.

The biggest slip-up of the night was a literal one, halfway through Act Two.

Caro stood in character on one side of the stage, her hands twisting the apron of her costume, listening in as Joshua's Freddie took the phone call that could change the whole direction of the story. Upstage, raised above the rest of them by the set design, Darcy stood in a facsimile of a red phone box, reciting her bitter lines down the receiver and having them echo through the auditorium via the magic of the sound engineers at the back.

'I can ruin your life, just by telling the truth,' Darcy/Jocelyn said.

Joshua took a beat before replying. He was playing the scene well, showing the conflicting emotions of the character, and there was complete silence from the audience as they waited to see what he would choose: the truth or the con.

'Then tell it,' he said, finally, and handed the phone to Caro.

Caro/Maggie stepped up to return his trust with her own. 'I'm sorry,' she told Darcy, 'I think you must have the wrong number.'

Amid the cheers and applause that went up as she slammed down the receiver again, hopefully the audience missed the crash that sounded from the edge of the stage a few moments later.

Caro's eyes widened as she looked at Joshua, who returned her unspoken question with an imperceptible shrug. Whatever was going on over there, they had to finish the scene before they could find out – and with everything coming to a head, Caro wasn't off stage from now until the curtain call.

'What do we do now?' Joshua/Freddie asked, as the cheers quietened at last.

'Now, we find a way to make it real,' Caro/Maggie replied.

There were several more scenes – frantic, exciting ones, where the whole community of the play drew together to make Freddie what he'd been pretending to be from the start – part of the family. Caro was on stage right until the last scene presented the happy ending, and the audience came to their feet as the curtain fell. Caro waited until it hit the boards, then dashed into the wings, towards where the crash had come from.

'Is everything okay back here? What happened?' She saw Darcy sitting upon a crate in the wings, Amber wrapping her ankle in crêpe bandage.

'It's the steps to that damn phone box.' Darcy wiped away frustrated tears from her eyes. 'I slipped on my way down. Like, my feet just couldn't grip them. Just as well it was my last scene.'

'It's not broken.' Amber tied off the bandage and stood up. 'I don't think it's even sprained that badly. Just needs rest. Now, you all need to get out there and bow for your adoring public!'

Darcy managed to limp back onto the stage for the bows, and with that their first post-Luke performance was over – and they'd all survived.

Caro had no idea where Rosalind had disappeared to while she was on stage, but with another mostly successful performance under her belt she was eager to get on with the investigation. Which meant talking to Darcy.

Caro had always planned to grab Darcy after the curtain call, before she could escape back to her dressing room, and her ankle could only slow her down. Caro suspected that nobody would be partying, or even going to the tapas bar for a quiet dinner, tonight – their first performance without Luke had been emotionally draining – so this would be her only chance to talk with her that night.

Piotr would probably have notes for them all, tweaks to how they did things to harmonise with their new male lead. But if he had any sense at all, he'd keep them for tomorrow.

Amber, Caro and Darcy headed for the dressing rooms. Caro slipped her arm through the younger actress's as they walked, for extra support for her ankle, and Amber took her arm on the other side to help. Darcy jumped at the contact, but then relaxed, giving Caro a grateful smile.

'It's an adjustment, isn't it? Performing with a new leading man in Luke's role, I mean,' Caro said. When Darcy only hummed an agreement, she went on. 'It wouldn't be easy under any circumstances, but knowing that Luke isn't coming back, ever. That he's . . .'

'Dead,' Darcy finished for her, when she trailed off. 'Yeah. It's . . . hard.'

'I'm sure Piotr would have let your understudy go on in your place tonight,' Amber said. 'You shouldn't have to be here if you're not feeling up to it. Everyone would understand if you needed a few days off.'

'I know. He offered. But . . .' Darcy blinked, her eyes looking damp and glassy again. 'It's easier to be working right now. To be someone else, instead of me, for a couple of hours. You know?'

'I do.' Caro felt much the same. The idea of going home and mourning her friend alone made her chest hurt. At least here she was being *useful*. Entertaining people and hunting a murderer.

There would be time for grief later.

Caro gave Darcy's arm a sympathetic squeeze. 'You two got together on this production, didn't you?'

Darcy nodded. 'I just can't understand why anyone would want to hurt him.' Her voice turned a little shaky. 'He was . . . everyone loved him so much. Not just me. I can't think of a single person who'd want him dead.' She glanced up at Caro. 'Well, except for Posy, I guess.'

Caro's throat tightened. 'I don't know if Posy wanted him *dead*. I think she just wanted him to leave her alone.'

'I guess she got her wish, then,' Amber said, as they reached the door to Darcy's dressing room. 'In a roundabout way.'

Darcy pushed open the door, and Amber stepped away, moving back down the corridor towards the stage again. Caro followed Darcy as she limped inside.

Darcy had managed to get a dressing room to herself – an advantage of the small cast for the play, Caro supposed. As Darcy settled herself at her dressing table to take off her stage make-up and let down her hair, Caro perched on the edge of an armchair, the back of which was draped with several pieces from Darcy's own wardrobe, including a fedora that Caro accidentally knocked to the floor and struggled to replace and balance.

She watched Darcy's reflection as she carefully went through her skincare, her eyes wide under the bright bulbs around the mirror. As her make-up was wiped away, the dark shadows under her eyes became all the more prominent.

'So, how *did* you and Luke get together?' Caro asked. 'If you don't mind me asking.'

'He pursued me,' Darcy said, with a sad smile. 'Said he fell for me the first day we met, and he couldn't resist. He was . . . he was so sweet. Brought me flowers and gifts, took me out places, told me how beautiful I was every single day. And, well, he won me over, I suppose. I fell for him – hard.'

'I know you must be heartbroken at his death,' Caro said, as Darcy sniffed and dabbed away a tear. 'And I'm genuinely sorry for your loss. I don't want to make this time any harder for you. But I was wondering . . . if I could maybe ask you a few questions?'

'I've already told the police everything I know,' Darcy replied.

'Yes, but . . . I'm hoping I might see something they haven't.' Caro met Darcy's gaze in the mirror and held it.

'You're doing this for Posy, I assume?' Darcy said after a moment, looking away. 'You realise that the whole world thinks she did it.'

'The police clearly aren't so sure or they'd have charged her by now.' It wasn't entirely a lie, even if Caro was fairly sure they were trying their hardest to gather up every scrap of evidence they could that might lead to a conviction.

'Still.' Darcy swept a cloth across her face, removing the last scraps of make-up from her flawless skin, then reached for a serum to start layering on the next products to keep it looking that way.

'Okay, yes, I'd like to clear Posy's name,' Caro admitted. 'So I'll be talking to everyone, not just you.'

'You're starting with me, though, aren't you? Because I'm the most likely suspect apart from her. It's always the girlfriend or boyfriend, right? Crimes of passion, or whatever.'

Caro didn't mention that *actually* they'd started with Joshua, since Darcy hadn't been around. 'You were closest to Luke. It makes sense that you'd know him best. I'm hoping you might have some insight on why he was at the Arcadia yesterday.'

'How would I know?' Darcy was suddenly very busy with the contents of her cosmetics bag.

'Because you followed him there?' It was only a hunch, but from the way Darcy's shoulders stiffened, Caro knew it was a good one. 'You did, didn't you?'

'How did you know that?' Darcy put down the moisturiser she was holding and spun on her stool to face Caro. Then she shook her head. 'It doesn't matter. I know I shouldn't have. I should have trusted him. He told me he'd changed – he *showed* me he'd changed. But then I heard Joshua talking about how Luke had cheated on his sister when they were dating, and Taran told me about his past with Posy and . . . I couldn't help but wonder, you know?'

'I know,' Caro said, simply.

'It wasn't even the first time.' Darcy's elbows dropped to her knees, her shoulders slumped and her head bowed. 'I didn't want to believe he would cheat, but I wasn't blind. He kept disappearing off to run "errands" but he'd never say what they were. So I followed him one time – a couple of weeks ago now – and saw him having lunch with some blonde and acting *very* friendly. I couldn't quite see her face, but it *could* have been Posy, now I think about it.'

'Blonde' wasn't exactly a deciding feature – there had to be thousands of blonde women in London who could have been having lunch with Luke Burrows. But since Caro had seen Luke meet another blonde just the other day, it definitely raised possibilities.

'You know Posy. Tell me the truth.' Darcy leaned forward, her forearms resting along her thighs and her eyes pleading. 'Was she sleeping with Luke again? Just tell me. Please.'

'No. No, I'm sure she wasn't. She's with Kit now – Kit Lewis. And she loves him. Posy wouldn't do that to him.' She was almost certain.

Darcy scoffed. 'Like that ever stopped anyone.'

Caro pulled out her phone and showed her the photo of the woman she'd seen Luke with the previous morning. 'Was this the woman you saw him with?'

Darcy squinted at the image, even when Caro enlarged it. 'It could be, I suppose. Like I said, I didn't get a good look at her face. Who is she?'

'That's what I'm trying to find out,' Caro admitted. 'She's the old friend Luke met before he died.'

Darcy stilled and looked up at her. 'You were following him too? Why?'

'Because . . .' Caro sighed. 'Because Posy didn't trust him and I wanted to prove her wrong.'

'And did you?'

'I don't know,' Caro admitted. 'I thought so. But maybe not.'

'That makes two of us, then,' Darcy said, with a half-smile.

'You realise this gives you a good motive for murder,' Caro said, after a moment. 'If you believed that Posy and Luke were together, you might have killed him in a jealous rage.' She might have tried to frame Posy, too – or at least get her out of the way while she did the deed by sending that message from Caro's phone. Yes, Darcy fitted the bill nicely as an alternative prime suspect to Posy.

Except that she looked genuinely surprised at the accusation. 'Why would I kill him, though? I'd rather make his life miserable than end it. Wronged woman could have played well on social media if I pitched it right. Besides, if I killed every guy who'd ever cheated on me I'd have been locked up long before this.'

Caro wasn't crossing her off her list just yet, but she had to admit, she believed her.

'After he left the Regent that day, you followed him to the Arcadia. Did you go inside?'

Darcy looked briefly uncomfortable. 'Only as far as the stage door – you can check the logs, I didn't go in. I watched *him* go in, though – and then I didn't want to hang around there any longer. I went for a walk. By the time I came back he was already dead.'

Caro stilled, running through that evening again in her mind. She'd *seen* Darcy there, hadn't she? Long before Posy came out with blood on her hands. And she'd already admitted to following Luke. Was she really supposed to believe she'd have stopped at the stage door? Especially since they knew someone else *had* gone in, disguised as Posy. Darcy's hair was too dark to pass for Posy's, but it wasn't as if it would be hard to find a blonde wig in a theatre, and they were a similar size.

Darcy turned back to the mirror and reached for her moisturiser again. 'Now, if that's all the gossip you wanted, I think we're done here.'

She didn't look at Caro again as she said her goodbyes and made her way out, back towards her dressing room to take off her own stage persona, hang her costume neatly for wardrobe to deal with, and finally make her way home – to an empty house, once again.

She didn't sleep so well without Annie beside her. But maybe that was for the best. After all, she'd lost so much time questioning people, she was behind on her edits.

So, author work tonight – after she'd called Rosalind to tell her they had a viable alternative suspect at last.

Rosalind

Since her return to London, Rosalind had been slightly regretting the romantic impulse that had led to her emptying her city flat of her personal belongings and selling it, while she and her stuff squashed themselves into the cottage in Wales with Jack. If she'd been thinking rationally, she'd have kept the flat – as an investment property or even to rent it out, or just as a city bolthole for them to use.

But she *hadn't* been thinking rationally, after the events in Scotland last Christmas. She'd been thinking romantically – or at least, emotionally – which, historically, was far less successful for her. And most people, actually. She'd been panicked after Jack's brush with death. So she'd put the home that had seen her through her widow years so far on the market, left everything in the hands of her estate agent, hired movers to pack and transport her stuff, and moved in with Jack, overlooking the river in Llangollen.

And it had been lovely. To start with.

She just wasn't the sort of person who was good at staying in one place, or focused on only one thing – or person. She needed space and variety and *alone time*. Something Jack seemed increasingly unable to comprehend.

So, her trip to London had been perfectly well timed – even if it had required a lengthy stay in a hotel. Something she'd cursed originally – missing her flat with her window seat and reading lamp, and her view over the park.

But as she reclined on her very comfortable super-king bed, with a tray full of room-service breakfast and the Sunday newspaper turned to the cryptic crossword, she admitted that hotel life really wasn't all that bad at all. If nothing else, it offered a welcome reprieve before she needed to return to refereeing Caro and Posy as they resumed their investigation. Assuming Posy would actually answer her phone calls today. She hadn't the night before.

She considered the clue for eleven down while she nibbled on some toast, waiting for her coffee to reach the right temperature – only to be interrupted by the ringing of her phone on the bedside table.

Jack's name scrolled across the screen and she took a moment to consider how that made her feel. Was there still the surge of irritation that had accompanied his every interruption of her morning ritual back in Wales? Or the nagging sense of guilt she'd felt for the first few days of her London escape?

No, actually. She smiled as she realised that, for the first time in a while, she was eager to hear from him – and enjoying that warm feeling that surrounded her heart again on seeing his name.

Maybe absence really did make the heart grow fonder.

'Good morning.' She could hear her smile in her words, and hoped he could, too. 'How are things at – in Wales?' She'd almost said *'at home'*. But that could only open up another discussion she wasn't ready for just yet.

'Good morning to you too.' A small shiver went through her at his husky morning voice. She wondered if he was still snuggled under the covers like she was? Probably not. He'd never been very good at staying in bed once he was awake – unless she had a very good reason to convince him. 'Wales is beautiful, as always. How about the Big Smoke?'

'Less smoky these days, thankfully,' Rosalind replied, thinking back to all those theatre fires she'd learned about on the tour – not to mention the actual fire at the Arcadia.

'And how are you?' A glimmer of concern sounded as his voice dropped lower. 'How is Posy, come to that? And Caro, I suppose? I know better than to think that the three of you aren't already halfway to solving this thing. But I told you, if you need any help, I can be down there in a few hours.'

'I know. And I appreciate the offer. But—'

'But you need some space.' Jack sighed. 'I know. And I know that's what I agreed to. But I *miss* you, Rosa, and thinking about you down there while yet another murderer stalks the streets you're walking . . . allow a man a little concern, will you?'

Since the last case they'd undertaken had led to *Jack* at risk of death, not her, she thought the concern was unnecessary. It had been *years* since she'd nearly been killed on a case. Well, two years, at least. And she wasn't sure the murderer had really meant to hurt her then, anyway. Probably.

'I'm fine,' she assured him. 'And anyway, it's not just that. Things here are . . . difficult.'

'Difficult how?' Jack asked, sharply. 'Is this to do with the murder?'

'Yes and no.' She sighed. 'Mostly it's to do with Caro and Posy.'

'Hmm. You said they weren't getting on so well? That's why Annie wanted you down there, right?' She could hear him settling back into his chair, ready to listen, to consider, and to offer his thoughts for her to mull over and make use of as she saw fit.

This was what she'd been missing the most, she realised. Someone who listened, supported, offered their views – but let her do things her own way in the end. If it could be like that all the time, maybe she wouldn't have needed to run away after less than six months of living together.

Oh, who was she kidding? She would have. This was who she was – and she'd been an idiot for trying to pretend otherwise. Even when she'd been married she'd spent half the year at least away from her husband filming or appearing on stage. She just wasn't built for staying in one place for too long.

'I might have been understating it,' she admitted. 'Especially since Caro more or less accused Posy of murder the other day.'

It was surprisingly cathartic to fill Jack in on everything that had been going on, without going into any real details of their stunted investigation so far. Just focusing on the issues between their friends, and trying to find a way to allow two headstrong women to back down and find their way back to friendship and trust again.

By the end of their call, she was feeling better about her chances of fixing the rift between Caro and Posy and therefore, she hoped, solving the murder, too.

'You're sure you don't want me down there?' Jack asked, as they said their goodbyes.

'Not yet,' Rosalind said, softly. 'But I dare say soon.'

She could hear his grin as he told her he loved her before hanging up.

Smiling too, she turned back to her toast and her crossword. Her coffee was almost the perfect temperature and—

The phone rang again.

With a frown, she glanced down at the screen, expecting it to be Jack with a 'one last thing' he'd thought of after hanging up.

Annie.

Or not.

'Annie? Is everything okay?'

'That's what I'm phoning to ask you.' Annie sounded strangely far away, for all that she was only in Suffolk. She also sounded more exhausted than Rosalind had ever heard her before. 'Caro sent me some strange meme at, like, four in the morning, so she's clearly not sleeping. And when I spoke to her just now she was all . . . distracted. What's going on over there? Do I need to come back?'

She knew Caro had already filled her wife in on Luke's murder – which meant Annie wanted to know how it was affecting Caro and Posy's already strained relationship, rather than what clues they'd turned up so far. With a sigh, Rosalind resigned herself to going over the same ground once more – although this time she tried to sound less annoyed with Caro as she did it.

When she finished, Annie let out a long breath. 'Well, that explains a lot. You know she doesn't *really* think that Posy could kill anyone, don't you? She's just . . . being Dahlia. You don't rule out any suspects without firm evidence.'

'*I* know that,' Rosalind replied. She did, really. Even if it didn't always feel that way. 'I'm just not sure Posy does.' But it was going to be up to her to convince her.

After reassuring Annie that she had matters in hand, Rosalind hung up once more and reached for her rapidly cooling coffee.

This time, she managed to eat an entire piece of toast and solve two crossword clues before the phone rang again. And at this point, she was almost expecting it.

Kit.

'Rosalind? Posy still won't let me come home but she sounds . . .' She heard him swallow over the line. He sounded closer than Annie, even though he was overseas filming. 'And the stuff they're saying online is . . . She wouldn't even answer her phone this morning. Have you spoken to her? You told me you'd handle this. I should come back, right? She needs me there?'

'She needs you not to make this situation any worse.' Rosalind tried to say it kindly, although she wasn't sure how well she succeeded. 'We talked about this, Kit. You know the minute you land in London and fly to her side the gossip blogs and the newspapers are going to be full of photos of you and stories about how she needs your support at this difficult time. And that just gives the whole story more airtime.' Not to mention potentially damaging *Kit's* reputation, which was the last thing Posy needed to be worrying about.

There was silence on the other end of the phone, followed by a long, shaky sigh. 'You're right.'

Of course I'm right. 'If it helps at all, I think she'd want you here, if that wasn't the case.'

'It does,' Kit replied. 'But please . . . tell me she's letting the two of you in, at least. She can't do this on her own.'

'I know that.' *Even if she doesn't.* 'You know what Posy's like. Always wants to believe she can go it alone. But we know better, don't we?' Because even if she *could* do it alone, even if she always had until now, the three Dahlias always, always did better together. 'Don't worry. We'll look after her.'

Her phone pinged with a text message, and she pulled it away from her ear to see the preview.

It was from Samantha. *Posy back in for questioning. Heading to station now.*

So much for her relaxing start to a Sunday.

She pushed away the remains of her breakfast, the crossword and the duvet, and swung her legs out of bed, holding the phone back to her ear.

No point worrying him any more than necessary.

'Don't worry, Kit. I've got this all under control.' Or she would have. Very, very soon.

Chapter Eleven

Johnnie tipped his head to the side as he considered the painting. 'What do you think it is, exactly?'

Dahlia sipped at her champagne. 'Why, darling, I think it's whatever you want it to be. That's the joy of art, isn't it?'

Dahlia Lively in *The Eye of the Beholder*
By Lettice Davenport, 1969

Caro

The police finally let people back into the Arcadia Theatre that day – and Caro and Rosalind were there before lunchtime to speak to Mal.

Caro had kept Rosalind apprised of her investigations, and they both agreed that they needed to see the CCTV footage of the fake Posy arriving at the theatre. Urgently.

'Mal might have been fooled, but I bet we can figure out who it was,' Caro said, with confidence.

'Hmm.' Rosalind tapped her jaw with a perfectly painted fingernail. 'I think I'd like to learn why he was so distracted he didn't notice it wasn't Posy in the first place.'

That, Caro had to admit, was a good point. One she hadn't addressed when she spoke with Mal on the night of the murder.

This was why they worked better as a team. The three Dahlias.

Except they weren't, at the moment. And it really didn't feel right.

'Do you think she's okay?' Caro's voice came out smaller than she'd intended.

Rosalind didn't pretend not to know who she was talking about. 'Samantha is with her. The most useful thing we can do for her right now is try and find out who really killed Luke Burrows.'

Caro didn't ask what they would do if the CCTV really did show Posy arriving twice. She'd said she didn't. They had to trust her.

Didn't they?

As early as they were to the theatre, especially on a Sunday when there was no matinee performance scheduled, Mal would be there earlier, probably eager to get his space sorted again and ready for performances to resume after the chaos of the past couple of days. Even on a normal day he'd be expected to be there before everyone else, ready to handle deliveries and such, and he'd stay there until the last person left the building at the end of the day. Which is why Caro hoped that if anyone knew what had really gone on at the Arcadia on the day that Luke died, it would be him.

He just might not realise it yet. In which case, it was their job to uncover the truth from his recollections.

The stage door at the Arcadia was controlled by a standard keypad, much like the one at the Prince Regent. Some of the theatres in the district had swipe cards, others just buzzers, but keypads seemed reasonably common and, as far as Caro could tell from talking to Eddie at the Regent, many of the theatre entry codes around the district were sort of an open secret to those who worked across multiple theatres over their career. They were there to keep the ordinary people out, not those who belonged to the stage world that Caro was briefly inhabiting.

'We didn't even have keypads back in my day,' Rosalind observed, as they rang the buzzer and waited for Mal to let them in. 'People just knew who was allowed in and who wasn't.'

Film and TV sets, in Caro's experience, were rather more secure. Perhaps theatre was just more trusting.

Which might have been what got Luke killed.

The door swung open, and they stepped inside. Behind his little counter, Mal looked up, obviously surprised to see them.

'If you're here to see Posy, I don't think she'll be coming in,' he said, awkwardly. 'We've been told her understudy will be covering the part for . . . well . . . the foreseeable future, I suppose.'

Caro shared a glance with Rosalind. That did not sound as supportive and trusting as Posy had probably hoped the team behind *Lights Out* would have been. Possibly as a result of the vicious social media coverage.

Or perhaps it just reflected the fact that they expected Posy to be in a police cell for a while.

'Actually, we're here to see you,' Caro said. 'I was hoping to continue our conversation from the other night?'

Understanding bloomed across Mal's face. 'You're still trying to prove her innocence, aren't you? Well, just let me know how I can help. Posy's always been good to me.'

Well, that was a start. At least they had someone on their side — and someone useful, at that.

'I assume the police have been very thorough in their investigations here.' Rosalind stood to one side of the counter, and Caro could see her noting the set-up, the computers, the iPad screen Mal apparently used to check people in and out . . . and the cameras, of course.

Mal nodded. 'They've spoken to everyone here, even those who weren't on site on the day. And searched every inch of the place twice, apparently. I think they'd have liked to have kept us closed longer, but one of our higher-ups had a word with one of their higher-ups and they picked up the pace.'

It was a high-profile case; it made sense they'd have a lot of people working on it.

'Do you happen to know if they had any success finding the murder weapon?' Caro asked.

Information like that shouldn't be shared with anyone outside the investigation, of course, but in Caro's experience it was nearly impossible to keep *anything* from the person in charge of the stage door.

'No sign of it yet,' Mal replied, with a shake of the head. 'Although apparently Pollie, our stage manager, is down a pocket knife that might fit the bill. She doesn't know exactly when it went missing from her kit, though.'

Caro flashed a glance at Rosalind. 'And where does Pollie usually keep her kit?' Amber's rarely left her side, in Caro's experience.

Apparently Pollie was less precious with her belongings. 'Oh, it's usually in the small production office by the stage left wing, next to the loos.'

'And is the office usually locked?' Rosalind asked.

Mal shook his head. 'Not really.'

Which meant that anyone in the theatre could technically have got to it, if it really was the murder weapon. And if Pollie didn't know *when* it went missing, it might not even have been the same day as the murder. *Interesting.*

Caro made a mental note to discuss it more with Rosalind after. But first, they had something else they needed to do.

'Caro mentioned there were some . . . discrepancies in the CCTV footage around the time of Luke's murder.' Rosalind gave Mal an expectant smile and, after a moment, he cottoned on.

'Oh! Yes. You'd like to see it, I guess?'

'Very much,' Rosalind confirmed. 'And the door log, if you please.'

'Right.' Instead of pulling down the iPad, though, Mal fished out a printed sheet that had been filled in by hand. 'Technically it's all in the computer system, but sometimes the iPad doesn't want to play ball, so I keep a written log too. Look, here. I logged her in the first time she arrived that day, but then when she came back in the second time I scribbled that one out and put in the later time instead.'

Caro took the paper log from him. There, under the scribbles, was Posy's name and a time – 17.35 – which was then replaced by 17.55. But above it was another entry. *Luke Burrows, 17.30.*

'You didn't think it was at all odd that Posy came into the theatre twice without leaving?' Rosalind had one eyebrow raised in disbelief.

Caro had asked him the same question, but she was interested to see if his answer had changed at all.

It hadn't. 'I figured she must have gone out front of house for some reason – maybe to join that meeting with Pollie and Keiko, the director – then come back round again.'

Caro heard what he wasn't saying. That Posy could have killed Luke, escaped out through the pass door to the auditorium, disappeared into the street then pretended to arrive again later. But why would she? It made no sense at all – the log would show her arriving twice, so what would she gain by it?

There was a niggle at the back of her mind, something from a half-forgotten Dahlia Lively story. Something Caro was trying very hard to ignore.

'Show us the CCTV, Mal.' The police had taken a copy, she was sure, but the original should still be on the computer system.

With unsteady hands, Mal pulled it up on the screen.

There was no sound, and the angle – from the camera above Mal's counter – made everything look odd. But as they watched, Caro saw Luke arrive, bursting through the door with his usual bonhomie, grinning for the camera he probably wasn't even aware was watching him. He stopped at the counter to talk with Mal, who was out of sight of the camera. After a moment or two, Mal must have sent him off towards the dressing rooms, because Luke turned and left. Obviously Luke's charm was more potent than Posy's strict instructions that he not be allowed in her dressing room again.

Then, just a minute or two later – Mal wiggled through the tape in between – another person entered.

With blonde hair gathered in a ponytail at the back of her head, a slim figure in a loose green utility jacket and a baseball cap pulled over her forehead, Caro had to admit it sure as hell looked like Posy. This woman never looked up at the camera, though – and didn't pause to talk to Mal, either. Instead, she waved a hand towards the counter and walked straight in as if she belonged there.

'You didn't talk to her?' Mal shook his head at Rosalind's question. 'Did you even see her face?'

His cheeks glowed pink. 'I . . . I don't remember. That day . . . I wasn't the most attentive. My boyfriend and I . . .'

Caro groaned. 'Getting back together or breaking up again?'

'Getting back together.' Which meant Mal had probably been sexting while Luke was murdered. Ideal witness, then.

'So a blonde woman in a baseball cap walks in, doesn't sign herself in but expects you to do it, heads off in the direction of the dressing rooms without a word, and you just assumed it was Posy?' Caro demanded.

'It was around the time she usually arrives . . .' Mal said, weakly. 'She's always early. Maybe not quite that early, but in the ballpark.'

Except that day Posy had been held up waiting for Caro, for a coffee date she knew nothing about. Had someone used their knowledge of Posy's schedule to impersonate her? To walk into this theatre without being questioned, kill Luke Burrows, then escape out the front of house before the real Posy Starling arrived?

It was starting to look like it.

The recording ran on, and together they all watched the real Posy arrive – and talk to Mal and sign herself in. Mal reached behind him and handed her the flowers Caro had seen Luke purchase that morning. With a look of disgust, Posy tore the paper off them and shoved the blooms into the nearest bin.

'You didn't think *that* was unusual?' Rosalind asked Mal. 'That she stopped and talked to you that time but not the first?' Caro hid a smile. None of them thought it was unusual that she'd thrown away the flowers from Luke.

Mal pulled a face. 'Honestly? I figured that she saw Luke arrive the first time and was in a hurry to yell at him. She moved through so fast I forgot to even stop her to tell her about the flowers he'd left for her.'

'Go back to the first time she arrived,' Caro instructed. She needed to look for signs it wasn't really Posy.

Mal wound back the recording and they all watched it again in silence.

The quality wasn't great – it didn't need to be, as a rule, it just needed to record. But now she watched it again Caro could see how the woman never raised her head even a little, presumably so she couldn't be recognised by Mal *or* the cameras. The utility jacket she was wearing over her black jeans would cover almost anything – Caro had assumed a slim figure because she was looking for one, but actually it was impossible to tell. Only the hair and the baseball cap stood out.

'Can you put the images side by side?' Rosalind asked.

Mal pressed a few buttons and the screen split with both Posys on view. Caro squinted at them. The first Posy looked a little shorter, perhaps? Maybe a little heavier? It was hard to be sure with the angle of the camera. The only obvious difference was that the second Posy wasn't wearing a jacket, but she could easily have taken it off.

'The police have this, you said.' Caro took a breath. 'Hopefully they'll be able to tell it's not Posy — not the same woman who arrived later.' They had special techniques and experts in this sort of thing, didn't they? Or at least better eyesight. They'd be able to tell.

'I'm sure they will.' Mal patted her hand, comfortingly.

But that didn't answer the question — if it *wasn't* Posy, who was it? Who had followed Luke into the theatre?

Outside again, Rosalind and Caro stepped back into the car that had been idling on the busy street, waiting for them. Rosalind instructed the driver to take them to her hotel, where hopefully they could make sense of everything before Caro had to be back at the Prince Regent for the evening performance. And maybe get some lunch while they were at it.

'What did you think?' Caro asked, as the driver pulled smoothly away from the kerb.

'The bit about the missing knife was interesting.' Rosalind stared out of the window, thoughtfully. 'Logistically, I mean. If the stage manager's bag with the knife in was in the production office by the wings, then our fake Posy wouldn't go past it on their way to the dressing room where Luke was killed. They'd have to have gone to find it then backtracked.'

'Or, our murderer came in through the front of the theatre, through the pass door from the auditorium into the wings — I think it has a keypad like the stage door, but the codes seem to be fairly general knowledge – went to the production office, picked up the knife then found Luke in Posy's dressing room.'

'It's possible,' Rosalind allowed.

But so were many other things. There was something else that was bothering Caro about what they'd learned from Mal. 'We're certain it wasn't Posy on that video – the first time, I mean. Right?'

'Aren't we?' Rosalind turned back to her with both eyebrows raised. 'She said it wasn't her.'

'It's just . . . doesn't it remind you of something?' When Rosalind looked blank, Caro took a breath and continued. 'That Dahlia Lively mystery. *Alibis and Afternoon Tea*.'

Rosalind's expression darkened. 'I know the one you mean. And no, I don't think so.'

'But in that one Lettice has one suspect arrive at the crime scene twice, once in a bad disguise as themself, so it looks like it couldn't have been them really, and—'

'I remember the book,' Rosalind said, crisply. 'But we can't think like that. Caro, nobody else has faith in Posy right now. *We* have to.'

'And do you?' Caro asked, softly.

There was just the slightest moment of hesitation before Rosalind answered. 'Of course I do.'

Rosalind

'Why, exactly, are we at a gallery opening?' Caro asked, as she selected a glass of complimentary champagne from a nearby waiter's tray the following evening. 'I assume not just for the free drinks?'

Posy still wasn't answering Rosalind's calls, and according to

Samantha the crowd of paparazzi outside her flat had only grown since she'd been released from questioning again, so Rosalind couldn't even go round there and bang on the door again without courting headlines. But she *could* keep investigating.

It hadn't taken long to track down Martha Burrows and the Silver Goose Gallery online and discover that, serendipitously, they were holding an opening for a new artist that night. Since it was a Monday, Caro didn't have a performance, so she'd shot her a text instructing her to put on her glad rags ready to hit the art scene.

'We're here for her.' Rosalind fluttered a hand towards the other end of the gallery as a woman in a deep burgundy gown stepped up onto a small platform and waited for silence, while a man nearby clinked a wine glass with a spoon.

'Welcome, everyone! I'm delighted that you're all here tonight to share in some incredible new artworks from one of our favourite artists, Bethany Kearns, and her new series, *HopeScapes*.'

Caro was squinting at the woman, as if trying to figure out why she was familiar. Rosalind supposed she did look just a little bit like Luke. Something in the eyes, perhaps.

'Luke's sister,' Rosalind murmured to her. 'Well, half-sister. Martha Burrows. She's the one who cleared out his dressing room.'

'Of course,' Caro breathed. 'I'll have to check, but I'm pretty sure she was the woman I saw following Luke into their dad's apartment building.'

'That makes sense.' And might explain why Luke had left so hurriedly, too, given what Amber had told her about the rift between the half-siblings.

Martha went on about the inspiration behind the works, the woman Rosalind assumed was Bethany Kearns blushing prettily to one side.

'Are we here because we think she might have killed her brother, or in case she found anything interesting in the dressing room to tell us who else might have?' Caro asked.

Rosalind shrugged. 'Both, I suppose.'

'Multitasking. Excellent.' Caro reached for a canapé from another passing tray.

'More than anything, she's the first person we've found in this case who – according to Amber at least – doesn't adore Luke. I want to know more about why.'

Martha finished talking and asked them all to raise a glass to the artist, then set them free to 'explore and experience' the work.

Rosalind found plenty of her old acquaintances in the room already, so started by making the rounds chatting away to the great and good of London art society. It wouldn't do to appear too single-minded in their focus and, besides, Martha was more likely to talk to them at length if she'd already had time with the people in the room who would actually add to the gallery's bottom line by purchasing one of the paintings.

Caro, meanwhile, had struck up a conversation with an exceptionally tall man with a moustache about a piece Rosalind *thought* was a painting of a boat, although she had to admit she wasn't sure.

'It's all about second chances, you see,' the man was saying when Rosalind passed nearby, while Caro nodded along thoughtfully.

Rosalind hoped that Annie liked *HopeScapes*, whatever they were. If they got out of there without Caro buying one it would be a miracle.

Finally, Rosalind deemed it time to start the conversation they were really there for. She caught Caro's eye across the room and, confident that she'd join her shortly, drifted closer to Martha Burrows in order to facilitate a meeting.

'Martha, darling! I don't believe I've seen you since you were a child!' Rosalind held out both her hands and clasped Martha's between them. 'It's so wonderful to see you again. How is your dear father?'

Luke's sister appeared taken aback at the greeting, but obviously recognised Rosalind, and had the social skills to go gracefully along with her. 'Rosalind King! What a treat for us here to have you join us tonight – and you brought a friend, too!'

Rosalind turned to introduce Caro, but Martha waved her away, reaching out to shake her hand. 'Of course I know Caro Hooper. *Everyone* knows the three Dahlias these days, don't they? Although I note there's only two of you tonight.'

'For obvious reasons,' Rosalind murmured, keeping her smile firmly in place. It was probably for the best that Posy *wasn't* with them. However contentious the relationship between Martha and Luke had been, bringing his suspected killer to her gallery would have probably been a bridge too far. 'We were just *delighted* to have the opportunity to visit your gallery and see such beautiful works.'

'Would you like me to introduce you to the artist?' Martha half turned towards where Bethany Kearns was talking with a small group of men, but Rosalind took her arm and pulled her back.

'Oh, don't let's interrupt her now. Actually, perhaps we could take a seat for a moment?' Rosalind gestured towards a few comfortable chairs set up around a low table that had just become free. 'At my age standing for too long just isn't advisable.'

She heard Caro stifle a snort behind her at that, but really, what was getting old good for if she couldn't use it to her advantage now and then?

Once they were all settled, Rosalind got right to the heart of things. 'We were hoping, in addition to enjoying the art, to have the opportunity to talk to you about your half-brother, Luke.' Rosalind schooled her expression into what she hoped was the perfect mix of sympathy and understanding. 'We are, all of us in the theatre world, so sorry for your loss.'

'Yes, well.' Martha looked away awkwardly. 'We weren't close. I don't imagine I'll be able to help you much.'

'But you were the one who emptied his dressing room, weren't you?' Caro's patience was obviously exhausted. Rosalind checked her watch. Right on schedule. 'Did you find anything interesting?'

'How did you know I did that?'

Rosalind flashed a long-suffering look at Caro. 'That was actually how I found out that you were his sister in the first place. I found a photo left behind in his dressing room and spoke to Amber, the stage manager at the Regent, about it. She sent me your way.'

Martha's eyes narrowed. 'You were asking about him? About *me*? Why? Are you investigating his death?'

'We're . . . interested parties,' Rosalind said, vaguely. 'And yes, we're hoping to find out exactly what happened to Luke.'

There was a long, silent moment as Martha studied her carefully. Rosalind stayed perfectly still and let her.

Finally, Luke's sister nodded. 'You don't believe your friend Posy did it, then? Is that just loyalty or do you have any actual evidence?'

'There are certainly enough discrepancies that the police aren't holding Posy, whatever the internet says.' Rosalind glanced at Caro, who nodded her agreement.

'You said you weren't close. Has that always been the case?' Caro asked, getting the questioning back on track.

'Yes. My father never actually married his mother – one of the few women he dated that he didn't, *you* know what he was like.' She sounded fondly exasperated, which Rosalind thought was surprisingly forgiving of her. Gregory had been a visionary director in his day, but that didn't always add up to being a good husband or father. Or person, come to that. 'I didn't even know Luke existed until about he was about seven years old, and even then, he wasn't really part of the family. Then when he turned eighteen, he and Dad had a falling out over something – I never knew quite what – and Luke stormed off to "make it on his own".' She put air quotes around the last phrase, pulling a face as she said it. 'Which actually meant living with his mother and new producer stepfather in LA, where I presume he kick-started his acting career through their nepotism instead of Dad's.'

That, Rosalind surmised, must have been a couple of years before he'd met Posy.

'What brought him back into the family fold?' Caro asked.

'Money, of course.' Martha's lips twisted into a snide smile. 'Isn't it always about money?'

'Your father is dying,' Rosalind said, low and sombre. She'd known it since she'd seen the yellowish tinge of Gregory's skin in that photo.

'He's been dying for years.' Martha's gaze flickered between the two of them. 'Mostly self-inflicted. But he does seem a bit more determined about it this time.'

Under the attempt to sound callous or unfeeling, Rosalind could hear a hint of pain. Martha cared more than she wanted them to know. But what was it, exactly, that she cared about? Her father or his money?

'So Luke reconnected with his father, knowing he was sick?' Caro sounded like she was trying to reconcile that information with the man she'd known.

Martha busied herself tidying a stack of gallery business cards and brochures on the table between them. 'Luke reappeared a couple of years ago, claiming he'd undergone some sort of Damascene conversion and changed his ways. Until then, all we really knew about him was what we'd heard from people who'd worked with him over the years and, honestly, it wasn't exactly encouraging. You know what this business is like.'

'Incestuous,' Caro said, nodding.

Martha frowned. 'Word gets around. Still, Luke was adamant he'd changed and, well, Dad believed him.'

'You didn't, though,' Rosalind guessed.

Martha patted the perfectly straight brochures and sat back, hands folded in her lap. 'The timing was . . . convenient. Dad didn't seem to notice that Luke only came back after an article appeared online, a review of Dad's work and the last play he directed, with a quote from him about how he was stepping back to enjoy his remaining time with his family.'

'He wanted to make sure he was in the will,' Caro said. Well, Rosalind supposed that was in keeping with the Luke Posy had warned them about.

'Presumably until then all of your father's money and possessions would have gone to you?' Rosalind tried very hard to sound perfectly neutral as she said it. 'And will again, now Luke is dead?'

Martha looked slightly taken aback, all the same. 'I . . . I suppose so. But you're not suggesting . . .' She trailed off. Rosalind remained silent, making it obvious that she was at least *hinting*.

Martha jumped to her feet. 'Well, I can stop you right there. I was here at the gallery late the day Luke was killed, until I got the call from the police as his next of kin. And actually . . .' She grabbed an appointments book from the desk behind her. 'Yes, look. There. I was meeting with some very important new clients of the gallery at the time they say he was murdered. They wanted some help choosing some interesting pieces for their new London townhouse and could only meet after hours.'

She shoved the book towards them, and Rosalind scanned down the sparse list of appointments to find the correct day.

There, in cursive black ink, was an evening appointment with *The Carpenters (Shannon and Henry)*.

'Obviously I've given the police their details and I'm sure they'll be following up.' Martha slammed the book shut again. 'Now, if you'll excuse me, I have actual clients to speak to.'

She jumped to her feet and strode away, leaving the book on the table. Caro flipped it open again and took a photo of the entries for the day of the murder, then turned to Rosalind.

'I'll send the names to Ashok,' she said. 'See if he can track them down, confirm the alibi. But until then . . . more champagne?'

Rosalind sighed. They weren't going to get any more out of Martha tonight, it seemed. 'Why not?'

Chapter Twelve

I think it's always so interesting to see my stories, my characters brought to life – be it on the theatre stage or even on the cinema screen, as has happened over the past few years with darling Rosalind playing Dahlia.

Stage or film, they're never quite as I imagined them, but that's not the point, is it? They're not made for me. They're made for all the people who come and watch the Dahlia Lively stories play out as if in real life. If they feel real to you, watching, then their work is done.

Interview with Lettice Davenport, 1985

Caro

Rosalind and Caro regrouped for brunch the next morning at Rosalind's hotel.

Caro, who'd already been up for hours working on the edits of *Seven Lively Suspects*, was ravenous by the time she arrived – but also more pensive than she tended to be of a morning. Or, she supposed, ever. Pensive wasn't her natural state.

But reading back over their adventures in Market Foxleigh the previous summer, she couldn't help but be reminded of how well they worked as a team. A team of *three*.

The two Dahlias just didn't seem to be having the same effect on this case. If anything, after meeting Martha the night before, they seemed to have expanded their suspect pool.

Caro found Rosalind already in the breakfast room, sipping on a cup of coffee.

'Ooh, I could do with one of those.' Caro signalled the nearest waitress as she slipped into her seat.

Rosalind raised an eyebrow. 'Couldn't sleep? I told you those brie canapés wouldn't agree with you.'

'I was up early,' Caro countered. 'Some of us still do actual work, you realise.'

'The book?' Rosalind asked. 'Which one is it now? Market Foxleigh?'

The coffee arrived, and Caro lifted it to her nose to breathe it in, hoping that just the scent would do the trick until it was cool enough to drink. 'That's the one. Sort of weird writing about the three of us solving a case right now.'

'And, of course, that case had much more to do with dredging up *your* past, rather than Posy's.' Rosalind's eyes were knowing over the rim of her coffee cup.

'I suppose,' she replied, as if that wasn't the exact thing that had been bothering her all morning.

She hadn't wanted to take that case. Hadn't wanted to go anywhere near Market Foxleigh and the memories it brought up. Just like Posy hadn't wanted anything to do with Luke.

Except Caro had never been in the frame for murder.

'Is there any news from her?' she asked, knowing she wouldn't have to specify who 'she' was.

Rosalind shook her head. 'Still not taking my calls. Or yours, I assume?'

'I haven't even tried,' Caro admitted. 'If she's not talking to you there's no way she'll talk to me.'

'Samantha is keeping me updated on the police side of things, at least. And I spoke to Kit again last night, after the art gallery.'

Caro looked up eagerly. 'What did he have to say? Is he coming home? He's spoken to her at least, right?'

'He's spoken to her. I don't think she's said much, though, because he still seems to be under the impression that we're making things better rather than worse.' Rosalind's coffee cup clunked back into its saucer, wobbling a little as if she'd dropped it the last few millimetres.

Caro took a moment to examine her friend more carefully. She looked . . . not just tired, but weary. Bone weary. The sort of exhaustion that came not from lack of sleep exactly, but from constant worry and feeling helpless. Caro knew that kind of exhaustion, too.

Posy's predicament was taking its toll on all of them.

She reached across and grabbed Rosalind's hand. 'We *are* helping. I know it doesn't feel like it right now, but we're going to solve this case and get Posy back. We are.'

Rosalind's gaze was empty as she met Caro's eyes. 'Are you sure? Does that mean that you're convinced of her innocence suddenly? Or that you're willing to manipulate the law and the evidence to get her out of any charges regardless?'

Caro dropped her hand, falling back against her chair in surprise. 'I'm not . . . I never wanted to believe she was guilty, Rosalind. I still don't. I just wanted to get to the truth. Whatever that is.'

'And if the truth is that Posy killed him? Say, in self-defence? What then?' Rosalind's expression remained perfectly blank. Did she know something Caro didn't? What had she found out?

'Do you think she did?' Caro asked, quietly.

'No.' Rosalind looked away, her shoulders slumping slightly, which – for someone with posture as perfect as Rosalind – was almost the same as giving up entirely.

Caro swallowed. 'We will solve this case,' she repeated, firmly, even though her throat was burning with the pressure of unshed tears. 'It might be the hardest one we've ever had, and yes, we have to do it alone, just the two of us. But we will. Whatever the truth turns out to be.'

'We will.' Rosalind's voice was soft, but she nodded and straightened her spine again, and that was enough.

Thank God. She didn't know what had caused Rosalind's crisis of confidence – maybe, like her, she'd simply realised that their suspect pool only ever seemed to grow, rather than shrink. But whatever it was, Caro was glad the moment had passed. They couldn't afford to lose faith now – in their investigative skills, if nothing else.

Caro picked up her coffee and took a sip, even though it was still too hot.

'So, what's next?' She looked to Rosalind for an answer, but the elder Dahlia wasn't listening. She was staring past Caro to the entrance to the breakfast room.

Caro turned to see what had caught her eye, and spotted two men with cameras, and a woman with a microphone just behind them.

'Think they're here for us?' Caro asked.

Rosalind gave a sharp nod. 'They can't get to Posy – her building has halfway decent security, at least, and she's not opening her door for anyone. So we're the next best thing. Honestly, I'm surprised it hasn't happened sooner.' She signalled for the waitress. 'We'll take our breakfast up in my suite, if you could have it sent up, please.'

Caro took one last swig of her coffee and left the rest behind.

They had to pass the reporters to get to the lifts to Rosalind's suite, but they both had experience of not answering questions, however demandingly they were asked. Rosalind slipped her hand through the crook of Caro's arm and together they strode straight past the now gathering crowd, in the direction of the shiny brass lift doors.

'Rosalind! Caro! Have you spoken to Posy Starling since Luke Burrow's death?' the first man called out. 'Do you believe she's capable of murder?'

'Caro! How does it feel to know your best friend might have murdered your co-star?' another voice shouted.

From there, the voices seemed to merge into one loud roar of questions. Hell, where were all these people coming from? Caro had always known the paparazzi sometimes moved in packs, but this was beyond anything she'd ever experienced before.

'Is it true you and Posy had fallen out before the murder, Caro?'

'Will you speak at Posy's trial?'

'Were Posy and Luke having an affair?'

'Where is Kit Lewis? Has he abandoned Posy in her time of need?'

One of the hotel porters standing by the lifts had already pressed the button to call it, Caro realised. Other hotel staff were trying to shield them, to form a barrier between them and the reporters. But still the questions came.

'Are you investigating on Posy's behalf?'

'Who do you think killed Luke Burrows?'

'Are you part of a cover-up to get Posy off the hook?'

Finally, finally, the doors of the lift snapped open just as Rosalind and Caro reached them, lurching inside and instantly pressing the button to close the doors, followed by the one for Rosalind's floor.

Caro sagged against the mirrored back wall of the lift, while Rosalind raised her arm and pressed the back of her hand to her forehead.

'The hotel security team won't let them up to my floor,' Rosalind said. 'We should be fine now.'

'Until we need to leave the hotel again.' How was this their life? And how were they supposed to help Posy if they were going to be followed by the press?

Rosalind was right. They were lucky they'd been left alone this long – apart from the usual few photographers who'd been catching images of all the cast and crew at the theatres ever since the murder. Obviously Posy's new hermit act wasn't getting them the headlines they needed any more.

'What do we do now?' The mirror was cool at Caro's back, and she pressed her hands against it to try and centre herself. She didn't want to turn and see her reflection. She suspected it would look just as rattled as Rosalind did right now.

'We go to my suite and eat breakfast,' Rosalind said, after a moment. 'We go over everything we've learned so far.'

'And when we have to leave? The reporters?'

Rosalind's lips hardened into a thin line. 'We carry on exactly like normal. Because we know Posy is innocent and so we don't need to worry. And we don't give those vultures a single hint that either one of us has ever thought otherwise, not even for a moment.'

It was the closest Rosalind had come to admitting that she'd had doubts too.

Caro nodded. 'That's it?'

'In public? Yes.' Rosalind met her gaze. 'You go to the theatre tonight and perform just as you would on any other day. I'll be in the audience watching. And between us . . . we keep asking questions. It's time to put some pressure on the other people involved in this case. We need to have a stronger suspect than Posy to put her in the clear.'

'Of course.'

The lift pinged and the doors opened at Rosalind's floor. The corridor seemed blissfully empty.

'In fact,' Rosalind added, as she stepped out, 'a confession from one of our suspects would be great, if you can manage it.'

Oh, so Rosalind just wanted the moon on a stick, then. As usual. 'I'll see what I can do.'

Posy

Posy smoothed the wrinkled newspaper out on her coffee table, relying on the reading lamp to see it since her blinds were shut, even though it was mid-afternoon. She wasn't risking anyone being able to see into her apartment right now, either from the building across the street or by using a drone camera or whatever. She didn't even want them to know for sure she was inside.

She just wanted this whole circus to be over.

She ran her hand over the newspaper again, reading the caption below the photo.

> *Socialite turned businesswoman, Shannon Carpenter (née Sharp), 32, has relocated to London with her millionaire husband – and is already causing a stir with her elegant but edgy outfits! Despite the rumours swirling about them in the American press, Carpenter appeared at*

There, the paper tore off, and Posy's gaze jumped back up to the image above it again.

Shannon Carpenter.

The name wasn't wholly familiar, but the face in the photo certainly was.

So many years later, and she could still see the teenager she'd befriended behind the honey-highlighted hair and the designer clothes. Still saw her face, and the betrayal on it, the last time Posy had left the apartment they'd shared in LA.

It couldn't be a coincidence that Luke had wrapped those flowers he'd left for her at the stage door in *this* newspaper. He'd been too sly for that. It had been a message. A warning – or a threat. She was sure of it.

She'd *been* so sure of it, at the time.

Now . . .

She needed to know. She needed to be certain, before she made her next move.

And now Luke was dead, there was only one way to find out.

Posy picked up her phone from the table. She'd been keeping it switched off, only turning it on once or twice a day to check for any important messages and make any essential calls. She'd used her laptop for research and sending emails instead, staying far away from any of the news or gossip sites. She hadn't been returning anyone's calls except for Kit's, and then only to stop him from jumping on the next plane to London.

There was nothing he could do to help her, and she wasn't about to tarnish his reputation any more than she already had.

She swallowed and turned the phone on, braced for the barrage of banners and notifications she'd been ignoring. She was going to ignore them a little longer, too.

The photo in front of her clearly showed the hotel Shannon and her husband were departing. It only took a moment to pull up their website then click through to call the reception desk.

'I'd . . .' Her voice came out scratchy as she tried to speak. Too long answering questions at the police station had made her throat ache. She cleared it and tried again. 'I'd like to leave a message for Shannon Carpenter, please?'

A pause. 'I'm sorry, there's no guest by that name staying with us right now.'

Of course not. She wouldn't use her real name. 'Um, what about . . .' Her gaze slipped across the table, past the newspaper to the script on the other side. 'Willa Andrews?'

Another pause. 'Of course. What is your message, please?'

'Could you tell her that . . . that Alice would like to talk. In person. I'll leave my number and she can text me the details of where to meet.'

As the receptionist took down the phone number, Posy tried not to think about having to leave the safe haven of her flat to meet Shannon. It had to be done.

It was the only way she was going to get the answers she needed.

Even if Shannon had no reason to give them to her.

Rosalind

When Rosalind appeared on the stage a lot more regularly than she had of late, interviewers would often ask her if she preferred film or theatre, or if she got bored performing the same role over and over, saying the same lines every night for sometimes months on end. They'd never seemed to understand that every performance felt different, even when the cast and lines remained the same. The energy altered from night to night, waning and waxing with the audience as well as the cast and crew, rather than the moon.

Watching the same play was a rather different experience, especially only a week after she saw it for the first time. But with a new actor in the title role, *Finding Freddie* was a different play.

Joshua had taken over the role of Freddie with style. Some actors might have been anxious about stepping into a dead man's shoes, but if Joshua felt any nerves he wasn't showing them. His take on the character played a little less for the laughs, and a little more for the pathos, and it worked.

But Rosalind had to admit, she was only half watching the play, and half watching the man beside her.

When she'd approached Piotr and asked if it would be possible to get a ticket for that night's performance, she'd hoped for exactly the answer she got – not just a ticket, but a seat next to the director himself. He'd been impossible to get hold of since the murder – she assumed that the death of a star put rather a lot of pressure on the production team – and so was the only one of the suspects that neither she nor Caro had spoken to since the murder.

From what she'd heard, Piotr had been sitting anxiously in the audience at all performances since *Finding Freddie* had reopened after Luke's death, and she was curious as to whether his concern was for Joshua's acting abilities, or the safety of the rest of his cast.

When the lights went up for the interval, she followed Piotr to the bar to collect their drinks.

'He's doing well,' she observed, as he took a sip of his gin and tonic. 'Are you going to keep him in the role or replace him with another big name?'

Piotr swilled his glass around thoughtfully. 'We'll see. Sales would like a big name, of course. But sometimes big names can be more trouble than they're worth.'

'Was Luke? More trouble than he was worth? Or had he really changed his ways?'

Piotr's sharp gaze landed on her. 'What have you heard?'

Rosalind allowed herself a small smile. Piotr had been full of praise for Luke the other day. Would that change now Luke was gone, she wondered? And if it did, would that make him more or less of a suspect? She wasn't sure.

'I spoke with his half-sister, Martha, last night. She seemed to feel that his sudden reformation was suspiciously timed, and maybe not entirely genuine.'

Piotr huffed a laugh. 'She would. I know Martha well enough, and she's the martyrdom type herself. Makes a fuss about being the only one to care for her father – even though last time I visited Greg he had two separate live-in carers, and she only stopped by once a week. Too busy with her gallery, and being a 'patron of the arts'. Now she's not working in theatre any more she likes to spend her father's money to make her still feel part of it. She's a patron here at the Regent and over at the Arcadia, plus half a dozen other theatres in London probably. Even gives tours sometimes. Not that I think Luke necessarily did any more for Greg, even after his prodigal-son return. They were all out for what they could get in that family. Isn't everybody in this industry?'

'I like to think not,' Rosalind said, quietly.

'Hmm, well. Maybe,' Piotr allowed, with an apologetic look in her direction.

'But that wasn't what you *thought* I'd heard about Luke, was it?' He'd reacted too quickly to her question about him changing his ways – and been too relieved at the suggestion that it was just Martha causing trouble. 'What were you afraid someone had told me?'

He started to bluster, but Rosalind cut in before he got too far. 'Come on, Piotr. We've been friends for too many years to play pretend now. What was going on? Did it have something to do with that discussion about Amber and the deputy stage manager I overheard the other day?'

'I don't see that it matters now.' He looked over her shoulder, clearly hoping that there would be somebody – anybody – more important that he he might legitimately need to go and speak to instead.

There wasn't.

Rosalind moved to block his line of vision, just in case. 'Not even if it could have something to do with Luke's untimely death?'

Now he met her gaze. 'If that were the case, the important thing would be for me to tell the police – which I have done.'

So whatever he was hiding *was* worth telling the police. 'What did you tell them?'

She could see the question on the tip of his tongue: *Why should I tell you?*

But she could also see the moment he realised that she'd keep asking if he didn't. And if *she* didn't, Caro would, and that would only be worse. The Dahlias found things out, one way or another. And if it was sheer perseverance that got them there, so be it.

Piotr sighed. 'Amber and Luke had a bit of a falling out, that's all. As far as I was concerned, Luke's behaviour was above reproach. But then, shortly after we moved from our rehearsal space into the theatre, Amber came to me because her DSM had expressed concern about Luke and Darcy's behaviour in the wings.'

'Inappropriate behaviour? During the show?' Rosalind dreaded to think how bad that behaviour would need to be to get reported up.

Piotr nodded. 'I was sure it was just the usual pranking and messing around – you know how that goes. But there appeared to be some . . . mutual nudity, and in this day and age anything remotely, well, sexual can get a person into a lot of hot water.'

'Amber's the company stage manager, right? She didn't talk to Luke herself?' Normally any messing around of that sort would have been dealt with by the stage manager at the time.

'She did. She said he laughed it off and she was concerned he wasn't taking it seriously. So she asked me to talk to him. And, like I guessed, it was just foolish hijinks. But then *Luke* got his back up because we were questioning his professionalism.'

'I can imagine, after all the hard work he'd put into proving he'd changed.' Fooling about in the wings wasn't exactly proof that he was the same man he'd always been, but if there was a formal complaint made by the DSM or Amber, Rosalind could see how it could have caused Luke problems. And if Martha was right and the falling out between Luke and his dad had been over his behaviour, and their reconciliation was congruent on his rehabilitated nature ... Yes, Luke wouldn't have been happy about any sort of character-based rebuke.

'Exactly.' Piotr sighed. 'So he hit back, and made a complaint against Amber. She'd had some childcare problems the previous weekend and brought her son to a rehearsal. Luke said it was inappropriate.'

'Ah.'

'I was just mediating between the two of them. By the time you overheard me talking to Luke it was more or less sorted, I think, with pride still mostly intact all round.' He shrugged. 'The director's lot.'

The bell rang to inform the audience that they needed to return to the theatre. She didn't have much longer. 'Things improved in the wings, I take it? With Luke and Darcy, I mean.'

'People stopped complaining,' Piotr said. 'I'm not sure if that's the same thing.'

But just because they stopped complaining to the management, didn't mean they were happy about it – and wouldn't find somewhere else to complain to.

'Last I heard the bigger problem was Luke and Darcy *arguing* backstage during the show. Loudly.' Piotr pulled a face. 'Actors.'

Apparently he'd forgotten who he was talking to. 'You must have been worried about the stories reaching the press. That wouldn't look good for the show.'

He gave her a knowing look. 'If you're insinuating that I had a reason to kill Luke Burrows I'd prefer it if you asked me the question outright.'

Piotr hadn't lowered his voice at all, and several passing audience members turned to them in alarm.

Rosalind ignored them, and raised one eyebrow at the director. 'Well? Did you?'

With a smug smile, he pulled a small, black notebook from his pocket. 'In the back of this notebook, I keep a running list of my enemies. A hit list, if you will.' He opened it to the relevant pages and held it out to her. 'You'll notice he's not on it.'

He was right, Luke's name wasn't there – nor were any of the cast and crew. But she was amused to notice a number of other, more famous names she recognised.

She handed the notebook back. 'And did the police feel this was satisfactory evidence of your innocence?'

The bell rang one last time. 'We need to get back in there.'

Piotr drained the rest of his drink, slammed his glass down on the bar, and headed for their seats, Rosalind following more slowly behind, still considering everything he'd told her.

'Just one more question,' she said, as they settled into their seats. 'The day of the murder, we were having drinks in the bar. You left after seeing something out of the window. What was it?'

'I don't remember.' The answer came just a little too fast for her to believe it. 'Maybe it was the fire engine.'

The lights dimmed before she could tell him that the alarms hadn't rung out until *after* they left the bar.

The second half of the play washed over her as she tried to piece together what they knew so far, without the benefit of Posy's notes, or Caro interrupting with little insights every few moments. There was something here. Something that linked everything together. But she was damned if she could put her finger on what it was.

Something she'd seen, maybe? Or heard?

On the stage, Caro/Maggie stood to the side, trying to look brave and unaffected when the whole audience knew the character was terrified of getting her heart broken, as Joshua/Freddie answered the phone. This was the moment of the play that mattered most – when Freddie made his decision about the path his life would take from here on in. And the rejigged cast was absolutely killing it.

She smiled as Joshua held the phone out to Caro, and she took it, shutting down Darcy/Jocelyn's attempt to betray them. Somewhere in the audience, a little whoop went up, and then there was laughter and clapping, and Rosalind knew that this show would continue to run, to be a success, even without a big name.

She was glad of it, for Caro's sake. And she wondered if the same would have still been true if Luke was alive. Would his reformed bad-boy image have slipped – before or after he inherited from his father – or was it a true change? If it had all been an act, if he reverted to the man Posy remembered, would his misbehaviour off stage have ruined things in the end? Led to an early close, however good the play?

She'd seen it happen before. And saving the play – for everyone involved – was as good a motive for murder as any of the others.

After a few more scenes, the play came to an end – with a roar of applause and a standing ovation for the cast. Rosalind joined in, smiling fondly as she watched Caro and the rest of the company unite at the front of the stage, hand in hand, to take their bows.

Then she blinked and looked again. Because there was something not quite right . . .

Someone was missing.

Chapter Thirteen

'She confessed, Dahlia.' Johnnie sighed wearily. 'That's the end of it.'
Dahlia eyed him mutinously. 'Not if I have anything to say about it.'

Dahlia Lively in *Impossible Crimes for Impossible Times*
By Lettice Davenport, 1972

Caro

After the chaos of brunch, the rest of Caro's day had gone surprisingly well.

Tuesdays were a two-performance day, which meant she'd gone straight from Rosalind's hotel to the theatre, ignoring any cameras or reporters she came across on her way. She had a job to do – and not just on stage.

Rosalind was right. They needed progress, fast. More than that, they needed a more believable suspect than Posy – and Caro was determined to find one.

Shortly after they came off stage from the matinee performance, Ashok had called with an update on a few things she'd asked him to look into, which was also promising.

'So, my police contact—'

'Are you ever going to tell me who that is?' Caro had interrupted. 'Or at least what you've got on them to make them help you?'

'No,' Ashok shot back, instantly. 'But you do want to hear what they told me. It's about the fire at the Arcadia at the time of the murder.'

'Wasn't it a cigarette in the bins?'

'Yes. That's been confirmed by the investigators from the fire department,' Ashok said. 'But they also found something else in the bins. A coat – a green utility jacket, partially burned and covered in blood.'

Now *that* was worth knowing. If the murderer had started the fire to dispose of the evidence . . . why hadn't they thought more about the fire before? *Because we got distracted by fake Posy on the CCTV camera.* The fake Posy wearing a green utility jacket.

'Still no sign of the murder weapon?' she asked.

'Not that I've heard,' Ashok replied. 'It wasn't with the coat, anyway.'

New information in hand, Caro had swung by the wardrobe department ostensibly on some small errand of little consequence, and managed to sneak into the wig room to establish that, yes, there was a blonde wig styled already in a ponytail that looked an awful lot like the one on the CCTV footage from the Arcadia. She'd snapped a few photos to share with the police.

She'd also had a word with some of the wardrobe staff, and triple checked that they'd all been together at the time of the murder, so were out of the frame. She also heard their thoughts on Luke, which had only left her more confused than ever. While most found him charming and professional, one or two were less complimentary.

When she pressed for more information, though, they clammed up. The most any of them would say was that they'd seen him backstage with Darcy, and they didn't like the way he was with her.

Before she left, Caro asked, as an afterthought, 'I don't suppose there's a coat missing from wardrobe is there? A green utility jacket?' It wouldn't have fitted with the costumes on *this* play, but the theatre wardrobe was far more extensive than just what was currently being used.

Milly, the woman in charge of wardrobe, frowned. 'Not as far as I know. Although . . . Hanna! What was that jacket you were complaining about losing the other day? The one you thought you must have left in the tapas bar?'

'My green one,' Hanna called back. 'The oversized utility one. With the pockets and the tie waist.'

Caro kept her face expressionless as she yelled, 'I hope you find it!'

So. Two small mysteries solved. The jacket and the wig must have come from the wardrobe department, one way or another, and the cap could have come from anywhere. She was more interested in the differences of opinion on who Luke was from the wardrobe staff.

She needed to talk to Darcy again and find out what they meant about the way he was with her.

It was only when she ferreted out Amber, to ask her some more questions, that she realised what might be behind the differences in opinion: some of the crew had been in the wings to help with costume changes, and others hadn't.

'I honestly don't know what to make of it.' Amber rubbed a hand across her forehead, wearily, leaving a small stripe of black behind – pencil, Caro expected. 'Luke was . . . he was professional and charming and genuine all through the rehearsals. He knew what his reputation was and he promised he'd moved past it – and he honestly seemed to have. You know this, Caro you were there.'

'I'm sensing a but,' Caro said.

'But the last couple of weeks . . . I'd had a few complaints from the crew – my DSM in particular. First, it was just pranks and messing around in the wings. But then someone spoke to me about the way Luke had treated Darcy off stage. Nothing physical that time, but they thought the way he spoke to her was . . . toxic. I tried to raise it, but the person didn't want to go on the record, and I hadn't witnessed it myself . . .'

'Was this person in the wardrobe department?' Caro guessed.

Amber looked surprised. 'You've spoken to them? Good. That's . . . good.' But despite her words she still looked troubled as she slid down to sit on the floor of the wings.

Caro crouched down beside her. 'What are you thinking, Amber?'

She took a breath, and stared out over Caro's shoulder towards the stage as she answered. 'I guess I'm starting to wonder . . . I wanted to believe he'd changed, but now he's dead I think more people are talking and, well, I wonder if maybe the Luke we saw – the cast, the management . . . maybe it wasn't the same Luke that some others saw. The people he thought were . . . less important.'

'I'm starting to wonder the same,' Caro admitted, softly.

'And that makes me worry about Darcy.' Amber leaned back against the wall, her legs stretched out in front of her. 'In my experience, guys like Luke . . . like he used to be, anyway, they are very tuned in to the people around them, and what they can get from them. He set his eyes on Darcy from the start – we all saw it, even you, I bet.'

Caro thought back to the early days of rehearsals, and nodded. Luke had always been there pulling out a chair for Darcy or handing her a water bottle. She'd thought it was sweet, romantic even, that he was so enamoured with her.

She hadn't thought that Darcy had returned the feeling, though, at least not to start with. She'd been surprised, she remembered, when they'd first appeared at the tapas bar one night hand in hand. But what had Darcy said? He'd worn her down.

'Once he'd won her, maybe the dynamic changed,' Amber said. 'I don't know. I guess other people's relationships are always a mystery.'

But passion was a motive, and so was hate or fear. Whatever had been going on between Luke and Darcy, it seemed like she might have a motive either way.

Caro needed to talk to Darcy again, that much was obvious, but the actress seemed to be going out of her way to avoid her. She'd almost cornered her twice before they called the half for that night's show, but each time she'd managed to slip away, or thrust someone else into the conversation so she could escape.

The evening's show went well enough. She tried to grab Darcy again in the interval, but she disappeared too fast for her to find, and there was no answer when she knocked on the door to her dressing room. Then they were back on stage again, in character, and no chance to talk until after the show.

Maybe it was for the best. Caro needed to focus on the show, to give it her all. And those closing scenes got the same uproarious reaction as they had every other night, leading into the happy ending. They'd nailed it.

Except, when it came to the final bow, Caro realised suddenly that Darcy wasn't there.

'Where's Darcy?' she asked, out of the corner of her mouth, over the wild applause of the audience.

Joshua gave a barely there shrug. 'She was on stage a couple of scenes ago. Maybe her ankle was giving her trouble again.'

The audience either didn't notice or didn't care that one of their company was absent, as the applause went on and on. Caro's muscles tensed as she forced herself to stay in place and smile, not run off and chase after Darcy, wherever she'd got to.

Finally, the cast took one last bow, then made their way off stage into the wings. Caro raced towards Amber, whose headset was askew, her red hair wild around her face, and her eyes wide.

'Where's Darcy?' Caro demanded. 'She wasn't there for the curtain call.'

'I don't know!' Amber was already striding towards Darcy's dressing room. 'She was on stage, then she disappeared after her last scene and by the time I realised she hadn't come back for the curtain call it was too late.'

Caro knocked purposefully on the dressing-room door and, when there was no answer, called Darcy's name. Still nothing.

Amber looked at Caro, who shrugged, and turned the door handle, pushing it open. 'Darcy?'

The room was in darkness. Amber flipped on the switch and, after a moment, the bulb overhead flickered to life.

For a moment, Caro's heart stopped in her chest, and she realised she was expecting to see another body. But the dressing room was simply empty.

'Her costume is here, all hung up,' Amber said, running a hand over the fabric. 'But I can't see any of her personal stuff – her bag or what have you.'

No, not quite empty.

'There's a note.' Caro moved towards the dressing table, where a folded piece of paper leaned against the mirror. There was no name on the front of it, which made it fair game as far as she was concerned.

Picking it up, she carefully unfolded it, read it twice, then laid it out on the table and took a photo of it.

'What does it say?' Amber asked, crowding closer.

Caro folded it up again. 'I think we need to get this to the police.'

Rosalind

'Tell me again. What did the note say?' Rosalind demanded.

On the other side of the table, Caro groaned and pushed her phone with the photo of the note towards her before reaching for her wine glass. 'Read it for yourself.'

Once the police had asked their questions, and it became clear that Darcy was no longer in the theatre, the rest of the company from the Prince Regent had decamped over to the tapas bar for alcohol, food and – obviously – gossip.

The note was short and simple.

I had to do it. Nobody knew what he was really like. I couldn't take it any more. I'm not sorry. He wasn't ever going to change.

But I can't live with it, either.

Goodbye.

'It's her handwriting, I presume?' Rosalind pushed the phone back across the table towards Caro.

'God knows.' Caro took back the phone and rubbed her forehead wearily. 'Who honestly knows what anyone else's handwriting looks like these days?'

'The police will check, I'm sure,' Rosalind said. Someone would have to be able to recognise it, wouldn't they? Her parents, maybe. 'Did she sign out at the stage door?'

'No, but she'd taken all her stuff with her. I imagine she slipped out the front through the pass door to avoid questions from Eddie or anyone else backstage,' Caro said. 'She could have easily hidden while we came off stage to look for her, then disappeared into the crowd.'

The audience would have been streaming out on all sides. Rosalind could have passed Darcy herself and not even noticed in that sort of a crush. Especially if she'd worn the same wig and hat she'd presumably used to sneak into the Arcadia disguised as Posy.

Suddenly, the restaurant door flew open again, crashing against the doorstop and rattling the blinds.

And there was Posy.

The youngest Dahlia had a light cotton scarf tied around her neck, one Rosalind suspected she'd been using to cover her hair and maybe her face on the way over. Her blonde hair was tied back in a ponytail, but it looked more dishevelled than usual, and her T-shirt and jeans seemed to be hanging off her. The purple shadows under her eyes when she pushed the utterly-unnecessary-at-this-time-of-night sunglasses up on top of her head spoke of long, sleepless nights since they'd seen her last.

Everyone stared, of course. Posy's eyes widened as she realised the attention she'd drawn, and she took a step backwards before, suddenly, Caro was at her side. Rosalind hadn't even realised she'd left the table.

'We're over here,' she heard Caro say, loud enough to cover the whispering. 'Come join us.'

The speculation now was rife throughout the restaurant. Rosalind was sure the contents of Darcy's note had already spread through at least those people backstage at the Regent, and probably further by now. Everyone would have an opinion on what it meant – especially for Posy's innocence.

Well, Rosalind had told Caro they needed a confession. And according to that note, they had one.

'I got your message,' Posy said, her voice soft, as she slid into the empty chair at their table. 'Can I see it? You took a photo, yeah?'

Caro handed her the phone and they both watched as Posy's gaze darted across the screen, taking it in before pushing it away again.

Then she sat back in her chair, shoulders curled in and her hands clasped together on the table.

'Was that what it took for you to believe I didn't kill him?' Posy asked tightly. 'Someone else confessing?'

Rosalind glared at Caro. This one was hers to answer.

'No,' Caro said, cautiously. 'I . . . Posy, I never thought you murdered Luke. Not seriously. I'm sorry if I led you to believe that I did. I just knew we needed to consider all the angles because the police *would*, and we needed to be armed with all the information we could find to solve this. But I will admit that I wondered, for a moment or two, here and there, if you might have done it in self-defence.'

'Because of the thing with the book,' Posy said, her voice flat. 'The night he surprised me in my dressing room.'

'And because in investigating his death, I think I've started to see that you might have been right about him all along. That maybe he hadn't changed as much as he wanted people to believe.' Caro took a breath. 'And I think, based on this note as well as some other conversations I've had, I think Darcy knew that too.'

Now, Posy looked up and met Caro's gaze. Rosalind glanced between the two of them, her jaw tense. This was it. If they were going to forgive and forget, it had to be now, surely.

Posy glanced away again and the moment was gone. Caro's face fell, and Rosalind took a quick breath to hide her sigh.

'You're not the only ones who've been investigating.' Posy pulled a familiar-looking notebook from her bag, flipping it open in her lap so the pages were hidden from them. 'I couldn't do much, locked up in my flat, but I sent emails and messages, made some calls. And I picked up some stuff at the police station. And . . . I spoke to Darcy. Yesterday.'

'How was she?' Rosalind asked. 'What did she tell you?'

'She was scared.' Posy looked up and met Rosalind's gaze. 'She said she suspected that Luke was cheating on her before he died but couldn't prove it. And if it wasn't with me she didn't know who with.'

'She told us the same,' Caro murmured. 'But I didn't get the impression she was *scared* of Luke, not then. Although talking to others . . .'

'He . . . Luke had a . . . a process, I guess,' Posy said. 'For a while, at the start, you were the only thing that mattered to him. He'd love bomb you, make you feel on top of the world while he was winning you. But then once he had you, he lost interest. And that's when things got hard. When the gaslighting started, among other things. That's what happened to Darcy.'

'She told you that?' Rosalind asked, surprised. Darcy hadn't mentioned anything of the sort to Caro, but then Posy was closer to her own age and obviously didn't like Luke. Maybe that was why she'd opened up to her. 'Did she tell the *police* that? If he was abusive, that explains her note . . .'

But Posy was shaking her head. 'Darcy didn't tell me. I told her. I . . . I needed to know if he was still that man. And from what she said . . . I'm pretty sure he was.'

Rosalind glanced at Caro, knowing from the hard line of her friend's jaw that she was as horrified by this revelation as she was. *She told her he didn't hit her*, Rosalind remembered Annie telling her.

But abuse didn't have to be physical.

She wanted to talk more about it, give Posy the chance to open up to them at last, to reassure her they were on her side. But Posy was already glancing around nervously at the other people in the restaurant, pulling her sleeves over her hands then shoving them up again. She was going to bolt again soon, Rosalind could tell.

They needed answers before that happened.

'How did Darcy respond?' she asked.

'She wouldn't hear it,' Posy said. 'She wouldn't admit what he was doing to her. She kept making excuses for him even when she described his controlling behaviour. I guess she didn't want to be considered a suspect – like me – by speaking out against him. But then tonight she sent me this.'

She pulled out her phone and turned the screen towards them, the message from Darcy clear.

You were right.

The time stamp was before the evening performance.

'Tonight? Right about what?' Caro asked. 'Did you accuse her? Was she saying you were right that she'd done it? Or that you were right about who Luke really was?'

Posy shrugged. 'No way to tell. I tried calling her back as soon as I saw the message, but it went straight to voicemail. But . . .'

'What?' Rosalind asked when she trailed off. 'What is it?'

Posy's eyes were wide as she answered, as if she couldn't believe she was saying it either. 'I don't think Darcy did it. I think she knew something, and I think she was scared and that's why she ran. But I don't think she did it. And so you have to keep investigating.'

Rosalind stilled as she watched Posy across the table. 'You realise this note, Darcy's confession and disappearance, it gives you an out. Even if the police can't find her to arrest her. You're off the hook if someone else has confessed.'

But Posy shook her head. 'It doesn't matter. The . . . the truth is what matters. And that's what we – what you – need to find.'

She pushed her chair back away from the table and jumped to her feet.

'Wait. Where are you going?' Caro asked. 'What are you going to be doing?'

Posy's smile was strangely crooked. 'I'm going to talk to an old friend, I hope.'

Caro

They'd stayed at the tapas bar debating what Posy had told them for at least another glass or two of wine, but by the time they called it a night, Caro and Rosalind still weren't settled on their next steps.

'We'll sleep on it,' Rosalind said, in the end, when Carlos looked like he might be about to personally throw them out of his restaurant so he could go to bed. 'We can meet tomorrow for lunch and talk it through again.'

'At least the paparazzi might have lost interest in us by then.' Somehow the news about Darcy's note had already leaked, and internet theories were once again abounding. There was an alert out to find her, and Caro had heard one of the officers mentioning searching the Thames. Whether that meant they were leaning towards the theory that Darcy had fled the theatre, headed straight for the nearest bridge and jumped to assuage her own guilt, she wasn't sure. Just the thought of it made her shiver, so she tried not to dwell. As far as she knew, Darcy was alive and well and – if Posy was right – innocent.

A full-ish night's sleep, or as much as she ever got these days, hadn't seemed to help, though. Neither did several cups of coffee and a few hours of edits on the book. Doom scrolling social media and seeing the even split between 'Justice for Posy' posts and 'it's all a giant celeb conspiracy' articles didn't make things any better either.

By the time she met Rosalind for lunch, Caro still didn't know what they should do for the best. Let Darcy's confession stand and hope that the police found the evidence to back it up – and Darcy herself, come to that – so Posy was exonerated, or keep chasing the possible alternative killer based purely on Posy's hunch.

But it was a beautiful summer's day, London was stunning and, for now at least, things seemed to be improving with Posy. Caro was going to try to take the win and enjoy lunch.

The terrace at the back of Somerset House looked down over the Embankment and out over the Thames. From the table Rosalind had chosen, hidden away behind the temporary bar and quite a lot of decorative greenery, she could see all the way across to the South Bank. She knew if she carried on to the end she'd be able to make out the National Theatre but from here it was hidden by trees.

This summer, a pop-up Italian restaurant had taken over the terrace, providing them with some excellent coffee and paninis for lunch. However, Caro couldn't help but note that it was just the two of them – again.

'Did you ask Posy to join us?' she asked, as casually as she could.

'I did. I called her this morning. Apparently she had another commitment she couldn't break.' Rosalind's mouth twisted a little at that, so Caro guessed she'd spent some time trying to convince the youngest Dahlia that she could, in fact, break whatever that commitment was.

'At least she picked up this time,' Caro said. 'And it is always easier to talk about her when she's not here.'

Rosalind huffed a laugh. 'This is true. So. What do you think, now you've slept on it?'

'Of Posy's visit? Or Darcy's confession?'

'Either. Both.'

Caro leaned back in her chair, stared out over the river and considered. 'Posy didn't do it,' she said, finally.

'I never thought she did.'

'Well, even if I had, I'm certain now that she didn't. She wouldn't have come to us last night and told us to keep investigating if she had. Besides, if Posy had killed him it would only ever have been self-defence, in the moment, and everything we learn makes it look more and more premeditated. Don't you think?' Caro smiled up at the passing waiter and they placed their orders for lunch, Caro choosing the first thing she fancied on the menu since she hadn't had a chance to consider. It didn't matter. She knew she'd barely taste it. Not when she was so distracted by the investigation.

'You mean the CCTV, the message to Posy to keep her away?' Rosalind said, once the waiter was gone.

Caro nodded. 'And the fire. Set in a bin close enough to set off the alarms but not so close as to do any actual damage to the theatre itself. I'd imagine they tried to time it just so nobody would go into the dressing room until the following day. If Posy hadn't been so annoyed at me, she'd have waited longer for me to show up, I'm sure.'

'Could Darcy have done all those things?' Rosalind asked. 'I know Posy doesn't think she did, but . . . theoretically?'

Closing her eyes, Caro ran the sequence of events like a film in her head, knowing that Rosalind would be doing the same. Did it make a seamless story yet?

'Almost,' she said, finally. 'She could have sent the message, taken the coat and wig, gone to the Arcadia and pretended to be Posy at the stage door. She'd have had to go past the dressing room to the production office to get the knife – if we're right about the murder weapon

– that's the only bit that's dodgy. Then she'd have had to go back to kill Luke, hide the weapon, stash the bloodstained clothes, go out through the pass door by the stage to front of house and then round the side to dump the clothes and set the fire. I saw her out front after the alarms went off, so she was definitely around.'

Rosalind hummed her agreement. 'But if she *didn't* do all that... why leave the note?'

It was all speculation now, Caro knew. But sometimes, talking through the possibilities was how they found the real answer.

'Maybe... maybe she *was* the fake Posy, but not the murderer,' Caro suggested, remembering Rosalind's earlier objection to limiting their suspect list to just the women. She could have been an accomplice. 'Maybe she felt guilty about helping the murderer and *that's* what she couldn't live with.'

'Or she was afraid the murderer would come looking for her next to tie up loose ends.' Rosalind gave a sharp nod. 'Yes, that tracks.'

'Should we be looking for her?' Caro didn't really have any desire to go playing hide and seek across London for a missing actress, but maybe she could get Ashok to do it...

Rosalind shook her head. 'Leave that to the police. We need to focus on what really happened to Luke. So. Who is still on our suspect list, either as fake Posy or Darcy's accomplice?'

'Piotr, Amber, Joshua, Taran and Martha,' Caro listed promptly. 'We've lost Darcy and Posy, obviously, and Mal was behind the counter when the fake Posy arrived – plus he wouldn't need an accomplice to get access to the dressing rooms.'

'Five suspects. All with varying degrees of motive. I suppose that's progress.' Rosalind sighed. 'I spoke to Piotr again last night, and you spoke with Amber. I think Martha's given us all she's going to. So I suppose we try to talk to Taran and Joshua again today? I can go to the Arcadia later while you're at the Prince Regent. Take one each.'

'That works.' Caro had to admit, investigating was a lot easier when there were three of them to share the questioning. But even with the investigative side sorted, she didn't feel any more settled than she had first thing. She bit the inside of her cheek, then asked, 'Do you think Posy's ever going to forgive me?'

She'd hoped for an instant, positive response, but instead Rosalind hesitated — so long, in fact, that Caro couldn't watch her face a moment longer, and found herself studying the faces of the other people on the terrace instead.

Until she unexpectedly spotted someone she recognised.

'That's her,' she breathed, just as Rosalind opened her mouth to respond.

'Who?' Rosalind started to twist to see where Caro was looking, but she caught her hand and stopped her.

'Don't be obvious. But at the far table over by the terrace wall. That's the woman that Luke met at that townhouse, the day before he died.' Ashok hadn't been able to identify her from Caro's photos, not with her face shaded by a hat and sunglasses. But seeing her in the flesh Caro was certain it was the same woman. She pulled up the photos on her phone to show Rosalind for confirmation, all the same.

One more loose thread — something else she didn't understand about Luke. Could she be the link they needed to make sense of everything that had happened?

Caro looked away and waited while Rosalind casually reached down for her handbag, twisting in her seat as if to make room for the bag on her lap while she rifled through it for something. In truth, Caro knew she was studying the woman in question.

And the second woman who joined her moments later, without glancing back in their direction.

Which was just as well, as they recognised her too.

I'm going to talk to an old friend, I hope.

'Well, I guess we know what Posy's prior engagement was now,' Caro said, softly.

Chapter Fourteen

Dahlia leaned against the railings and looked out over the River Thames, with its bridges and boats and mysteries.

'London is a wonderful place, Johnnie. My favourite city in the world.' She turned to look at him. 'But sometimes it can be so cold.'

'And deadly,' Johnnie said, wrapping his coat around her shoulders.

Dahlia Lively in *Midnight in London*
By Lettice Davenport, 1962

Posy

It had been years since Posy last saw Shannon Carpenter, née Sharp, other than in the grainy photo in the newspaper wrapped around the flowers that Luke had left for her, the day of his murder. She'd tossed the flowers in the stage-door bin before she headed to her dressing room, but she'd kept the newspaper, folded safely in her pocket to consider later.

She hadn't been sure Shannon would return her call or agree to meet. But she'd been certain that she'd know who was calling when she gave her fake name, even after so long. There was only one person who could be the Alice to Shannon's Willa.

It was fortunate that most of the paparazzi outside her flat had left since Darcy's confession became public knowledge. A few had lingered, of course, but she'd taken care to cover her hair and wear her biggest sunglasses, and walked past them without even a no comment. Paired with a silk cami, light jacket, sandals and jeans, she hoped she wouldn't stand out anywhere. Today was not a day for fans *or* haters to recognise her.

The woman waiting for her at the table on the terrace at Somerset House looked just like she had in that newspaper photo: glossy, expensive and perfect. Shannon today was a far cry from the giggly teenager Posy had known back in LA, but she'd still have recognised her anywhere. Or maybe that was just shame and regret talking.

Posy and Shannon had met when they'd been co-starring in the summer teen movie, *The Switch Up*, thirteen years earlier. The timing had been convenient, as Posy had just discovered that her parents had betrayed her, embezzling all of her funds from her earlier films. She'd disowned them and walked away – and Shannon had let her stay with her in the flat her father owned in LA. They'd quickly become fast friends, along with Shannon's boyfriend, their other co-star – Luke. He'd been playing Posy's love interest for the film, but they'd barely had to share more than a brush of the lips on screen. Off screen, it was he and Shannon who had fallen fast and hard for each other, before Posy even arrived on the scene.

In the movie, Shannon and Posy had played almost identical girls, Willa and Alice, who met on a plane and swapped summers, a sort of coming-of-age story with added London and Italian scenery and, in Posy's recollection, a lot of gelato.

In reality, of course, most of the movie had been filmed on a studio set in LA and the surrounding Californian countryside, with moody establishing shots of London filmed later. Shannon, playing Willa, had flown to London for a couple of weeks of actual on-location filming, leaving Luke and Posy back in LA.

Which was when their on-screen romance had bloomed into something more.

Back then, the two girls' features had been similar enough to pass for each other, their nineteen-year-old figures equally waifish in their denim cut-offs and T-shirts. For the movie, they'd covered Posy's lighter hair with a long, dark wig to match Shannon's natural locks, and called the transformation good. Not twins, but close enough for film work. Ironically, today Shannon's hair was highlighted to within an inch of blonde, a honey tone not unlike Posy's.

Back then, they'd been friends. The same. A pair.

Now, though, Posy felt like she was sitting opposite an alternative universe version of herself. The woman she could have been if she'd followed a different path. Maybe the woman she would have been if she hadn't let Luke into her life.

If things had gone differently between the three of them, maybe Shannon would have been the one to spend years in the wilderness, in and out of rehab, vilified in the tabloids. Maybe Posy would have been the one to marry a millionaire businessman and give up her own career to be the perfect society wife.

She almost laughed at the idea. No, she would never have been that. And she was proud of the woman she'd become, despite the mistakes she'd made on the way. Right now, her life might not be quite so sunny, but she had faith that it would be again – once she'd solved this case.

Facing Shannon in her designer dress and delicate – but expensive – jewellery, with her perfectly smooth hair and immaculate lipstick, it would be easy to feel like a child by comparison. A teenager who hadn't grown up when all her peers had. Here she was, in trouble again, while Shannon looked like she'd taken on the world and won.

Probably because she had.

If Shannon wanted to underestimate her that way – and the faintly pitying look on her face as Posy sat down suggested she did – that was fine by her. It would make it all the easier to take her down.

Posy had spent years feeling nothing but shame and guilt about how her friendship with Shannon had ended – one of the main reasons she hadn't wanted to tell Caro the whole story of her history with Luke, back when he was just Caro's latest co-star rather than the subject of their latest murder investigation. But now, she couldn't help but feel that Shannon's presence in London, right at the time Luke was killed, couldn't be a coincidence.

Maybe she wasn't the only one with something to feel guilty about.

A waiter brought Shannon her coffee, and she thanked them with a small nod before focusing on Posy. 'I have to admit, I was surprised to get your message. How did you know I was in London?'

A second coffee was placed in front of Posy. She hadn't ordered it, but Shannon must have. Shannon hadn't added anything to hers – no milk, no sugar – so neither did Posy. It was petty, but she wasn't going to give an inch she didn't have to.

She *wasn't* a child. She wasn't here to be looked down on or pitied, not any more. She'd turned her life around and she wasn't that person, the one Shannon knew back then. The girl whose life had been falling apart and had almost taken her with it.

'Is that why you came?' Posy asked. 'Curiosity?'

'Among other things. I imagine rather a lot of people are trying to talk to you right now.'

It had been too much to hope that Shannon wouldn't have heard of the latest scandal attached to Posy's name, she supposed.

'Luke told me you were here,' Posy said, answering her initial question. 'He seemed to think I'd want to know.'

Shannon's lips curved in a small, secret smile. 'He was meddling until the end, then.'

'I suppose so.' She just didn't understand *why*. Had he just wanted to torment her? To threaten her? To scare her? Was it purely to demonstrate the power he held over her? *I know your secrets and I could out them whenever I want, and then where would you be?* So much of her past was already public property, but there were at least a few stories she'd managed to keep hidden. Until now.

The things she'd done with Luke, for Luke, were some of them.

It was another motive, she knew. Another reason she might have wanted to kill him.

But it was just possible that he had meant it as a warning. If Caro was right, if he had changed – if Darcy had been lying, in that last text message . . . Maybe he'd wanted to warn her that there was someone else in London who might be looking to take her down.

'Of course, I should have guessed you were in town before that.' Posy lifted her coffee cup to her lips, watching Shannon over the rim the whole time. She sipped the bitter drink, then placed it down again. 'The sudden increase in stories about my horrible past was the first clue. Usually with the same reporter. Most of them focused on my time in LA.' The stories had varied, and many of them had been covered often before online or in the press. Once one paper started including them others followed suit, but Posy had noticed that the most cutting and damning pieces were always in one place first – a Theatreland gossip blog. From there, they got picked up by one paper, and then the others, until the stories were everywhere.

Shannon's eyes widened innocently. 'I don't know what you're talking about.'

'I thought it was Luke, at first,' Posy admitted. 'Playing both sides. Pretending to have changed, to be everyone's best friend, then feeding the gossip pages ancient stories about me behind their backs. But then, of course, he was murdered – and I discovered that someone had tried to frame me. Disguised themselves as me convincingly enough to sneak into the theatre and kill Luke in my dressing room, setting me up to discover the body and be the first and only suspect.' Posy took another sip of coffee, revelling in Shannon's silence. 'I thought to myself, who in the world hates me enough to do that? And I only came up with one name. Yours.'

Shannon glanced away. 'I understood that someone else had already confessed to the murder. Luke's girlfriend, I believe.'

'She didn't do it.' Posy couldn't explain the visceral feeling that told her that was true. 'I think she saw you and recognised you, somehow. I think you threatened her then paid her off – told her to leave and gave her the money to do it. God knows you're rich enough to bribe anybody.'

Shannon's expression shifted, and suddenly she was staring right into Posy's eyes, searching them for something.

'It's an interesting theory,' she said, finally. 'And I can see why you'd cling on to it. I mean, it would make it a lot easier to forgive yourself, wouldn't it, if I was guilty of a worse crime? If you could just hate me, maybe you could love yourself again. Is that it?'

Posy forced herself to keep her face neutral and her gaze on Shannon's face, looking for any hint of guilt. 'I just want to catch a murderer.'

'Well, I'm afraid you're looking in the wrong place.' Shannon reached for her coffee and took another sip. 'I'm honestly kind of insulted you think I've had nothing better to do with my time here in London than think or talk about you, let alone leak stories to the gutter presses. Quite aside from the fact that the worst stories *I* know about your youth aren't ones I would want to be spread around since they also concern *me*.'

She had a point, not that Posy was willing to admit it yet.

Shannon continued. 'And as for the murder accusation – which, if you repeat to anyone else I will obviously look into suing you for – I had an appointment elsewhere in London the evening Luke died, nowhere near the Arcadia Theatre. I'll happily give the police the details if they need them.'

'They will,' Posy said, with more confidence than she felt. She'd been so sure it had to be Shannon . . .

'But even if I didn't have an alibi, your little theory does rather fall apart when you realise that Luke and I made up years ago. If he was meddling, reminding you of our one-time friendship, I imagine it was because he was trying to force a reconciliation.' Shannon sighed over her coffee cup. 'He always was the most romantic of the three of us – and I mean that in the purest sense of the word.'

'A reconciliation?' Of all the possibilities that had occurred to her since Luke appeared in her dressing room and gave her that old script, a reconciliation with Shannon hadn't been one of them. Mostly because she knew that neither she nor Luke deserved it.

'Yes.' Shannon shifted in her seat, uncrossing her legs only to cross them the other way instead. Her attention seemed to be half on Posy, half on the river rushing past below. 'You see, Luke and I had . . . reconnected over the past few years. We bumped into each other in New York some time back and, well, we talked. And we both listened. After that, whenever we were in the same place for a time we'd get together. We made our amends, made peace with the past and found a way to be friends again, at least. Like things were at the start. Perhaps he wanted the same for us.'

Shannon and Luke had become friends again. How had she not known this?

Except, why would she? The time when the three of them had been each other's worlds was a long way in the past. And it wasn't like she'd given him an opportunity to tell her since he'd been back in her orbit.

'You met up here in London?' Darcy had said she'd seen Luke with a blonde, having lunch. She hadn't sounded convinced when Posy insisted it hadn't been her. Could it have been Shannon?

'Often. For lunch, or what have you. We talked a lot about what happened,' Shannon went on, still not quite meeting Posy's eye. 'You might have heard that after I left LA, I never went back.'

Of course she'd heard. The gossip had been everywhere. The daughter of a prominent Broadway actress and a rich businessman, Shannon had grown up in theatres and turned of age on screen. Her future was supposed to be bright, and lit up in neon. Instead, she disappeared.

'I heard you went back to your family,' Posy said, carefully. 'Next thing I knew your engagement was being announced in the papers.' An engagement to a much older man, a business associate of Shannon's father, as far as Posy had been able to find out.

'I went back to my family because I was pregnant, and my boyfriend was sleeping with you, and I didn't know what else to do.' Shannon's words were blunt but quiet. Merely stating the facts.

They cut into Posy's heart all the same.

She'd done so many stupid, ill-advised things during what Caro called her wilderness years. But none of them had hurt another person the way she'd hurt Shannon.

After Shannon, Posy had only really ever hurt herself.

'I heard rumours, later. About the pregnancy. And . . . and a miscarriage.' She hadn't known if they were true. There were always rumours, and when Shannon hadn't returned to acting after her early success as a teen . . . well, there had to be a reason.

She'd blamed herself, anyway. Blamed herself, and blamed Luke, even while she stayed with him, as if leaving would be admitting just how wrong she'd been all along. She'd let him gaslight her, believed the things he told her about who she was, like he could know her better than herself. She'd let him take control of her life – her remaining money, her friends, her career . . . and she'd sunk deeper and deeper into herself, into self-hatred, until she'd finally run away again covered in shame and disappointment.

She'd stolen her best friend's boyfriend, only to finally realise she should never have wanted him in the first place. She'd always believed that was her punishment, until now.

Being framed for Luke's murder felt like a much more efficient punishment.

'It was an ectopic pregnancy,' Shannon went on. 'Things went badly and, well, afterwards the surgeon told me I'd never be able to have my own children.'

'I'm sorry.' It wasn't enough. Nothing she could say or do would be.

Shannon's slim shoulders rose maybe an inch and dropped again, not quite a shrug, more an acceptance of fate. 'An ectopic pregnancy is not a miscarriage. It would have happened regardless. I didn't miscarry because of the stress of finding you and Luke in bed together, or whatever story you've been telling yourself all these years. It was a medical inevitability. A tragedy, perhaps – but mine, not yours.' Her tone was sharp and unforgiving, even as she told Posy it hadn't been her fault.

Plenty had, though.

She'd told Caro that Luke couldn't be trusted because he was a liar and a cheat. She hadn't had the courage to tell her that she was, too. She'd wanted her friends still to think the best of her, even after everything they *did* know. To not know how badly she could betray a friend, in case they thought she could do it to them. Turned out the lie – of omission, but still a lie – had been wasted. Caro had still thought her capable of murder.

Rosalind might have understood. Caro . . . never. Posy wasn't even sure *she* understood her actions back then.

Maybe she'd done worse things in her wilder days, but that betrayal of her only friend, the one who stuck by her when things went to hell with her parents, gave her a place to live . . . that was the one she struggled to accept about herself.

'Some days I can even convince myself it was for the best.' Shannon gave her a knowing look. 'I think we can *both* agree that Luke would have been no use as a father.'

'You told Luke all this?' Posy reached for her coffee again mostly to give her something to do with her hands. It was too bitter to drink.

'Mmm.' Shannon nodded. 'It was . . . cathartic. For both of us, I think.'

'Hence the reconciliation.' They'd been children back then, as much as she would have denied it at the time. And hadn't Posy spent the last few years trying to prove that people could change, that it was possible to move on?

But as Caro had pointed out, she hadn't been willing to give Luke the same chance.

Had she been wrong? Caro had hinted last night that she hadn't. Darcy's last text message, and the note she'd left, suggested the same. But now Luke was dead, would she ever really know for sure?

'I take it that possibility hadn't occurred to you?' Shannon looked amused at Posy's lack of insight. 'Of course it hadn't. You always expect the worst from people. Which is why his plan would never have worked.'

'You don't think we could be friends again?' It wasn't that Posy was surprised by that – their worlds were very different now, for all that Posy's star had risen once more. What could they possibly have in common these days?

Shannon looked up, over Posy's shoulder, and a faint smile graced her lips. 'I think we both have enough friends these days. Don't you?'

She got to her feet, leaving her coffee half drunk, a lipstick ring on the cup, and stepped away from the table, towards the doors back into Somerset House. Posy turned to watch her go – and felt her breath catch in her lungs.

'Rosalind King, Caro Hooper.' Shannon held out a hand to each of them in turn. 'It's a pleasure. I'll leave Posy with you.'

And then she was gone – leaving Posy facing two Dahlia stares, two raised eyebrows, and a lot of explanations ahead.

Chapter Fifteen

'Was there something you wanted?' Dahlia looked coolly up at Johnnie as he lingered in the doorway.

He sighed. 'I've come to ask for your help.'

'Oh, really?' Dahlia raised an eyebrow.

'Yes, really,' he replied, impatiently. 'Now, would you like me to beg, or would you rather get on with solving this murder?'

She tilted her head to the side as if she were considering, and Johnnie rolled his eyes before hitching his trousers at the thigh ready to bend his knees.

Dahlia jumped up from her chair. 'Oh, all right. Let's get on with the investigation.'

If she let him get down on one knee the idiot might go and propose again by accident, and they really didn't have time for that nonsense.

Dahlia Lively in *Violet Murder*
By Lettice Davenport, 1964

Rosalind

In Rosalind's experience, it was always easier to get people to talk when they were walking. Something to do with not having to look the other person in the eye as they spoke. And heaven knew the three of them needed to talk, so she dragged the others across Waterloo

Bridge to the South Bank, and blessed the late June weather that made it so perfect for a relaxing stroll.

They passed the statue of Laurence Olivier in silence, walking under the trees that lined the river, and past the National Theatre, where Rosalind had once spent a very happy season appearing in *The Importance of Being Earnest*. She had to admit, performing in front of over a thousand people on stage was less intimidating than persuading all the tourists they passed that all was well in the world of the three Dahlias.

She walked between Caro and Posy, the tension in the air vibrating over her, belying the concept of 'relaxing stroll'. This was ridiculous. One way or another, she was going to sort this today so they could get back to what really mattered: solving a murder.

'So. You've been busy, I take it.' Caro spoke across her, at Posy. 'You told us last night you'd been investigating. I assume that was the old friend you were talking about? You know she met with Luke the morning of his murder. I saw them. If you'd told us about her before we could be further along already. But I guess you were trying to solve this case on your own.'

'It's hard to know who to trust to help you when everyone thinks you're a murderer,' Posy shot back.

Rosalind sighed. Of course they weren't going to make this easy.

They were drawing attention, though. The three of them together always did – they were far more conspicuous as a trio than individually. So far it was just tourists pointing and whispering, 'Wait, is that . . .' as they passed, and the odd click of a camera phone. It probably wouldn't be long before someone approached them for autographs or a selfie – and the last thing they needed was more photos of Caro and Posy glaring at each other appearing on the internet.

Rosalind looped her arm through Caro's, then repeated the movement on the other side with Posy's. The South Bank was wide enough to let them walk three abreast, and even with all the summer tourists, they were given space to continue that way for now, at least.

They were starting to get a little gaggle following them, however, and that would never do. Rosalind spied their escape up ahead, though. In her experience, most fans were pleasant enough if you gave them what they wanted – attention. They just wanted to be noticed.

So first, she paused against the railings of the river, keeping a firm grip on both Posy and Caro, and turned to talk to the small gang following them. They posed for photos – Posy and Caro managing passable smiles as she dug her nails into their arms – and signed a couple of autographs, and then it was time.

'Thank you so much for stopping to talk with us.' Rosalind beamed broadly as she fumbled for the catch on the gate in the railings behind them. 'Enjoy the rest of your day!'

The gate swung open and she ushered Posy and Caro down the steps that led to the beach beside the river – and shut the gate politely behind them when others tried to follow.

The narrow beach was mostly deserted, and the sounds of the river – the boats, the lapping of the water, the seabirds – masked their conversation anyway.

Rosalind turned to face the other two. 'Right. We're going to move on from this, right now. Posy, Caro knows you didn't kill Luke. We know you better than that, but we also had to consider all the angles to the case. And Caro? Posy is entitled to her own life and her own secrets, just like you and I are. Okay?'

She glared at them both, giving them little room to quibble. Unsurprisingly, they both nodded.

'Good.' Rosalind let out a breath. 'Then let's walk and talk. Caro, you start.'

Caro pulled a face. 'Fine. Posy, I'm sorry I thought you could be a murderer—'

'Not that,' Rosalind interrupted. 'We're moving on, remember? Posy, we need to know who that woman was, and why she was meeting with Luke the day he was killed. So start talking.'

They meandered slowly along the beach as Posy filled them in on her conversation – and history – with Shannon.

'So you stole your best friend's boyfriend,' Rosalind said, flatly. 'That's it? That's the big secret you couldn't tell us about your history with Luke?' There was something else there, though. Something she hadn't quite grasped yet . . . *Luke had a . . . a process*, that's what Posy had said. The way she'd described her relationship with him . . . she couldn't be *ashamed* of the way Luke had treated her, could she?

Posy shrugged stiffly and looked out at the river. 'It was more . . . the whole person I was back then. It was while I was working on that movie that I found out about my parents embezzling my money, and Shannon took me in. She was . . . much better to me than I deserved, and I betrayed her. And until today I thought I'd ruined her life. Literally caused her miscarriage – and sent her rebounding into marrying some business associate of her father. So, yeah. I didn't want you guys thinking that about me when it had nothing to do with what happened to Luke.'

Rosalind could understand that, she supposed. Posy had worked so hard to rebuild her life after addiction and bad choices, and letting in the other two Dahlias had been a big part of that. Rosalind suspected she'd worried they'd think she might betray them too, one way or another.

And Caro . . . Rosalind could admit that Caro didn't always have a great deal of tolerance for others' personal failings – especially when it came to things like cheating. She eyed her carefully, waiting for her response to what Posy had told them.

'This was right after your parents?' Caro said, after a moment. Posy nodded, chewing on her bottom lip. 'And what you told us last night, about how you thought he'd been treating Darcy . . . that was how Luke treated you, wasn't it?'

Rosalind held her breath, waiting to see if Posy would answer. If she'd tell them everything, at last.

'I was nineteen,' Posy said, softly. 'I didn't know what a relationship was supposed to look like. And he'd been . . . he was so sweet to Shannon, at least as far as I saw. When we first . . . started, I wasn't sure, I tried to back away. But he was . . . he said he was bewitched by me. That he knew it was wrong, but he couldn't help the way he felt around me. He made me feel beautiful, wanted. But more than that, he made me feel powerful.'

At a time when all her power had been taken away from her by her parents stealing her money, Rosalind could understand how attractive that must have been.

'But then once we were together and Shannon was gone . . . I had to leave the flat we'd shared, and I didn't have anywhere else to go. So I moved in with Luke.' Posy pushed her hands into her pockets and stared out over the water rather than looking at them. Rosalind glanced over at Caro, taking in her pained expression as she listened to Posy's story.

'I didn't even realise at first that anything was wrong. I thought we were both just adjusting to living together, that I was being a grown-up for the first time. Except soon I noticed that *I* was the only one adjusting – compromising, to keep the peace. He wanted to know where I was, who I was with, all the time. The movie had wrapped, and I was auditioning for new roles, and he had opinions about all of them. Then opinions turned into orders. Before I knew it, he was controlling what I wore, who I could be friends with, my career . . . even my money.'

'How did you get out?' Caro asked, in a low voice.

'I got a new role, and the actress playing my mother . . . she saw what was going on. She told me to get out and, eventually, I did. But I guess the damage was done.'

Rosalind frowned. 'What do you mean?'

'I think . . . looking back, it's easy to see it, but I didn't then – just like I didn't really see Luke's actions for what they were until it was too late,' Posy explained. 'But I think being with Luke, betraying Shannon, coming so soon after everything happened with my parents . . . it destroyed my self-belief, my sense of self, even. I was so *ashamed*. For trusting my parents, trusting Luke, hurting Shannon. I didn't even want to be myself any more. And, well, that was around the time I met Damon.'

The boyfriend who'd really helped her to destroy her life by introducing her to drugs, and the party scene – and then almost done it again when he visited the UK shortly before the Dahlias met for the first time in Aldermere. Of course. Suddenly Rosalind could see that whole, horrible progression.

Caro sighed. 'If you'd told me that, I'd have hated him with you from the start.' Always loyal, that was Caro. Even if she hadn't seemed it recently.

'But you couldn't,' Posy replied. 'Whatever I'd said. Because you had to work with him. I figured, we'd get through this run and then it wouldn't matter, because we'd all be off doing other jobs and I wouldn't have to think about him again. And maybe you'd never need to know about that girl I'd been. But I just didn't want you to get sucked into his orbit, either – that's why I warned you away. Luke . . . like I told you, he was a cheat and a user. He took what he could from people and then left them sucked dry.'

'Except this time he's dead.' Rosalind took a deep breath of Thames air, then regretted it. She needed to see how this all fitted in with everything else they'd learned. 'You thought Shannon was the woman at the theatre on the CCTV, pretending to be you, yes?'

Posy nodded. 'I mean, we literally got cast in a film together because we looked so alike. It seemed reasonable. But . . . she sounded pretty believable when she talked about making up with Luke.'

'They didn't look on the outs when I saw them together,' Caro confirmed. 'But that doesn't mean anything. They're actors – or they were, in her case.'

'She hasn't forgiven Posy, though,' Rosalind pointed out. If she *was* still holding a grudge against Luke, framing Posy for his death would fit. On the other hand, it wouldn't be unheard of for a betrayed friend to forgive the man but not the woman.

'We hold other women to higher standards than we hold men,' Caro admitted.

'Shannon also told me she has an alibi for the evening of the murder,' Posy went on.

Rosalind stopped walking as the something that had been niggling at the back of her brain suddenly jumped to the forefront. 'Wait. Shannon. Shannon Carpenter?'

'Yes?' Posy blinked at her.

'Caro. Give me your phone.' It only took a moment to flick through Caro's camera roll and confirm her memory. 'Shannon's alibi is Luke's half-sister. They had a meeting at her gallery in Islington that night.'

They all looked at each other. 'That can't be a coincidence,' Caro said. 'Can it?'

'It doesn't feel like it,' Posy admitted. 'How does Luke's sister feel about him?'

'Like he was trying to steal her inheritance and faking his change in personality to do it.' Rosalind sighed. 'Okay, well that puts another spin on things.' And Shannon was now another suspect added to their bulging list, especially if there was a chance that she and Martha were in it together. 'We're going to need a new plan. Come on. Posy, we'll fill you in on what *we've* learned on the way.'

Rosalind led them towards the steps at the other end of the beach, back up to the South Bank. She looked away to hide her smile when Caro took Posy's arm as they walked.

Caro

Their walk along the South Bank continued past the Tate Modern, past the wonderful curved shape and thatched roof of the Globe Theatre – where Caro was now determined to perform one day, after her recent stint on the stage – and past the *Golden Hinde*, that recreation of Sir Francis Drake's Elizabethan galleon, the first British ship to circumnavigate the globe, now strangely moored between a Caffè Nero and a looming brick office building.

Posy's confession weighed on Caro like a raincloud, ready to burst. As she took in her surroundings, she revisited each part of it, trying to reconcile the Luke Posy had described with the one she'd known, wondering how much of his reported change was real and how much was an act.

Wondering how different things might have been if Posy had told her everything from the start.

She understood why she hadn't, though, even if she didn't like it. Posy had been ashamed of her own actions, and maybe embarrassed at the person she'd been, letting Luke get away with so much. Caro got that. She hadn't always been the person she'd hoped to be, either, and it was always hard to admit that.

Whatever had happened in the past, they were where they were now – and they still had a murder to solve. With a nod to herself, Caro packed up the history of Posy and Luke and parcelled it off to the back of her mind to deal with later, once this was all over. The only part she cared about now was Shannon, and that suspiciously convenient alibi.

The path was teeming with tourists still, and although they managed to avoid posing for any more photographs, Caro was sure plenty were being taken without their knowledge. If they started talking murder again, they'd probably end up being recorded, too.

She considered suggesting they retired to Rosalind's hotel room, or Posy's flat – not her and Annie's house, though, since the kitchen table was currently covered in edits, and the lounge in surveillance photos. They could duck into Borough Market, she supposed, although if she had any more coffee her nerves would start jangling.

Or . . .

As they turned their backs on Sir Francis's ship, another building came into view – its tower and arched stained-glass windows far more beautiful than the offices, and surrounded by picturesque gardens.

'Let's duck in here,' Caro suggested. 'See if we can get a little privacy.'

'Southwark Cathedral?' Posy asked, doubtfully. 'Are you sure?'

Caro shrugged. 'We can claim we're praying. It's probably good for our souls, or something.' It seemed they'd already done the confession part, anyway.

Inside, the cathedral was cool and calm, and quite honestly a bit of a relief from the summer day in the city outside. The vaulted ceilings rose high above them, and the stained glass let in coloured light that danced in the sunshine on the stone floors. There were other visitors, of course, but here they were lost in their own thoughts or prayers, and too respectful to interrupt anyone else's.

It was perfect.

The three Dahlias took a moment or two to explore, admiring the decoration and design, before settling into three of the wooden chairs in the nave to talk. A bushy black and white cat stalked past them, looking perfectly at home. Caro smiled. It was always good to see the Southwark cat.

Posy pulled out her notebook, and Caro felt a flash of relief as she realised they weren't solely relying on her own ability to record information any longer. Still, she pulled out a few loose pieces of paper from her own bag and passed them over, so that Posy could add the timeline she'd scribbled down to the official case notes.

Together, the three of them looked over what they already had, nodding silently when they'd digested it all.

Posy frowned. 'So our first working theory is that Darcy took a wig and coat from the Regent to pretend to be me and follow Luke into the Arcadia, then let her accomplice backstage through the pass door. The accomplice either brought their own knife or picked up the one from Pollie's bag in the production office, and killed Luke, getting blood all over Darcy, presumably because of where she was standing. They both then stashed the bloodstained clothes, escaped out front, then set fire to the coat in the bin but hid any other clothes and the murder weapon elsewhere. Is that right?'

Caro nodded. 'That's theory number one, yes.'

'And theory number two is that *Shannon* pretended to be me to get in through the stage door and frame me, let Martha in through the pass door and they killed Luke together, everything else being the same as the first, and then they fake alibied each other. And in that theory, Darcy saw something and was threatened and/or bribed into leaving that note and running.'

'Yep. So. Questions?' Rosalind said, her voice low.

'Could any threat or bribe be enough for Darcy to take responsibility for a murder?' Posy's uncertain voice, given her recent experiences as a murder suspect, gave Caro a slight twinge of guilt. She pushed it aside to focus on the case in hand.

'Who was Darcy's most likely accomplice?' Caro said, promptly. 'Piotr, Taran, Amber or Joshua?'

'If it *was* Darcy and an accomplice,' Rosalind said, thoughtfully, 'one of those four people – all of whom claimed that they believed Luke was a changed man – must have been lying. They had to have still hated him, either for something in his past *or* his present.'

'So we need to find the person with the best motive,' Caro said, encouragingly. 'That's all. We've done it before.'

'Exactly. Now, any more questions?' Rosalind asked, crisply.

'I might have one.' Caro frowned down at Posy's notes as she tried to figure out exactly what was bothering her about them. Finally, it clicked. 'You said you told Mal not to let Luke into your dressing room any more. So why did he let him in that day?'

'I . . . I don't know.' Posy met her gaze with her own frown. 'One more question to ask, I guess.'

'Then let's get into it.' Caro got to her feet. 'Come on. It's time to bring this investigation to a close. Together, this time.'

Chapter Sixteen

It's always difficult, solving a case you're closely, personally involved with. The professionals have their dispassionate disconnection – objectivity, I suppose they call it. We Dahlias, on the other hand, rely on our instincts and experiences. But this time, it turned out that mine had been very wrong.

Seven Lively Suspects
By Caro Hooper

Posy

They each had their assigned tasks for the evening ahead. Posy had offered to tackle the Arcadia, and speak to Mal and Taran. The fact that neither Caro nor Rosalind objected to her questioning suspects without them said a lot – first, she hoped, that they no longer suspected her even a little. And second, that they really didn't want her with them on their own fact-finding missions.

Caro, obviously, would be at the Prince Regent – performing, now with understudies in both Luke *and* Darcy's roles. 'If we lose any more cast members we're done,' Caro had grumbled. 'But for the time being, the show is bloody well going on.' While she was there, she planned to talk to Joshua again, see if there was any more she could get out of him about Luke.

'I just wish I knew what to ask beyond "So, how did you feel about Luke *really*?"' she'd sighed, as she'd left.

Meanwhile Rosalind was going back to Islington before the gallery closed to talk to Martha, somewhere Posy was very sure she wouldn't be welcome. There might have been little love lost between Martha and Luke, but bringing one of the primary suspects for his murder around for tea was going a little far, Rosalind had felt. Posy agreed.

They made plans to regroup at Caro's the following morning, and went their separate ways.

Except this time, Posy didn't feel like she was saying goodbye for good.

It was strange, arriving at the Arcadia again, knowing she wasn't supposed to be there. She couldn't really blame the team for deciding that the production of *Lights Out* was better off without her until the whole murder thing was settled. It was possible to take that 'all publicity is good publicity' thing too far, and if the crowds that had been gathering outside her flat were anything to go by, all keeping her on stage would have achieved was a lot of negative press and probably some eggs thrown at her. Maybe worse. It wasn't fair to ask the rest of the cast to put up with that.

Still, it was hard to walk up to the stage door knowing she wouldn't be performing that night. So she waited until she knew the play was already in session before she approached. It would be easier to talk to Taran after he'd finished on stage anyway. Hopefully, he'd be more relaxed – and more willing to answer questions.

Mal's eyes widened at the sight of her as she let herself in through the stage door, glad that nobody had changed the key code. Mind you, she was fairly sure it hadn't been changed since it had been installed.

'Posy . . . you know you're not supposed to be here, right?' Mal came out from behind his counter, apparently ready to stop her going any further physically, if required. 'Even if . . . I know about Darcy's note, but all the same. Management says—'

'I know, Mal,' she assured him. 'I'm not planning on staging a coup and demanding my dressing room back.' She shuddered at the thought of that room, images of the last time she'd been in there, with Luke's body, filling her brain unbidden. For all she knew, it was probably still sealed off by the police, anyway.

'Then why *are* you here?'

'I wanted to ask you a couple of questions,' she said. 'And then . . . I was hoping you'd let me through to talk to Taran.'

His shoulders sagged, and he rolled his eyes. 'You realise you're as bad as Luke was for this, right?'

'That's actually my first question,' she replied. 'The day Luke died . . . he was in my dressing room. But I'd told you not to let him down there again – and you hadn't. You'd made him leave the flowers with you at the stage door just that morning. So what did he say to convince you to let him in later that day?'

He blinked at her in confusion, a frown settling between his eyebrows. 'He didn't. I mean, I wouldn't say I *let* him in that first time, either. He had the door code same as you, and he just barged in while I was dealing with something else and told me it was fine because you were expecting him.'

'I wasn't.'

'I figured that out when you threw a book at his head,' Mal said, drily. 'But the night he was killed? He . . . I didn't tell your friends this? He wasn't here to see you. He said he was going to wait in Taran's dressing room, because Taran had asked him to stop by because he needed to talk to him about something.'

'Taran. Luke was here to see Taran?' If that was the case, how had he ended up in *her* dressing room? Suddenly, all the questions she had for her friend and erstwhile co-star took on a new slant – and a new urgency.

She gave Mal a pleading look. 'I really need to talk to him.'

Mal stepped back with a sigh. 'Fine. Go wait for him.' She dashed past him, towards the dressing rooms, his final words echoing after her. 'But don't say I didn't warn you about what happened to the last person I let do that!'

Taran looked surprised – but pleased – to see her waiting for him when he came off stage.

'I was hoping we could talk,' she said, vaguely, and he smiled.

'Sure,' Taran replied, with an easy smile. 'How about we get a late dinner? Just let me change and I'll meet you at the stage door?'

He didn't act like someone with something to hide. But Posy knew well enough that meant nothing at all when it came to suspects – or actors.

They ended up, unsurprisingly, at the tapas bar – although Posy was relieved to see that none of the *Finding Freddie* cast seemed to be there tonight. She didn't want any interruptions.

Gabriella was serving again, her eyes still a little red and raw, her father glaring at her from the kitchen doorway, but she managed a smile for them as she took their orders and brought their drinks.

Finally, over a glass of good red wine for him and a tonic water for her while they waited for their food, Taran called her out.

'So. As lovely as it is to join you this evening, I realise you've got an ulterior motive for asking me here.'

Posy tilted her head in admission. 'I do.'

Taran's answering grin looked devilish in the candlelight. 'Is it nefarious?'

Only if you don't like being suspected of murder. 'I'm . . . trying to figure out exactly what happened to Luke the day he died.'

'Clearing your name.' Taran nodded. 'That makes sense. Although I thought the police had a confession now? Besides, where do I come into it? I didn't even see him that day.'

No, of course he hadn't. Because Taran had been outside the theatre when she'd emerged after the fire alarm, waiting with the others to see if it was a real fire. He'd been the one to tell Caro that the fire brigade thought it was a lit cigarette tossed in the bin out the side of the theatre. Luke might have been waiting for him, but Taran hadn't gone in through the stage door to meet him.

'You didn't go inside the theatre at all that day?' She needed to confirm the specifics for her timeline. 'Even through the front?'

'Nope.' Taran reached for his wine glass again. 'The alarm was already going off when I got there.'

'So you didn't speak to Mal. Not outside the theatre, during the alarm?'

'I don't think so.' He frowned. 'Should I have?'

She sighed. It might have made life easier if he had. 'Did you know that Luke was at the Arcadia that day to see *you*?'

'Me?' Taran's eyebrows leaped up. 'Then why was he in *your* dressing room?'

'Just another part of the mystery I'm trying to solve,' she said. 'So you didn't . . . ask him there?'

'Why would I do that?' While it was entirely possible that Luke had lied to Mal about meeting Taran just to get in there, Posy couldn't help but notice that Taran's response wasn't a denial.

'That's what I'm asking you.'

Suddenly she was certain, without knowing exactly why, that Taran *had* asked Luke to the theatre that day. She just didn't know if he'd done it in order to kill him.

'I . . .' He broke off, looked away, and swore softly under his breath. 'I am apparently incapable of lying to you, which is more disturbing than I'd have thought.'

'I find it quite reassuring.' Even if she suspected it was just another act he was putting on. Almost everything in this case seemed to be. 'You *did* ask him to come, then?'

'Yes.'

'Why? And why didn't you tell anyone?'

Taran sighed. 'Because he had something I wanted. And I'm greedy that way. And I didn't mention it because . . . well. *I* didn't want to be suspected of murder.' That much, at least, she could understand.

'Something you wanted?' she pressed.

He shook his head. 'It doesn't matter now.'

Posy was pretty sure that it did, actually. So she tried another tack. 'You knew Luke at drama school, you told Caro?'

'Yeah. And then we worked on a production together, five or six years ago. He, uh, dated a friend of mine, back then.'

'A close friend?'

'Very.'

Okay, well Posy knew how *this* story went – from her own experience if nothing else. 'Let me see if I can guess. You were dating this girl first and he stole her from you?'

Taran sipped at his wine before answering, lounging back in his chair with his legs stretched out towards her under the table. 'That would be the standard, wouldn't it? But no.' He straightened up, and put his glass down. 'I never dated her. I *wanted* to, sure, but no. We were just friends, and probably better for it. But when she started seeing Luke . . . it was like the girl I knew started to fade away, day by day. He chased after her, wooed her even, charmed her . . . you know what he was like.'

'Too well.' Posy swallowed a gulp of her tonic water and tried not to think about drinking anything stronger. 'He was . . . he was that way with me too.'

She hadn't realised it at the time, had been too naive to even realise what was happening. That all those friendly gestures and warm smiles were anything more than him being nice to his girlfriend's new friend and roommate. Until they found themselves alone more and more often, and suddenly kissing him felt inevitable. Somehow, almost not like a betrayal at all, but something fated.

Later, she'd never been able to understand how he'd made her feel that way.

'But then, once he had her, it was like she couldn't live up to the ideal he'd had of who she'd be in his head. Nothing was good enough. And she tried so damn hard to make him happy . . .'

Taran's hand shook as he took another gulp from his wine glass. His eyes were dark and shadowed, like the memories had made everything grey. There was more to this than a bad break-up, she was sure.

'What happened?'

He looked down at the dregs of his wine glass, then raised it in Gabriella's direction. She nodded, and hurried across with the bottle.

'They broke up. But he couldn't accept it. He basically stalked her afterwards, until she cut ties with almost everyone and moved away. She was terrified. Not that she told us that then. She was too scared of him to speak up.' Taran's voice was low and quiet, but Gabriella, pouring his wine, gasped anyway.

'Did you ever see her again?' Posy asked. Gabriella, she noticed, was now wiping the table behind Taran. Very, very slowly.

'Not for years. Not until *this* year, actually.' Taran shrugged. 'Turns out that social media is good for something after all. We . . .

reconnected. She's living in the States now, married, with kids. She's happy. But . . . she told me things about Luke, about their relationship. I mean, I was worried about her at the time, but like I said, I had no idea about the truth of it. Nobody did. She didn't even tell her parents or her younger brother to start with, and then apparently she swore them to secrecy. And when he started getting more and more well known . . . she was scared he'd come looking for her. She didn't even want to risk getting back on social media until a couple of years ago.'

'But she's okay now?' Posy asked, aware that Gabriella had stopped even pretending to clean now, as she waited for Taran's answer. She'd adored Luke, according to Caro. He'd been helping her with drama school applications. This had to be a horrible shock, learning about who he really was.

'Yeah, she's fine.' He gave her a reassuring smile, and Gabriella finally moved away. 'Living her best life. She even set up a private support group online for people who'd gone through the same thing. And the stuff she told me about Luke . . . it could have ruined him, if it came out, especially now he's more of a name. If I convinced her to talk to the press, I'm sure there are more women like her who'd come forward.'

Posy was certain there were, too. Her, for a start. She'd bet that none of those other women would believe he'd changed, either.

And if Luke was relying on his changed nature to secure his inheritance . . . 'You were planning to blackmail him, weren't you? For what? Money?'

She'd thought Luke had been planning to blackmail *her*, but she'd got it the wrong way round. If Shannon was right, he'd been trying to make amends. Had Luke been hoping for the same with Taran?

'Not money.' Taran shifted in his chair, looking uncomfortable. 'Even I wouldn't sink that low. I just wanted . . . his influence, I guess. We started out at the same time, auditioning for the same roles, but with his family connections he'd always got the bigger parts, heard about better opportunities first. I just wanted some of that – for him to mention my name in places it mattered. He . . . put in a word, helped me get this role, and that was great. But I wanted more. To try and get a break into TV, maybe. That was all.' He looked up and met Posy's gaze. 'I know it doesn't paint me in a great light, but you have to believe me. Luke Burrows was worth much more to me alive than dead, given what I knew.'

Posy stared into his eyes, taking in everything she saw there, then nodded. 'Okay.' Taran's shoulders relaxed instantly, and his familiar smile re-emerged. 'That's why you punched that poster after you heard he was dead? Caro told me about that.'

Taran winced. 'Yeah. I know. Making his murder all about me. On brand, right? I just . . . I finally thought I was getting somewhere and then . . .'

'Is there anything else I should know?'

And now the tension was back. 'Actually . . . yeah. I don't know if . . . you might already know this. But the woman I talked about? She was Joshua Griffin's older sister.'

Posy startled in her chair, scraping the legs against the wooden floor. 'Luke's co-star Joshua?' Caro had mentioned they'd dated, that the break-up had been bad, but this was something else.

Taran nodded. 'They had different surnames. I don't know if Luke realised, or recognised him. It was years ago, and he'd have been a lot younger. But I . . . kept in touch with the family. Looked after Josh a bit when he first started out.'

'Did you talk to him about how he felt working with Luke? Did he know about everything with his sister?' Because he sure as hell hadn't mentioned it when Caro and Rosalind spoke with him, according to their notes.

'Yeah, a bit. I mean, he just said it was a job, you know? He was cast before they brought Luke in, and he wasn't going to back out of his first big role because of it, even if he had been demoted to understudy and a smaller part. He told me he would just ignore Luke, as best as he could.'

Except he'd been laughing and joking with him at rehearsals right before Luke left for the Arcadia the day he died, according to Caro. Had Joshua really believed Luke had changed? Or had it all been an act?

She checked the time on her phone. Caro would probably have spoken to Joshua already, but just in case . . . she sent her a message with what she'd learned, so she could follow up.

This was why they worked better together than apart.

Rosalind

Rosalind's second conversation with Martha Burrows wasn't much more successful than her first.

'Look, I told you. I had an appointment with a client the evening Luke was killed. I was here, in Islington, so really, I think you'd better go harass someone else before I call the police. You might be a National Treasure, Rosalind King, but that doesn't put you above the law!'

Martha's voice grew shrill at the end. Rosalind waited patiently for her to calm down.

'It was actually your client I wanted to speak to you about,' she said, finally. 'Shannon Carpenter. Were you aware that she was a close friend of your half-brother's?'

From the blank look on Martha's face, she hadn't been. 'I didn't . . . she didn't . . . no one even mentioned Luke. I had no idea!'

'I see.' Either Martha was a better actress than anyone had ever given her credit for, or she genuinely hadn't known about Luke's connection to Shannon. Which meant it was either a coincidence or . . . 'But you were definitely with her at the time of the murder? Here, at the gallery?' Rosalind pressed. 'And I'm asking for *her* alibi now, not yours.' No need to explain the 'in it together' theory.

'Definitely,' Martha said, firmly.

So. Either they were both lying or they were both telling the truth. And Rosalind was no further along than she'd been *before* she traipsed all the way to Islington.

She just hoped that Caro and Posy were having more successful evenings.

They'd agreed to meet at Caro's house the following morning for a proper debrief.

'Bring breakfast,' Caro had told them. 'I've no food in.'

'I miss Annie,' Posy had sighed. 'Not *just* for her cooking, but . . .'

'Agreed,' Rosalind had replied.

But on arrival that morning at the townhouse Caro shared with her wife, Rosalind had to admit that Caro was clearly missing Annie more than they could – and that Annie hadn't been entirely wrong to be worrying about the effect of her absence when she called.

'Make yourself at home,' Caro announced, after she answered the door to them both, before disappearing back up the stairs. 'I'll be right down.'

'Was she wearing a bathrobe?' Rosalind wrinkled her nose. She'd never seen Caro in anything less than a full coordinated outfit before, unless she was on surveillance and in disguise. A faded towelling robe really wasn't her style. Even Posy's self-professed 'lounge wear' that she wore around her flat was in better condition than that thing.

'I think it was Annie's.' Posy shut the door behind them with her foot, carefully juggling the bag of pastries and tray of coffees they'd picked up on the way over. 'Come on.'

Posy headed for the kitchen, murmuring something about mugs. Rosalind started to follow, but paused at the door to the living room as she passed.

They'd spent enough time in Caro and Annie's house over the past few years, for Christmas celebrations and Sunday dinners, that they both knew their way around well enough to feel comfortable even in their hosts' absence. Rosalind had even stayed over once or twice while the sale of her flat went through. Annie had suggested she stay this time, rather than the inconvenience of an hotel room, but since the whole point of Rosalind coming to London was for some much-needed personal space, she'd politely declined.

Now, staring into the living room, she wondered if Annie's offer had been more for Caro's benefit than her own.

The square coffee table in the middle of the room was covered in large, glossy photos of people that had obviously been taken at a distance with the kind of lenses the paparazzi used to get their sneaky shots. Dotted around the photos were Post-it notes and empty mugs.

The kitchen, when she reached it, wasn't much better. A couple of years earlier Caro and Annie had added an extension to their period home, including a glass roof and doors that opened up to make the space almost part of the garden — and which also made room for a large wooden table that served them well for the Sunday roasts Annie was famous for.

In her absence, however, the table had clearly become a secondary desk for Caro, since it was covered in what looked like pages from her recounting of their adventures in Market Foxleigh the summer before.

Rosalind paused to scan the top page, and scoffed. 'I'm not sure that's exactly how it happened.'

'Step away, Rosalind,' Posy teased from the kitchen island – which was mercifully free of paperwork as Posy was using it to plate up pastries. 'You know she hates anyone reading her writing until she's done editing.'

Which was all well and good, but when she was writing about their lives Rosalind felt they should get some sort of say in things.

'She's trying to do too much.' When she glanced up at the kitchen cabinets, she noticed that several of them had Post-it notes stuck to them. Peering closer, she realised that some were lines from *Finding Freddie*, presumably left over from when she'd still been in rehearsal, while others appeared to be notes to herself about Luke's murder.

Could any of the male suspects have passed for Posy on the CCTV? read one bright pink note.

On the counter below were the last couple of days' newspapers. Rosalind scanned the headlines, before spotting more stories about Posy on the inner pages.

'We could sit outside.' Posy opened the doors to the garden, letting the summer breeze in. It wasn't hot out there yet, but the seating area got a good dose of morning sun. And at least the table wasn't covered in notes or photos.

'Good idea!' Caro breezed in, now more appropriately attired in a pair of linen trousers, a square-necked camisole, and a patterned kimono floating over the top of it all. 'Have to make the most of the summer weather.'

'And the space,' Rosalind murmured, tucking the newspapers under her arm and following her outside.

They settled at the bistro table in a sunny patch towards the back gate, the smell of rosemary filling the air, along with the heavy scent of the roses that ran along the garden wall. Posy picked apart a pastry as she waited for her coffee to cool, and Rosalind tried not to wince at the crumbs going everywhere.

'So, how did we all get on yesterday? Shall I start?' It didn't take long to fill them in on her conversation with Martha – or the lack of conclusions she'd been able to draw from it.

Posy and Caro seemed to have had slightly more profitable evenings. Posy recapped her chat with Taran, then Caro took over.

'It's just as well you messaged,' she told Posy. 'Because I was getting nowhere before that.'

'So? What did he say?' Posy asked.

'That it was water under the bridge, and Luke had changed. Apparently nothing Luke had done since joining the show had set off any alarm bells.' Caro sighed. 'He said he spoke to his sister when Luke got the role and she told him to be careful but otherwise take the opportunity. Apparently she might have mentioned that most actors were, well, something not very complimentary, and if he tried to avoid all of them he'd never work again.'

'Hmm.' Rosalind weighed Caro's report against Posy's. 'Are we convinced?'

'I don't know,' Caro admitted. 'Someone in this case is lying about believing Luke had changed. Someone had to be still holding a grudge – or have experienced his bad behaviour now, despite his whole reformed bad-boy act for the sake of his father and his inheritance. And they had to hate him enough to kill him for it.'

Rosalind sat back and steepled her fingers in front of her. 'Piotr and Amber both had an inkling that Luke wasn't as reformed as they'd hoped, because they heard it from people on the crew.'

'But they both also wanted the show to be a success, so seemed to be more or less ignoring it,' Caro put in. 'Although Amber might have been worried for her job, reading between the lines. If Piotr had to choose, he'd pick Luke over her, I'm sure.'

'And if Piotr thought Luke was more of a threat than an asset he'd just fire him,' Rosalind said. Heavens knew she'd seen him do it before. 'Although he was more . . . conciliatory to him than I'd have expected when I heard them talking. And certainly sang Luke's praises more before his death than afterwards. It felt like he . . . needed Luke. Or was afraid of him.'

'Taran knew that Luke was a bastard but was using it to his advantage,' Posy said. 'And Joshua knew but apparently decided the career opportunity was worth more than revenge.'

'Although Luke's death has also *increased* his career opportunities,' Rosalind noted. 'He's playing the lead now, after all.' *That* definitely counted as a motive.

'True.' Caro narrowed her eyes. 'And Darcy. Darcy knew he wasn't the man he was pretending to be. From what we've heard about his treatment of women, she's still the strongest suspect on that front. Not least because she's actually confessed.'

Posy clearly still believed that Darcy was innocent, though, because she jumped in immediately with another option. 'What about Martha and Shannon? It has to be both or neither of them. Right?'

'Martha never believed Luke had changed in the first place, and definitely had a financial motive,' Rosalind said. 'She is also a patron of the Arcadia *and* the Prince Regent, and seems to know her way around the theatre world pretty well. She could have got into either.'

'Shannon seems adamant that he *had* changed, though, and they were friends again.' Posy peered at the newspapers where Rosalind had placed them on the table. Then she reached over to snag the nearest one and shook it out to read the whole article.

'What is it?' Rosalind leaned forward to try and see what had Posy frowning so hard. But before she could figure it out, Caro's phone started ringing, that blasted TV theme tune blaring out across the garden.

'It's Piotr.' Caro jumped to her feet before she pressed the screen to answer.

Rosalind couldn't hear the director's words. But she could tell by the look on Caro's face as she paced to and fro across the garden that the news wasn't good.

And she was right.

Moments later, Caro hung up the phone.

'They've found Darcy,' she said.

Chapter Seventeen

'I just can't shake the feeling that we're so close, Johnnie,' Dahlia gripped her glass tighter, until her knuckles turned white.

Johnnie took it from her, obviously afraid it might break. 'We'll get there,' he said soothingly. 'We always do.'

She looked up at him, holding his gaze with her own. 'But will we get there soon enough?'

He didn't answer.

Dahlia Lively in *The Devil in the Details*
by Lettice Davenport, 1946

Posy

Posy looked up from the newspaper that had caught her attention and stared at Caro.

She wanted to ask if Darcy was okay, if she was alive, even. But she didn't have to. Caro's face said it all.

'How?' Her throat felt too tight to force the word out. 'Where?'

Caro slumped back down into her garden chair. 'At the theatre. Down in the bowels, by one of those tunnels that they're planning to excavate once our run is over. Apparently it's a site of archaeological interest.'

'And police interest,' Rosalind murmured.

'Anyway. One of the crew was clearing out some of the old props and staging that were being stored down there, ready for the archaeological team. There was a locked trunk – like an old steamer trunk – and it was too heavy so he forced it open it and . . . found her. He called for help, and people started flooding down there.'

'Which the police will be thrilled about,' Rosalind muttered. Jack's ex-DCI sensibilities were rubbing off on her.

'Piotr was next on the scene and cleared them all out and called for the police. It looks like . . . it looks like she never left. She'd been dead . . . a while.' Caro sat up a little straighter, clearing her throat. Trying to be a professional again, Posy supposed, rather than a grieving friend. 'The police have sealed the whole place off. Piotr's notifying all the cast.'

'Suicide?' Posy asked, even though it was hard to imagine how it could be.

Was it wrong that Posy had almost hoped that it *was* suicide? That maybe *she'd* been wrong and Darcy had been guilty all along? That this might all be over now?

But it wasn't.

Caro shook her head. 'Not . . . not suicide. At least, the police are treating it as suspicious. That's all Piotr knows.'

'Until they get the post-mortem results, they won't want to assume anything at all.' Rosalind brushed a rogue biscuit crumb off the table. 'But dead in a steamer trunk? It doesn't *sound* like suicide.'

'Someone must have forged the note,' Caro said. 'I mean, in this day and age, who would recognise their own handwriting, let alone anyone else's? Nobody writes any more. Well, except Posy. No offence.'

But Posy wasn't really listening. Because they were both missing the more important point.

'Wait. If she never left the theatre... where was she when you found her note? When you were all looking for her?' Posy looked between the other two but got only blank looks in return.

'She must have been down there all along,' Caro said. 'We looked everywhere – and so did the police. But we were looking for her *alive*, and there are a thousand hiding places in that theatre. Not to mention so many boxes and suitcases and crates. Plus, the area by the tunnels has been blocked off for ages for safety reasons. Nobody would have gone through all that junk down there...'

'Not until the body started to smell.' Rosalind wrinkled her nose. 'The killer must have planned to get her out of there before then. Maybe even down that tunnel, if it's still connected to the river.'

'You're still not getting it,' Posy said. 'Your notes said Darcy disappeared *while you were on stage*. During the second half of the play, right?'

'Yes,' Caro confirmed. 'She was on stage for the phone-call scene, but gone before the curtain call.'

'Then that knocks out most of our suspects in one go!'

'She's right,' Rosalind said. 'Piotr was sitting next to me in the audience. Joshua was on stage the whole time – or near enough. Certainly he wasn't off long enough to kill anyone.'

'Amber was in the wings that night,' Caro confirmed. 'I saw her, and so did a dozen other people back there.'

'And Taran would have been on stage at the Arcadia at the same time,' Posy finished. 'So that just leaves Martha and Shannon.'

The revelation hung heavy between them.

'Are we sure?' Rosalind asked.

'They must have done it together,' Posy said. 'Just like we thought.'

'But how do we *prove* it?' Caro frowned, and looked at Posy. 'What did you see in that newspaper. Before Piotr called?'

'Oh!' Posy picked up the newspaper and shook it out to the relevant page. 'It was just another article about the case, and me. Saying that there was now another suspect, but still managing to insinuate that I'm a terrible person. But there was one bit . . .' She scanned through the text, trying not to take any of it as personally as it felt. 'Here. It talks about a party in LA where the police were called, and the details it gives . . . Luke wasn't there that night. It was before everything really went to hell. And none of this information was ever in the press at the time. Only Shannon knew that stuff.'

She'd suspected Shannon was behind the stories. It didn't hurt any less to be proved right.

'So she *was* the one leaking the stories about you to the press,' Caro said, breathlessly. 'It's not proof of murder, of course, but perhaps evidence that she hated you enough to frame you?'

'And it means she's getting sloppy,' Rosalind put in. 'None of the other stories were traceable directly back to her. If I had to guess, she called her pet reporter directly and gave them that one after your lunch yesterday.'

'Yes . . .' Posy put the paper down, hoping they wouldn't notice the way her hands were shaking. 'Maybe if I confront her . . .'

'No.' Rosalind's voice was firm. 'Not alone.'

'I'll go with her,' Caro offered. 'But I think we need to try something else before an actual confrontation. I know, I know, me being the voice of caution isn't our usual dynamic. But in this case . . . I think we should watch her. Follow her. See if she goes to Martha now she's seen you. Or anywhere else – like that house I followed Luke to. I can't shake the feeling that there's something else going on here, and I want to know what it is before we go in all guns blazing.'

Posy nodded. 'Okay. Then let's get going.'

Caro

It felt good to be *doing* something again – and even better to be doing it with Posy by her side. Caro wasn't foolish enough to believe that everything had been solved by one conversation and a walk along the Thames, but it was a start.

Once this whole mess was done with, they could see about rebuilding the trust between them properly.

For now, they had a killer to catch.

They started at the hotel where Posy knew Shannon had been staying, situating themselves in the cafe across the road to keep an eye on the entrance. Posy had already been inside to see if she could get any information from the staff about whether Shannon was even still in the hotel at present, but no one would talk. Instead, Posy called from outside and left a message for her old friend, asking her to meet again, hinting that she knew more now about Luke's death, and that they needed to talk.

She'd named another cafe within walking distance of the hotel and said she'd be waiting there in an hour, if Shannon wanted to show. Now, they just had to hope she'd take the bait – and see if there was anywhere else she went first. Like Martha's art gallery, where Rosalind would be waiting close by, just in case.

'There she is,' Caro murmured, as Shannon emerged from the revolving doors of the hotel.

'Then let's go,' Posy replied.

Caro pushed her sunglasses into place as Posy donned her cap. They waited until Shannon had scanned the street and set off alone before leaving the cafe and following her, ensuring they kept enough people between them that they wouldn't be spotted – easy enough on a busy London street.

Harder was making sure they didn't lose their target in the crowd. Shannon seemed to know exactly where she was going, moving swiftly and determinedly forward without pause.

'She's passed the cafe,' Posy said softly. 'The one where we were supposed to meet. It's down that street.'

'She has something she needs to do before she sees you, then,' Caro surmised. 'That, or she's standing you up.'

Fortunately for them, Shannon didn't get on the tube, or a bus, or even call a taxi. And it didn't take long for Caro to realise that the turns and side streets they took led inexorably towards the townhouse she'd followed her to with Luke during her previous surveillance.

She wasn't much of a believer in fate, but she did feel that everyone was due a lucky break now and then – and this case was certainly *overdue* one.

Caro and Posy hung back again as Shannon made her way up the stone steps to the front door and slipped inside without waiting for anyone to let her in. She belonged there, then, it seemed.

And then they waited.

There was still no discreet gold plaque to tell them what the place was, and Caro's googling hadn't given up any more information than Ashok's research had. The best chance they had of finding out what was going on behind that door was talking to someone who came out of it – someone *other* than Shannon, she expected.

That, or knocking on the door and asking.

If it were a case with Ashok, Caro knew she'd have to be cautious and do the former.

But since this was a three Dahlias case, and they were so close to solving it . . .

'Come on.' Caro grabbed Posy's arm. Apparently her caution and sensibility had worn out for the day. 'We're going in.'

Posy

Inside, the townhouse looked like an incredibly upmarket therapist's office. They were met at the door by a receptionist in an expensive cream suit and high heels, with highlighted hair carefully styled in a chignon, who obviously didn't want to let them in at all – not that Caro gave her much choice in the matter. Posy tried to hide her smile as Caro played the exuberant actress role and swept in as if her admittance couldn't possibly have ever been in question. It was almost as effective as Rosalind's National Treasure mystique. The receptionist hurried after her as Caro made her way into what had once presumably been the living room of the house.

Decked out with two cream leather sofas, and a glass coffee table loaded with high-end photography books showcasing interior design, fashion and travel, it really could have still been a living room, except for the slim and elegant desk at one end, offset from the fireplace, where the receptionist retook her seat at her top-of-the-range laptop.

'Um, if you'd both like to take a seat. You said you were here to see . . .'

'Shannon Carpenter,' Posy said, with a guileless smile. 'We're old friends. I was actually supposed to be meeting her later, but there's been a change of plans and I couldn't get hold of her.'

'But then, total miracle!' Caro exclaimed, eyes wide and smile wider. 'We saw her come in here and I said to Posy, that's fate that is! So we knocked.'

'Right. Of course. If you'll just give me a moment.' The receptionist gave them a very tight smile then hurried out of the room rather than making use of the phone on her desk.

Left alone for a moment or two, Posy turned to Caro and said, 'What do you think? What's the deal here?'

Caro sank onto one of the cream sofas, scatty actress persona gone. 'I'm not sure. Did Shannon mention a company she was working with while she was in London?'

'No, nothing. I got the impression that she was just following her husband here for *his* work.' Posy tried to think back to what that initial article Luke had left her had said about Shannon being in London, but as far as she could recall it had mostly been about her clothes.

'She doesn't seem like the sort to work in an office, even one as upmarket as this one. So what's she doing here?' Caro stared at the door as they both mused on the question.

Posy couldn't bring herself to sit, so instead she toured the room, taking in the presumably original artworks, maybe from Martha Burrows's gallery. With a quick check of the doorway to ensure no one was coming, she slipped behind the desk and took a look there, too. The computer screen had locked, but there were a few papers on the desk itself. A receipt from Martha's gallery. A menu for an event next week. A glossy photo of a manor house with a crowd of people in black-tie attire in front of it. And underneath, more candid shots of the party that must have gone on inside.

Before she could whip out her phone to capture any of it, there was a noise in the hallway and she slid out again to join Caro by the sofa.

'Posy! Caro! This is a surprise!' Shannon didn't *look* surprised as she entered the room, her hands out in welcome, her smile fixed in place. If anything, behind that smile she looked annoyed. 'Posy, I thought we were meeting later? At the cafe?'

'We were,' Posy said apologetically. 'But I'm afraid something came up. Caro needs my assistance with a task this morning, you see. I left a message for you at the hotel, but you'd already left. And then . . .'

'We happened to be in the area and – what luck! We saw you entering this building,' Caro said, partially truthfully. 'You see, we're retracing Luke's footsteps the day before his death, and we know he came here too, so we thought it was worth checking out what goes on here. Seeing you was an added bonus! So, what exactly is this place?'

She waited, patiently, for Shannon to explain the purpose of the townhouse office. Shannon looked to Posy, and she smiled patiently too.

Silence. It was the best way to trap people into talking, they'd found.

It only took one long, awkward moment for Shannon to start talking.

'Oh, well, that's easy.' She manoeuvred past the coffee table and sat on the sofa opposite them. 'This is an events agency. They specialise in *very* high-end, luxurious events – especially parties and galas. I employ them sometimes when I'm in London for my own charitable events, or those my husband is associated with.'

'And Luke worked with them too?' Posy asked, innocently.

Shannon glanced down at the table. 'Oh, he was just here for me. I had an appointment here anyway and he didn't have much time, so it was nothing more than a convenient meeting place.'

'That makes sense,' Caro said. Because, of course, it did.

It just didn't feel like the truth.

She'd come here to confront Shannon about killing Luke with Martha. She'd been so certain they'd got it right, that their solution was the only possible one.

But when she'd spooked her, hinting in her message that she knew more than she should, Shannon hadn't run to Martha. She'd come here. A place within walking distance of her hotel – maybe the reason for choosing that hotel in the first place?

'Posy. You said in your message that you had something you wanted to talk about?' There was a tension in Shannon's shoulders, like she was ready to defend – or attack – as needed. She was *expecting* something. An accusation. But for what?

Somehow, Posy was sure it wasn't murder.

She thought back to the photos on the desk and played a hunch.

'Uh, yes. I was going back over our notes about people's conversations with Luke before his death, and someone mentioned that Luke had talked about bringing another friend here, a young actress?' Posy said, ignoring Caro's puzzled look. Because no one had mentioned that at all. Nobody knew about this place except for them. 'Do you have any idea who that might have been?'

'None, I'm afraid.' Shannon's answer was too quick, too ready, to be the whole truth. And the sharp smile that accompanied it only confirmed that Shannon now realised that Posy knew nothing. Had nothing. 'But I know that the company are always on the lookout for waiting staff of a certain calibre. Maybe he was helping a friend find work?'

Given what Posy had spotted in the photos, she was almost certain that was the case. It also told her exactly where they needed to go next.

Shannon wasn't going to give them anything else. Posy got to her feet and smiled politely at her old friend. 'Thank you for clearing that up for us. It really gives us a much better idea of the timeline leading up to the murder. You never know when these tiny pieces of information are going to come together to make a bigger picture.'

'I'm sure,' Shannon murmured. 'Now, let me show you out. I'm afraid I have a meeting I need to get back to about next week's gala.'

Posy could feel Caro glaring at the back of her head as they made their way out of the front door, and back onto the London street.

'What was that about? I thought we were going to confront her? And I had more questions!' Caro demanded, as Posy stuck her hand out for a passing cab.

'She wasn't going to answer them. Besides, I got us everything we need.' The cab stopped and she leaned in to talk to the driver, then opened the door for Caro to get in first.

'You did?' Caro had her eyebrow raised as Posy fastened her seatbelt and the driver pulled away from the kerb. 'What did I miss? Where are we going now?'

'We're going to pick up Rosalind, and then we're heading to the tapas bar,' Posy said, answering the last question first. 'You were right about there being more going on here. There were photos on the desk, of one of their fancy events, I guess. Gabriella was in them. And she wasn't the only one.'

Chapter Eighteen

Dahlia jumped from her seat. 'This is it, Bess! This is what we were missing. If I'd only realised sooner that they knew each other, that they had history...'

And then she was out of the door, leaving a confused Bess staring after her.

Dahlia Lively in *All That's Hidden*
By Lettice Davenport, 1947

Rosalind

Rosalind got Posy to go back over exactly what she'd seen on the desk at the townhouse the moment they picked her up from her hotel in the cab. Caro had called to warn her they were coming, with a vague summary of what had happened, but Rosalind needed details. Lots of them, if a murder accusation was going to hang on a few photos nobody except Posy had even seen.

'Couldn't she have been there as waiting staff, as Shannon suggested?' Gabriella had told them that Luke was helping her with her applications to drama schools. Maybe he'd also helped her find extra work to supplement her income from the tapas bar, in order to save for her studies.

'She wasn't wearing a waitress outfit,' Posy explained. 'She was in a green evening gown, holding a glass of champagne, hanging on the arm of some guy in a tux. Older, rich, but not exactly silver-fox territory.'

That didn't sound like waiting staff. 'What do you think was going on, then?' Rosalind had her own ideas, but she didn't like any of them.

'That's what I'm hoping Gabriella can tell us,' Posy said, grimly. 'I only spoke to her a few times before everything happened, but she always seemed happy and engaged. She liked hanging out with the cast after hours, I think. But when I was there with Taran the other night, she looked upset, and she was eavesdropping on everything we said about Luke.'

'You think she knows more than she's been saying?' Caro asked.

'Well, someone does,' Posy replied.

The taxi pulled up on the side street by the tapas bar, and Rosalind let Posy pay while she and Caro got out. It took her longer to unfold from the seat, after all.

It was mid-afternoon – just past the lunch crowd and too early for the pre-theatre diners. The perfect time to ask their questions.

Gabriella was wiping down tables when they entered, her father observing from behind where the kitchen opened up onto the restaurant, so that patrons could see the chefs sautéing and tossing and chopping and whatever else it was they got up to in there. Rosalind knew it occasionally involved brightly burning flames, and that was about it.

She let Posy make the approach; she was closest in age to Gabriella, and perhaps less alarming because of it. She was also the only one of them that had seen the evidence they were trying to understand. Soon, the three of them were seated together at a small table below the mural that spanned one wall of the restaurant.

'What is it you want to know?' Gabriella sounded bone weary as she slipped into the last seat at the table, which only served to emphasise the dark shadows under her eyes.

Posy shot a quick look at Rosalind before starting. Rosalind sat back in her chair, giving the youngest Dahlia free rein to take on the questioning. Because as interested as she was in the answers, she was more interested in the way Gabriella's father – Carlos, wasn't it? – was now watching them from the kitchen doorway.

What's he afraid she's going to tell us?

But then another chef called him from further inside the kitchen and he turned and moved away, out of sight and earshot.

Good. Rosalind was certain Gabriella would speak more openly without her father listening.

'You and Luke were close, yes? Closer than you let on when we spoke last time.' There was no censure in Posy's voice, Rosalind realised. No hint of shaming the other woman.

Gabriella gave a slow, jerky nod. 'I know . . . I know he was with Darcy, but things weren't good between them. It wasn't going to last much longer. And he said . . . he said he couldn't talk to her, like he could to me. So sometimes he'd come by without any of the others and we'd . . . talk.'

'Just talk?' Posy asked, gently.

'To start with. Like I told you, he was helping me with my drama school applications. And then . . . it turned into something more.' A blush spread across Gabriella's olive-toned skin. 'If you're asking if we were sleeping together, the answer is yes.'

Rosalind exchanged a glance with Caro. If they'd wanted definitive proof that Luke hadn't changed as much as he'd claimed, they had it. But Rosalind was certain this wasn't the end of it.

'I wanted to talk to you about something else Luke may have been involved in.' While Posy explained to Gabriella about the townhouse, and Luke's visit with Shannon, and the photos she'd seen on the desk, Rosalind listened carefully, piecing together the evidence with everything they already knew. Was whatever Shannon was up to in that townhouse the reason Luke had to die?

'Can you tell us about the party you went to?' Posy prompted. 'Why you were there, and what happened?'

Gabriella's eyes were wider than ever, her complexion paling as she looked between them both.

'I . . . Luke knew I wanted to earn some extra money, for moving out into my own place, when I go back to university – drama school.' The words came soft but stilted. 'He told me he knew a way I could make really good money working for an events firm his friend owned. They had a party that night they needed staff for. I figured it was just waitressing, and I know how to do that, so I went along. But . . . but it wasn't waitressing.'

There was something heavy in Rosalind's chest. A rock, maybe. Or perhaps just her heart. Every time she thought this world had sunk as low as it could go, it found new depths.

Posy's expression beside her was grim. 'What was it, Gabriella? What did they want you to do?'

The girl looked haunted, lost in her own memories. They weren't going to rush her to an answer. 'When I arrived at the townhouse, they were so kind and friendly, the people working there. They had a dress all ready for me – this beautiful, emerald-green gown. I said something about worrying about spilling stuff on it while I was serving, and the woman helping me laughed. She said I wasn't there to serve food or drink. Then another woman – Shannon – came over and told me that my only job that night was to look pretty. She said that . . . that was why Luke had recommended me. Because he thought I was so beautiful. I figured . . . if Luke thought I could do it, it must be like an acting role. That it would be fine.'

Rosalind already knew it wasn't going to be fine. They waited in silence while Gabriella took a sip of water from the glass on the table before she continued.

'They took us – me and a few other girls – to this fantastic manor house in the middle of nowhere. I was shown to a bedroom and told to wait there for my 'date' – and that was the first time I got really nervous. When I asked questions, they acted like I was being ridiculous. Told me it was all for show, that all I had to do was smile and enjoy the party and be good company for my date. And when he arrived, that's what I did. He was older than me – a lot older – but I figured maybe he liked being around young people because we were more fun. And everyone at the party seemed to be having fun. I . . . I relaxed, I guess, because I really didn't think Luke would have got me into anything bad.'

That, if Rosalind had to guess, must have been around the time the photo Posy had seen had been taken. She'd said that Gabriella was smiling in it.

'But then the party started winding down, and when I asked about how I was getting home my date laughed and told me the night wasn't over yet. And suddenly I was back in that bedroom and he was yelling about getting what he paid for and . . .'

Gabriella broke off on a sob, and Posy grasped for her hand across the table.

'I told Luke the next day that I was never going back there. That I hated what he'd got me into. That it couldn't be legal, that I'd tell the police . . . but he showed me that photo, the one with me smiling, and told me that the police wouldn't believe me. And then he gave me the money I'd earned and . . . I'd never make that kind of money anywhere else. We both knew it. And I was too ashamed to tell anyone about what had happened.'

'When was this?' Posy asked, softly.

'A month or so ago, I think. It was before they moved into the Prince Regent, when they were still rehearsing in their other space around the corner – I remember because they ordered lunch the day before the party and I delivered it. It must have been that long because . . . last week, I found out I'm pregnant. And I was so ashamed, I couldn't tell anyone how it really happened. I don't even know . . . I don't know if Luke was the father or my date at the party and then Luke died and . . .' Her words dissolved away into tears and suddenly Carlos was back, emerging from the kitchen doorway where Rosalind hadn't even seen him return. He wrapped his daughter up in his muscled arms, holding her close. Rosalind didn't know how much of her story he'd heard, but it must have been enough.

It only made Gabriella sob more, burying her head in his shoulder as he whispered what sounded like reassurances to her in Spanish.

Finally, when Gabriella's tears had subsided enough for them to hear each other speak, he looked up and met Rosalind's gaze.

'*I* will take her to the police. We will make sure these people pay for what they've done to my little girl.'

Rosalind nodded, and got to her feet. 'Then we will leave it in your capable hands.'

But Posy hesitated by the table, and Rosalind suddenly realised that there was a question she hadn't asked, yet. Gabriella hadn't been the only person she'd thought she recognised in the photos.

Posy gave the girl a gentle smile. 'Gabriella, I'm sorry to make you remember. But at the party . . . did you talk to anyone else about what happened, or see anyone else from either the Arcadia or the Prince Regent theatres there?'

Gabriella looked up, and nodded. 'One. He was a guest there, like my date. I don't think he noticed me, though.'

'Who was it?' Rosalind asked, hoping against hope that Posy had been mistaken in what she thought she'd seen in that photo.

Gabriella told them. And another part of the mystery of Luke and Darcy's deaths tumbled into place.

Posy

The Arcadia seemed strangely quiet when Posy arrived the following afternoon. Or maybe that was just because she was entering through the front door, rather than the stage door. There was no matinee planned, and the front-of-house staff was minimal, the bar not currently open and no theatre tours booked.

They had the place to themselves: the Dahlias, and their suspects.

They'd set up camp at Caro's house again, after Gabriella's revelations at the tapas bar. Posy hadn't had much time to process what it meant or how she felt about Shannon running some sort of elite escort ring with at least one unwilling participant, or the fact that Luke had been helping her. The initial horror was still the most overwhelming feeling.

She knew later the guilt and the questions would sink in – the biggest one being, would Shannon have still ended up on this path if she hadn't run away from LA after finding Posy and Luke together? But she couldn't think about that now.

They had a murder to solve. Two, in fact.

So they'd hunkered down at Caro's kitchen table, edits shoved to one side, and gone back over everything they'd learned and every assumption that they'd made.

It was then that Posy finally saw what they'd missed.

And a new theory started to form.

It had taken a few phone calls, and some internet searches to confirm her suspicions, but by the time midnight came around, they had it all.

'We're certain, this time?' Rosalind had asked, clearly exhausted.

Posy checked with Caro and got a nod before she said, 'As certain as we can be.' The information was good.

They knew who killed Luke Burrows, and Darcy Coleman. They even knew why.

But they didn't have *proof*. Which meant they needed to get the murderer to admit it.

'We need to find a place to do the *J'accuse*,' Rosalind said.

'The Arcadia. It has to be. For one night only,' Posy joked. 'Leave it with me. You two put the call out to our suspects.'

She'd spent the morning running the last of her errands, before meeting the other two at the Arcadia. As she walked through the heavy front doors and up the marble steps to the red-and-gold-carpeted foyer she spotted Caro on the stairs, talking with Pollie, the Arcadia stage manager – her own last task.

Caro looked down, spotted her, and gave her the nod, letting Pollie go to take her seat up in the box. After all, it wouldn't be a proper performance without someone cueing the curtains, lights and everything else, and Pollie had volunteered.

Today, the stars of the show would be sitting out in the audience, for a change, while the three Dahlias took centre stage.

Rosalind was waiting for them by the entrance to the stalls seats, on the side of the theatre with the pass door to the wings.

'They're all here,' she murmured, trying not to draw attention to their arrival. 'But they're not happy about it.'

Caro looked out over the assembled suspects who, to Posy's eyes, appeared to be on the edge of revolt – and of walking out.

'Maybe we should have come in through the stage door,' she murmured.

'Too late now.' Posy pushed open the pass door that led into the wings and held it for the other two to go through. 'Time to put on a show.'

It felt odd, standing on the same stage where she had performed nightly, with the same setting and props, but not as her character, Nicki, with her seventies style and brash, American accent. She wasn't even standing there as Posy, not really. The Posy who'd stood on this stage back during their first rehearsals at the actual theatre had been dressed in jeans or yoga pants and stretchy tops, her hair pulled back in a ponytail, her face bare of make-up. That Posy had been focused on proving she could perform, could make this part her own, could hold an audience in the palm of her hand even when the lights went out.

That Posy hadn't been accused of murder by the internet and the world's press.

This Posy . . . this Posy was ready to hit back. To expose other people's secrets and shames instead of her own for a change. To tell the truth and catch a murderer.

To be *Dahlia* again.

It was a heady feeling.

Of course, this Posy had also ended up staying the night at Caro's, not for the first time, and unlike Rosalind hadn't had the presence of mind to bring an overnight bag. (In truth, Rosalind had directed the car she'd ordered past her hotel on the way to Caro's, where a porter had been waiting with a perfectly packed bag in hand. Posy wasn't sure she would ever have that sort of control or power over the world around her.)

The consequence of this was that she'd been dressed that morning, much like a doll, by the other two Dahlias, in clothes from Caro's second wardrobe, where she kept all the things that didn't fit her any longer. The resulting look was a very modern Dahlia – and far smarter than anything Posy would have picked herself for a general off-duty look.

Still, she supposed she *was* on duty – Dahlia duty – and the wide linen trousers and waistcoat did fit the bill nicely for that. She was in costume, her make-up was on, and she was ready to perform.

But first . . .

'Thank you, both,' she said, softly, as they stood in a line in the centre of the stage with the curtain still lowered. 'For helping me prove my innocence.'

'Of course,' Rosalind said. 'You're one of us.'

'And I'm sorry I wasn't as supportive as I should have been,' Caro said. 'You told me the truth about Luke and I didn't believe it.'

'Because you like to see the good in people, despite everything.' There had been plenty of time to think it over, trapped in her flat by the paparazzi outside, or waiting in a cold police interview room. Posy had drawn her own conclusions days ago about Caro's motivations. 'You believed me when I said I'd changed, and you wanted to do the same for Luke.'

'Except Luke *hadn't* changed,' Rosalind said, drily. 'Not in the ways that mattered.'

'No.' Posy felt a wave of sadness at the realisation. He hadn't changed, and it had got him killed. Worse, almost, he'd turned one of those people out there in the audience into a murderer.

She straightened her spine, and turned back towards the curtains. 'Are we ready?'

A nod to one of the assistant stage managers Pollie had roped into coming in early, and the curtain went up. Spotlights on.

And their audience, waiting. Staring.

Showtime.

Chapter Nineteen

'Love, hate, greed, revenge, fear . . . don't we ever get any new motives around here?' Dahlia asked.

Johnnie huffed a laugh. 'The human condition, my dear. Sometimes, I think they're the only things we really care about.'

Dahlia Lively in *For the Love of Money*
By Lettice Davenport, 1960

Rosalind

Normally, stage lights were a comfort. Not being able to make out faces in the audience when she was trying to perform was good. Today, though, Rosalind needed to be able to see their suspects.

Posy was certain they had this – that their deductions and conclusions held up. Even Ashok, brought in via video call at almost midnight the evening before, had agreed.

But until Rosalind could look them in the eye and see their guilt first hand, there would always be an element of doubt. So, as the whispers in the small audience turned to shouts, she stepped forward, to the edge of the stage where the lights weren't so blinding, and looked down.

There, in the third and fourth rows of the auditorium, were their suspects: Joshua, Taran, Amber, Piotr, Shannon and Martha. Darcy would have sat beside them if her body wasn't cold in a police morgue somewhere.

There were others in the theatre – witnesses, she supposed. Some of them had a part to play in what would follow, others had no idea they were even part of something at all.

But those six, they were the ones that mattered.

They'd been directed to their rows by the usher, who'd been paid a little extra to come in early and perform the service. But they'd chosen their own seats, and it was interesting to see how they'd arranged themselves.

Joshua sat towards one end of the row – still close enough to the middle for a good view, but with a reasonable gap from him to Amber and Piotr, who sat further along with only one chair's space between them. Taran sat in the row in front, as close to the other end as Joshua was to his. Martha and Shannon had seats next to each other a little further along.

Rosalind looked down at the six of them, and smiled.

'I suppose you're wondering why we've called you all here.' They wouldn't be, she knew. They'd all watched enough old Dahlia Lively repeats to know how this went now.

'You think you've solved it, then,' Piotr called up from his seat. 'Another murder under your belt?' He sounded sceptical.

Caro stepped forward, stood with one hand on a hip, her opposite foot pointing out. 'We *know* we have. We've only invited you all here as a courtesy. Before we go to the police.'

That was a risk, letting them know that they planned to tell the police what they'd discovered. But it was also a security. There were enough people here in the building that their suspect couldn't try anything without being seen. That was important. They could try to run but that would be an admission of guilt.

In Rosalind's experience, a person who'd killed twice already wouldn't hesitate to kill again. But if that second murder was only to try and get away with the first . . . they'd also try to brazen it out before giving away their culpability.

Which meant they had to play this exactly right if Posy's plan to expose them was going to work.

'Wait, I thought Darcy left that note saying *she* killed Luke.' Joshua looked genuinely confused about what had happened. It wouldn't take long to change that.

'That's what the killer wanted everyone to think,' Rosalind said. 'It's why they killed her. She was the perfect scapegoat – after Posy. Everyone knew that she suspected Luke was cheating on her. It made sense that she might have followed him and confronted him at the Arcadia. She had a built-in motive.'

'Speaking of scapegoats . . .' Posy moved towards the edge of the stage now. She looked pale in the stage lights despite her make-up, her soft blonde hair caught up at the back of her head with one of Caro's sparkling clips. Her cheeks were bloodless, but her jaw was set. She was ready, Rosalind could tell.

'You'll indulge me, I hope.' Posy's voice carried far beyond their suspects in the front few rows. She wasn't only speaking to them, Rosalind suspected. If she was proclaiming her innocence, she'd want everyone to hear. 'Because I know that for a while every one of you suspected *me* of killing Luke Burrows. Well, everyone except the person who really did kill him. So I hope that you'll allow me a moment to talk about why.'

That, at least, seemed to have piqued some of their interests. Joshua was no longer lounging back in his seat, one arm across the chairs beside him, his ankle resting on his opposite knee. He'd sat up, straight, giving her his full attention. And he wasn't the only one.

'In some ways, I think this case started weeks before Luke died.' Posy had moved towards the park bench, a piece of the set of *Lights Out*, and taken a seat. She leaned forward, her wrists on her knees as she addressed the audience. Caro and Rosalind moved as one towards the opposite bench on the other side of the stage. Posy had them all hooked; she didn't need them yet.

But they'd be ready when she did.

'I thought it started the day he surprised me in my dressing room,' Posy went on. 'The night I accidentally split his head open with a book. Or maybe when Caro brought him along to the press night of *Lights Out* and I saw him again for the first time in so many years. But actually, it started even earlier than that. It really began the day that Caro told me an old friend of mine had been cast opposite her in *Finding Freddie*. I remember it vividly, because we were attending a friend's wedding, and she said the words so nonchalantly. But I felt a chill go through me all the same. Because Luke and I weren't friends. And I knew he'd bring nothing but trouble into all our lives, just like he had done before.'

Rosalind scanned the faces of their suspects and saw understanding on every one of them. They'd all pretended they believed Luke had changed. Rosalind had thought it was a matter of finding the one person who was lying about it.

But it turned out they all were.

Caro stood up again, pacing to the centre of the stage before speaking. A spotlight found her, and Rosalind hid a smile. How typical.

'That has, I think, caused the biggest confusion in this whole case,' Caro said. 'And it became the central question as we tried to solve it. Who was Luke Burrows? We each thought we knew who he was, but kept tripping up over other people's ideas of him. To me, he was a friendly, amiable co-star. Charming and endearing. A changed man. It took me a while to realise that was only an act, another part he was playing.'

But she had, eventually. Rosalind had to admit that Caro was getting better at admitting when she was wrong.

Well. Slightly better.

Posy joined Caro in the centre of the stage. 'I was certain I knew exactly who Luke was. But even I started to doubt myself. In the end, though, what mattered more was who he thought *I* was.'

'And who was that?' Shannon called from the audience, her voice cold. 'Because I don't think Luke thought about you at all.'

Posy shifted to face her old friend, and Rosalind willed her on silently. 'Oh, I think he did. And he thought I was the same scared, easily led girl I was when you and he first met me. I realise now that what he wanted to do was scare me into silence about the man I knew him to be. That's why he came to my dressing room, why he left me reminders of our time together, why he wanted me to know you were in town too. He wanted me quiet, so he could get away with whatever he wanted over and over again.'

She stepped back, widened her stance, her arms out just a little from her sides. She took up space. She belonged on that stage. Rosalind didn't hide her smile this time.

'But ultimately, it didn't matter,' Posy went on. 'Because I wasn't the girl he remembered. And more importantly, I wasn't the only person in this case who knew the Luke of old – who knew the truth about who he was.'

Rosalind stood up. Her turn.

'We peeled back the layers of your histories – and your presents – with Luke.' Pacing across the front of the stage, she addressed them each in turn. 'Joshua. You lost your chance at stardom when Luke took over the role you'd played and you were relegated to a bit part and understudy duties. But that wasn't your first interaction with Luke, it emerged. He'd also dated your sister, years ago – and behaved badly enough that she felt the need to disappear completely to get away from him. Taran told us that.' She nodded in his direction, knowing every eye was on her as she moved across the stage. 'He hoped that information would buy him some of Luke's influence, some of his fame even. But little did he know what thin ice that fame was – and that what little influence Luke had might be gone soon if word got out of his behaviour behind the scenes of *Finding Freddie*.'

Caro took over the narrative as they discussed her play. 'Amber, you thought Luke had changed, but slowly had to acknowledge that his behaviour towards Darcy, and the crew, when the bigwigs weren't looking told another story. Worse, when you tried to address it with Piotr, Luke turned on you – threatening your job. And Piotr took his side.'

'Piotr, I watched you change after Luke died,' Rosalind said. 'Before his death, you were conciliatory towards him, and full of praise when talking about him. Afterwards, you became more honest about the liability he'd become. Once he was no longer a threat to you, that is. Because what Amber didn't know was that you had no power over Luke, because Luke knew all your secrets too.'

'What secrets?' Amber asked.

Piotr folded his arms over his chest. 'They don't know what they're talking about.'

'We do. Because it wasn't just your secrets he was keeping,' Posy said. 'For Shannon, Luke was an old friend, a fixer, a man who could get her what she needed, as long as she wasn't too queasy about his methods. Isn't that right, Shannon?'

'I have no idea what you mean.' Shannon glanced away to the side, her perfect hair swinging with her.

'I think you do,' Rosalind said, softly, but still pitched to carry. 'And I think the police will too, by now. Gabriella and her father went to talk to them last night. I'd expect a visit soon.'

She was rewarded by a flare of panic in Shannon's eyes, but it didn't last. They both knew full well that she and her husband probably had enough money and influence to make a solitary accusation go away.

They'd need more than one. And if they managed to tie her and her 'events business' to a murder in the national press . . . maybe that would do it.

'We'll see,' Shannon said, mulishly.

'We will.' Posy sounded firm, confident. It was good to hear. 'You see, Shannon and her husband were already under suspicion for their activities in the US, which I imagine is why they decided to relocate. But they also brought their illegal activities with them. An elite escort service, dressed up as charitable events, run from a townhouse right here in London. And Luke, always keen to connect people and earn favours, was able to find at least one naive young woman for your use, wasn't he?'

'He might not have attended the parties himself, but his relationship with Gabriella meant he heard all about at least one of them – and who was there.' Caro looked straight at her director. 'Like you, Piotr.'

His face was flushed almost purple, and he gripped the back of the chair beside him, eyeing the exits. 'You have no proof.'

Amber stared at him in horror. '*That's* why you always took his side?'

'That's why. But we'll be leaving that whole business to the police. Because as loathsome as it is, it's not why we're here. We're here to find out who killed Luke.' Rosalind turned towards Martha. 'Which brings us to our last suspect: Luke's half-sister, who saw Luke as an interloper, a user, only after the family money that would come his way once their father succumbed to his long but terminal illness.'

Caro joined her. 'You'd been the one who had looked after your dad for years, who'd been the good and dutiful child, and suddenly Luke was the favoured kid, the prodigal returned, isn't that right?'

'It's not an unusual story,' Martha said, uncomfortably.

'It was unusual that you were with Shannon at the time of his murder, though,' Rosalind said, thoughtfully. 'I'm not a big believer in coincidence, so that one gave me pause.'

'As it happened, though, it wasn't a coincidence, was it Shannon?' Caro said. 'In fact, it was just another example of Luke connecting and manipulating people for his own ends.'

'What do you mean?' Martha looked genuinely confused.

'Tell her, Shannon,' Rosalind urged.

Shannon rolled her eyes. 'Luke asked me to stop by your gallery to buy the art for the London townhouse, that's all. He wanted to try and win you over so you'd stop whispering poison about him to your father. I was supposed to mention casually that he'd recommended you when I came to settle up for the final pieces and arrange delivery. It *was* a coincidence that our appointment was . . . when it was.'

'The exact time that Luke was killed.' Caro clapped her hands together and smiled. 'Which brings us to our next phase. The events of that day.'

Caro

Caro loved all parts of the *J'accuse*. The build-up, the motives, the moment when it became clear that they were right . . . Normally, the timeline didn't interest her much – that was more Posy's bag, with her notebook or her Post-its.

This time, though, the timeline was everything.

'That afternoon, we were rehearsing for previews at the Regent. Before that, however, Luke visited his father – only briefly, because they were interrupted by Martha – and then he went to meet with Shannon at the townhouse where she runs her "events" business from.' Caro was pleased to see several disgusted looks sent Shannon's way at the reminder of her enterprise. 'He bought some flowers and dropped them at the Arcadia stage door, then arrived at the Regent where Piotr told him everything was sorted with Amber and the DSM. But something else happened around then, too, that I didn't even realise until later. I lost my phone.'

'Someone call *Crimewatch*,' Piotr muttered, and the people around him chuckled.

Was *Crimewatch* even a thing any more? Surely it had been taken over by true crime podcasts.

It didn't matter. *Focus, Caro.*

'Except it wasn't really lost,' she went on. 'Someone had taken it, to send Posy a message, on my behalf, asking to meet that afternoon at a coffee shop conveniently far away from the theatre.'

'I went, of course, only to get stood up,' Posy put in.

'We thought, as the police must have after they found Darcy's note, that it was a ploy to get Posy away from the theatre when Luke was due to meet her there, so that Darcy could confront him about his cheating. It would have been easy for Darcy to access my phone and send the message, and even easier for her to slip over to the Arcadia and pretend to be Posy to gain entry, as the CCTV cameras showed someone did. It all made sense, except for one thing.' She left it for Posy to complete the thought. After all, she was the one who'd been framed.

'Luke wasn't going to the theatre to meet me. He was meeting Taran.'

'Maybe Darcy didn't know or didn't believe it, maybe she suspected something else, but it was enough to give us pause,' Rosalind said. 'Because if she *had* followed him, she'd have seen him walk into Taran's dressing room, not Posy's – even though his body was found there.'

'The point is, Luke left the Regent at the break and headed over to the Arcadia, followed by Darcy,' Caro said, dragging them back on track. 'And shortly after that, a woman disguised as Posy got past the stage door and headed in after him.'

'Luke was killed around then, we think. Slashed across the neck with a short knife, cutting his carotid artery, according to reports.' Posy managed to sound completely unemotional as she described it – even though Caro was fairly sure she felt anything but. She might not have liked the man, but murder was hard to not feel *anything* about, even when you *hadn't* found the body. 'He must have been killed in my dressing room, as there was no blood trail anywhere else, and his body was hidden behind the chair. Realistically, I expect he was attacked from behind, by someone he trusted, otherwise there would have been more signs of a struggle.'

They knew from Ashok's police contact that the professionals agreed with that basic assessment. Caro was sure they knew much more than they did – forensic details and such, whether it really was a slash or a stab, how much force was used, all the things they'd need to build a case. But the Dahlias didn't work that way. That was enough for them to be going on with.

'At this point the murderer must have been covered in blood,' Rosalind said. 'So we imagined they'd stashed their coat with the murder weapon somewhere, and started to make their escape.'

'We're guessing, of course, now,' Posy went on. 'But since I arrived at the theatre shortly afterwards, I know there wasn't anyone else in that dressing-room corridor, and I didn't pass anyone near the stage door. I also know that the fire alarm went off before I reached the room, meaning Luke's body wasn't discovered for another hour or so.'

'Given where the fire started, and how, we have a pretty good idea of what happened next.' Caro grinned at their audience, their attention flicking between the three of them as they seamlessly told the story. 'The police found that the bin where the fire started, in the alley beside the theatre, contained a bloodstained coat. We assumed that the killer must have ditched it there while making their escape, and set it on fire to try and destroy it. But then we realised what was just above that bin. The ladies' backstage bathroom.'

That was when she'd been certain that Posy was right – when she'd gone over the blueprints of the Arcadia they'd found online and seen where those bathrooms were – and what else was near them.

Talking to Pollie that morning had just cemented it.

'So the killer was a woman,' Taran said, quickly. 'That's good to know. Puts three of us out of the frame.'

'Perhaps,' Rosalind said. 'We couldn't be certain, though. It was possible that the fake-Posy was a decoy – or an accomplice who let the real killer backstage through the pass door in the auditorium.'

'It could have been *anybody*,' Piotr said, angrily. 'Theatre security is a joke. Anyone could have got in if they wanted to.'

'It's true,' Caro admitted. 'It was possible. But it didn't seem likely. The timeline was too tight, for a start – who else would know Luke would be going over there exactly then, and prepare to keep Posy out of the way? Who else would have access to my phone? Who else could pretend to play Posy for the CCTV?'

'We were certain it had to be someone from either the Arcadia or the Prince Regent, or with enough connections to Luke or Posy to get into those places,' Rosalind said. 'In fact, when we started investigating, we quickly realised that most people involved with the two theatres already had alibis. Except for the four of you, and Darcy. Martha and Shannon were the only two outliers who also fitted the profile.'

'It was easy to uncover motives for each of you, too,' Posy said. 'You all had a plausible reason to want him out of the way. But to start with, Darcy seemed like the strongest suspect – either working alone or as an accomplice to the killer.'

'We kept digging, though,' Rosalind went on. 'I was in the audience the night that Darcy disappeared, I saw her on stage, and Caro found her note in her dressing room as soon as the play ended. It seemed that everyone at the theatres had an alibi for the time she went missing. But when her body was found in the bowels of the theatre . . . we were more certain than ever that there was foul play afoot.'

'We uncovered more secrets.' Posy looked directly at Shannon as she said that. Caro smirked. 'We went back over who was where when, the timeline, everything. And then we realised.'

Well, Posy had realised. But luckily she was happy to share the credit, so Caro took over. 'Darcy was on stage in the second half of the play, yes. But her only appearance was in the phone box, upstage, up on the higher part of the set that made up the hill. And if our killer – or their accomplice – had already pretended to be Posy, surely they could have played the part of Darcy, too. Which meant she could have been killed in the interval – when any one of you could have done it. All it would take was a good knowledge of the theatre – which all of you had.'

All of them knew the Regent Theatre, even the outliers. Martha had been following her father around at work since she was a toddler, and then worked in costume design, before becoming a patron of the theatre and giving tours. Shannon had spent enough of her early career in theatres to make it possible, especially if she was working with Martha. And the rest of them had made their livings on the stage or behind it. If they were determined enough – and with their own life and freedom on the line, Caro would bet they were – they could have hidden the fact that Darcy had never made it back onto the stage at all.

Taran was the only one who might have struggled, but they'd checked the timings and the intervals of both plays lined up. It was *just* possible he could have slipped out of the Arcadia and over to the Regent to kill, but he couldn't have played Darcy on stage in the second act. But an accomplice could – and could have cleaned up after him while he dashed back to the Arcadia to get back on stage.

Caro looked over their audience. They were starting to get restless.

'I don't see where you're going with this.' Martha had picked up her handbag and was holding it in her lap, as if she were about to make a move at any moment. 'Nothing you've said has given us any information about who the killer is.'

Of course, that was intentional. Caro looked up and caught the eye of Mal, the stage-door keeper, standing at the back of the auditorium. He gave her the agreed signal, and she smiled. It was time to move into the endgame.

They'd put on a show. Now it was time to bring the house down with a grand finale.

'You're right,' she said. 'And that's because, last night, we really did believe that any one of you could have killed Luke, and then Darcy.

Some of you were more obvious suspects than others, some motives more convincing. But in the end, it all came down to one thing. The murder weapon.'

'Pollie told Mal, shortly after Luke's murder, that her pocket knife had gone missing.' Posy was at Caro's side now, Rosalind close by too. 'We assumed that it must have been taken by the murderer to kill Luke. Except, when? There was no space in our timeline for a theft like that. So it seemed more plausible that the lost knife was a coincidence, and the murder weapon something the murderer brought with them to the theatre.'

'But do you know where Pollie kept that knife?' Rosalind asked, a rhetorical question that none of the audience even bothered to try to answer. 'In her stage manager's kit bag, in the small production office just off the wings. Next to that ladies toilet over the bin where the fire started.'

'Because the killer didn't take the knife to kill Luke,' Caro concluded. Her conversation with Pollie before had confirmed that for her. And now, as she looked at their killer's drained, pale face, she knew she was right. 'They shoved their bloodied coat out of that bathroom window, having first set it on fire, stashed the wig and hat they'd worn, then went and took Pollie's knife to hide the fact that they'd used their own to kill him. Because they knew that the knives were identical – because they'd bought them together, when they were both starting out as stage managers. Hadn't you, Amber?'

Chapter Twenty

'No!' Their suspect darted down a narrow alleyway that led to the river. 'Johnnie, stop him!'

But they both already knew he was too far away. It would take a miracle to catch him now.

Dahlia Lively in *Forever Summer*
By Lettice Davenport, 1952

Posy

'I . . . I don't know what you're talking about.' Amber was penned in, between Joshua and Piotr, her gaze darting this way and that for a way out. Would she try to brazen it out, or would she run? It didn't matter. One way or another, she was finished.

Normally, it felt good to catch a criminal – to solve a murder and put a killer behind bars. Today . . . Posy just felt sad about everything and everyone involved in this case.

The evidence they had wouldn't hold up in court – it was all circumstantial and late-night guesswork. But Posy had no doubt that the police would *find* the evidence they needed. Amber wasn't a master criminal. And despite what they'd first thought, this wasn't a carefully thought-out perfect murder where she'd covered all her bases. There'd be DNA, forensics, all that stuff coming back any day now, she was sure.

They'd just got there first.

'It wasn't just the knife, Amber,' Posy said, softly. Yes, establishing that Amber owned her own version of the presumed murder weapon had clinched things. But it was only one of many things that had led to their confusion. 'You're a single mum, right? Of a seven-year-old?'

Amber nodded jerkily. 'So?'

'Eight years ago, Luke was working here in London, on a play at the Arcadia, as it happened. And so were you.' Caro's words were blunt. 'On the stage that time, rather than behind it. But after that . . . you disappeared. No work for the next three or four years, until you reappeared working backstage as a part-time production assistant in the suburbs.'

It had been an accidental discovery at first, made when they were looking into the timeline of Luke's actions before and after he'd been dating Joshua's sister. But after that, Caro and Ashok's PI research skills had come to the fore to figure out the chain of events.

'It's hard to find work in theatre as a single mum.' Amber looked straight at them now as she spoke. 'Go on, then. Tell them all the rest.'

'It was the argument Joshua heard you having with Luke that did it,' Caro said. 'We misunderstood it to start – so did Joshua. We thought it was about Luke's behaviour in the wings. But we asked him last night to remember exactly what you'd said, and that's when it became clear. *You can't get away with that sort of behaviour*, you said. And he told you, *you'd be surprised what I can get away with. I'm the one with the money, the fame, I can get the whole world on my side if I need to. Even a judge.*' They'd thought it was about indecent behaviour, to start with.

But then they'd realised. He'd meant a judge in family court. Deciding custody.

'Luke was your son's father, wasn't he?' Posy made it sound like a question, even though it wasn't any longer, not to her mind. And if they were right about this . . . they were right about everything.

Amber stared at her for a long moment, indecision clear on her face. She was searching for a way out, a lie to tell, a counterclaim to make.

She didn't find one.

Her pale face crumpled, and she sank back into her velvet seat, her shoulders hunched over.

'Wait, what?' Martha was on her feet now, staring over at her friend. 'You never told me you knew Luke. I've *met* Milo and you never said . . . I never knew he was my *nephew*! Is this why you sought me out when we worked on that show together? Why you wanted us to be friends?'

Amber blinked at her, uncomprehendingly. Posy didn't blame her. Somehow, Martha had managed to make things about her, even when Amber was potentially confessing to murder. That was a talent.

Posy dragged them back on track, ignoring Martha and addressing Amber. 'Did you tell him, back then? Or did he find out recently?'

'I told him I was pregnant at the time. He didn't believe it was his – or said he didn't.' Amber's hands were clutched tight in front of her. 'I was . . . I was his Darcy, on that show. But I was stupider than she was. I didn't even realise how little I mattered to him.'

'You saw him pulling the same stunts this time as he did eight years ago and you realised he'd never changed, is that right?' Rosalind asked. 'Did he even remember you?'

'Yeah, he remembered.' Amber's smile was bitter. 'I thought he wouldn't, but he did. And he thought . . . he thought I'd have got rid of the baby – that's what he said. But when he found out I was a single mum, and when he met Milo, the weekend I had to bring him with me to rehearsals, Luke put it all together. Said he'd changed. That he was sorry. He wanted to be a part of his son's life now, all these years later. He said he wanted to make up for lost time.'

'But you said no,' Caro guessed. 'And that's when he turned. Started threatening your job through Piotr.'

'He said he'd fight me for custody,' Amber said. 'Tell the judge that I'd hidden his child all those years. That he'd changed now and he deserved a second chance.'

'You didn't believe him.' Posy hadn't. Turns out they'd both been right.

Amber shook her head. 'Would you? Men like Luke don't change. I suspected he only wanted Milo as another way to persuade his father he was worthy of his inheritance – and then as soon as he got his hands on the money . . . I was scared of what would happen to Milo then.'

Posy could imagine. Luke would ship him off to boarding school, just to keep him away from Amber as a further punishment to her. The boy would grow up traumatised by his narcissistic father, and gaslit into believing his mother had abandoned him. She could see it all so clearly – the same way Amber must have done.

After all, they both knew him too well to believe anything better of him.

'I saw him with Darcy, heard him bragging about his past with you, Posy,' Amber went on. 'And worst of all I saw what he did to Gabriella when she told me she was pregnant. I found her sobbing in the loos at the tapas bar, terrified. She didn't want to admit it was Luke's, at first, but I'd watched him with her. I recognised the signs.'

It was so easy to see how Amber had been driven to her breaking point. Betrayed and badly used by a manchild who never seemed to face any consequences – that might have been enough. But when he came for her son . . .

'A family court would usually decide in favour of the mother, though, wouldn't they? Especially when the father had refused to be involved in the child's life for years.' Rosalind was right; murder seemed an extreme answer to the problem, however much hatred Amber harboured towards Luke.

There was more to this story.

'He had something on you, didn't he?' Posy guessed, thinking back to those passive-aggressive gifts Luke had left for her before he died. The ones she'd thought were a warning. 'He was threatening you.'

Amber seemed too tired even to lie any more. 'He'd put a PI onto me, the moment he realised Milo was his. Following me everywhere, waiting for me to make a mistake, to do something Luke could use against me. They . . . they dug up everything I'd ever done wrong in my life. Every time I ever took drugs at a party in my twenties, the credit-card debt I got into when I first moved to London . . . the fact that I struggled with post-natal depression after Milo was born, and my mother had to basically raise him for the first year because I was struggling.'

Posy could hear the shame in Amber's voice, even for things that weren't her fault. 'I know how awful that must have felt.' Much like reading all of her own past transgressions in the paper thanks to Shannon's pet reporter had. 'But I'm sure a fair judge—'

'I couldn't risk it,' Amber interrupted. 'My mum has been sick lately and . . . there were times where she couldn't watch Milo and I couldn't get off work. Most times I could get in a babysitter, or ask a neighbour to keep an eye on him, so I didn't have to bring him with me. But Mum . . . she's not getting better, and she's not going to get better. She has cancer. Stage four. It was only a matter of time before the PI followed me to the hospital with her and figured it out. And . . . I just knew Luke would use that against me, too. Prove I couldn't manage my job and my child alone. He'd take him from me and I just couldn't . . .' She trailed off into a sob.

Posy's eyes closed for a moment, her jaw tightening. Amber had been so scared, and dealing with so much. She didn't want to be sympathetic or understanding of a murderer. But in a way . . . she was.

When Posy opened her eyes again, Amber seemed to have collected herself. She tossed back her red curls and carried on her story, her fists clenched against her knees.

'The worst part was, even though *I* knew Luke hadn't changed, everyone else genuinely seemed to believe that he was this new man. He'd convinced his own father, and you, Caro, despite Posy's past with him. If he could make all of you believe it, why would a judge be any different? I didn't have any proof, he covered his tracks too well – or he had enough leverage over people like Piotr that I knew they'd speak up for him.

'I had to play him at his own game. I tried to track down other women he'd treated the way he treated me, but I couldn't find anyone willing to speak out. Not even Darcy, or Gabriella. They all wanted to get on with their lives. Or they were scared because he had videos or photos of them he'd use. Besides, who would believe them over him? Luke Burrows could get away with anything because he was charming, handsome, rich and famous. They knew they'd be the ones vilified in the press. We all know the power of celebrity. But I couldn't let him get away with stealing my child out of spite.'

'Is that why you framed me?' The last piece of the puzzle fell into place. 'Because I never spoke up, either? Or because you hoped I would, now?'

'I tried to raise it with you once, your history with Luke, I mean. You brushed me off.'

Posy tried to remember the conversation, but couldn't. She'd run the other way whenever anyone had tried to talk about Luke.

'But I wasn't trying to frame you.' Amber's eyes were wide, sincere, and Posy found herself believing her despite herself. 'I wasn't . . . I didn't even mean to kill him.'

Rosalind stepped forward, towards the edge of the stage. 'We thought initially that this was a cleverly planned and plotted murder. The phone message to Posy, the disguise, the fire . . . But that's not how it happened, is it, Amber?'

Amber shook her head.

Caro joined Rosalind. 'Why don't you tell us what *did* happen?'

Posy waited to see if Amber would deny it, try to lie again, but it seemed they'd broken her. In a dull monotone, she told them everything.

'I overheard Luke on the phone before we started rehearsals, arranging to meet Taran at the Arcadia. I was already planning to confront him, to try and scare him with everything I knew after talking to Gabriella, so he'd drop the idea of trying to get custody of Milo. But I needed to catch him off guard, to talk to him away from the theatre where anyone might overhear us and, well, this seemed like my best chance. I was just going to follow him . . . but I was worried about the private investigator he'd got following *me*. I didn't know for sure if he was outside the theatre, but then he'd definitely been there other times when I'd never noticed him.'

'That's the job,' Caro said, sadly. 'If the target spots you, you're doing it wrong.'

'The Arcadia was perfect because the PI wouldn't be able to follow us in through the stage door,' Amber went on. 'But if he saw me follow Luke he might give him the heads-up. The roads around here are such a warren, and I didn't know where the PI might be hiding, so whichever route I took he might see me. So I was trying to figure out how to do it without being spotted when I saw your phone sitting in the wings.' Amber glanced up at Caro. 'And it was like the idea came to me fully formed. I knew from Mal that Posy was always the first at the theatre, and I knew from working with him before that Taran was always late. Nobody would be surprised if Posy slipped in early – and if I left here in disguise, the PI wouldn't notice me.'

Amber might not be the one on the stage, but Posy could tell that she held their whole audience in her hand.

'Your phone wasn't even locked. I just . . . sent a message to Posy from you, to keep her away from the Arcadia just a bit longer, then told Luke that Taran had left a message asking him to stop by a bit earlier than planned. He didn't question it. Then before rehearsals finished I nipped up to the wardrobe and make-up departments and grabbed a blonde wig and a coat to sort of hide the rest of me, and then I just waited until Piotr called for a break. I was worried about the wig, though – they never look quite right on me. So I grabbed a baseball cap on my way out and when Luke left the theatre . . . I changed into my disguise, slipped out through the front of the theatre and followed him.

'It was easy enough to get past Mal on the stage door – he didn't even look up from his phone. And then I saw Luke go into Posy's dressing room instead of Taran's, planning on leaving another one of his gifts for you probably, and . . .' Amber's voice broke. 'I didn't mean to kill him. You have to believe that. I just . . . I was so *angry*. And frustrated. He wouldn't listen. He laughed when I tried to tell him what I had on *him*, about Gabriella's baby, the other women. He said no one would believe someone like me. And I had my knife in my pocket from earlier and I just . . . I pulled it on him and he laughed some more. He even turned his back on me and I put the blade to his throat . . .' She looked down at her shaking hands. 'He turned on me, suddenly, but I didn't give way. And the blade . . . I must have been pressing harder than I thought because . . . there was blood everywhere. All over my coat, all over the room. He just . . . dropped. I couldn't . . . there was nothing I could do.'

Even if there had been, Posy wasn't sure Amber would have done it. Yes, it might have technically been an accident – although she wasn't certain if that was just a story Amber was telling herself. The post-mortem might have some answers on that, she supposed. Either way, Amber had put a knife to his throat, threatening him. In a way, it felt inevitable.

Amber swallowed, her throat bobbing before she looked back up at the stage again. 'You were right about the rest of it. I was panicking – I knew I couldn't go out there covered in blood. Luckily the coat had covered most of me, so I stripped that off and ran for the ladies to wash the rest off my hands and face. I shoved a lit cigarette inside the coat and pushed it out of the window into the skip below, and then I raided the production office next door because I knew Pollie kept a couple of spare changes of clothes there for emergencies, and she probably wouldn't miss them for a while. But then I saw her knife in her kit and I thought . . . I don't know what I thought. Maybe it would buy me some time if they thought *Pollie's* knife was the murder weapon. So I took it and pretended it was mine. I threw my real one in the Thames on my way home that night.'

The story was horrific, made worse by the toneless, almost emotionless way Amber told it. Like she was describing a play she'd seen, rather than something she'd done. Maybe that was the only way she could cope with it.

And it did explain some things that had been bugging them about the sequence of events. Posy tried to find even a hint of pride that they'd got this one right, but couldn't. She'd almost rather she'd been wrong.

'What about Darcy?' Rosalind asked, her voice sounding scratchy. 'Was her death an accident too?'

Amber nodded. 'She saw me leaving the Arcadia that day. It was her hat I was wearing – she'd left it backstage. She was asking questions, working things out . . . I tried to scare her into silence, but it wasn't enough. She kept pushing. She knew there was something going on between me and Luke and she wanted to know what. She kept saying that if I'd seen something I had to tell somebody. I told her I hadn't, that I'd never gone inside the Arcadia.'

Darcy, in her delusions about Luke cheating on her with some blonde, must have seen Amber in a blonde wig and jumped to all sorts of conclusions. But apparently, not the right one. Maybe she hadn't believed another woman was capable of such a bloody murder – or she'd just believed Amber's lie. Darcy had told them that she'd left as soon as Luke went inside, and Amber must have hung back until she was gone.

'Her fall from the scaffolding, that first night we reopened,' Caro guessed. 'That was you scaring her?'

'It was a warning, that was all. I didn't want to kill her. But she was threatening to go to the police and tell them what she'd seen if I didn't do it myself. I told her everything Luke had been up to – about Gabriella and the baby . . . but it didn't make any difference. She told me she was going to go to the police as soon as that night's performance was over. So I dragged her down to the tunnels in the interval so we could talk again, in private. But she still wouldn't listen. She tried to leave, so I tried to stop her and . . . she fell and she landed badly. I think she caught her head on the corner of something sharp, I don't know. She was just . . . She didn't move. And I couldn't find a pulse. The second half was about to start so I . . . hid her. Until I could figure out what to do next.'

The text message Darcy had sent her must have been after Amber's first lot of revelations, Posy realised. Maybe she'd believed her more than Amber thought.

'You posed as her in the phone-box scene, then went and left the note in her dressing room, right?' Caro guessed. 'But what did you plan to do with the body?'

'I didn't *have* a plan!' Amber yelled, jumping to her feet. 'I told you, I didn't want to kill her. I just needed her to stay quiet. I couldn't . . . I can't go to jail.' Amber's eyes widened, desperate and wet with tears as everything became real for her at last. 'I have a kid. I can't . . .'

Posy's heart almost broke for her.

Almost.

But it was too late.

The doors at the back of the auditorium opened, Mal stepping aside to allow the police entry. The cameras they'd asked Pollie to set up would have caught everything, and Mal had called for police assistance the moment the curtain had gone up.

It was all over now.

Posy stepped back and collapsed onto the bench, the sound of a police officer reading Amber her rights echoing around the silent theatre. Posy felt the warm weight of Caro's arm settle around her shoulder as she sat beside her, while Rosalind stood behind them, a solid, supportive presence.

It was over.

Rosalind

Annie's roast dinners were a thing of legend.

'Jack is going to be most unhappy he missed this,' Rosalind told her, as she stole a crispy bit of roast potato from the serving bowl.

'He should have come down for the weekend.' Annie carried the potatoes over to the large table – no longer covered in Caro's book edits – and added it to the growing feast.

'There didn't seem much point,' Rosalind admitted. 'Not when I'm heading back to Wales tomorrow.'

'You're going back? Already?' Posy appeared in the doorway, her phone still in hand. She'd gone to take a call from Kit almost thirty-five minutes earlier – and from the look of it, she wasn't quite done yet. Rosalind nodded towards the phone, and she held it out. 'Oh, he wants to talk to you.'

Rosalind took the phone. 'Yes, Kit?'

'That's what you call having everything under control?' He sounded almost amused, which she took as a good sign.

She rolled her eyes. 'We caught the murderer, didn't we?'

'And Posy's really fine? She says she's okay but . . . this one cut close to home, didn't it?' There was worry underneath his lighter tone. Which was good. Posy deserved someone who would worry about her.

Someone other than her and Caro.

'She will be,' she said, after a pause. No point lying to the man. 'When are you home next?'

'Another week and I'm done for a month or so,' Kit said.

'Then I think she'll be just fine.' She handed the phone back to Posy to let her say her goodbyes, and looked up to find Annie watching her.

'It's been a long couple of weeks for you three, hasn't it?' Caro's wife said.

'It has.' But they'd solved a murder, fixed the rift that had started to grow between Caro and Posy, and—

'The book is done!' Caro held her arms wide for applause as she entered the kitchen, kimono flapping behind her. 'All seventy gazillion pages of edits are back with my editor and I am free!'

'Free to write the next one?' Rosalind asked, one eyebrow raised.

Caro glared at her. 'Don't tease, or we won't ask you back for Sunday dinner next week.'

'She won't care. She's going back to Wales tomorrow.' Posy had snuck back into the kitchen in the wake of Caro's editing triumph.

'Really?' Caro's gaze snapped to Rosalind's face. 'Why?'

'I imagine it has something to do with that rock on her left hand,' Annie said, casually. 'Her fiancé is probably missing her by now.'

Posy and Caro crowded her in seconds, Caro grabbing her hand and holding it up to the light. Rosalind sighed and let them ooh and ahh at the diamond as they saw fit.

'You said yes, then,' Posy said, redundantly.

'Obviously.' And they called themselves detectives.

'When?' Caro asked, rather more shrewdly.

'A while ago,' Rosalind admitted. Not long after that awful Christmas, back when living together hadn't seemed quite enough, and before it became too much. 'I just . . . needed some time away before we went public.'

'Public like an announcement in *The Times*?' Annie leaned on the counter opposite to watch Posy tilting Rosalind's hand in the spotlights over the island.

'Public like wearing my ring to Sunday dinner.' Surely that was enough? Who else really needed to know?

She'd called Jack the night after the police had taken Amber away, and told him everything that had happened while she'd been in London. He'd sighed, but taken it as probably inevitable at this point.

'Jack's not expecting you to give up investigating once you're married, is he?' Caro narrowed her eyes at her. 'This wasn't like a last hurrah kind of thing, was it?'

'He knows me better than that,' Rosalind assured her. 'He knows you and Posy better than that, too. No, we've come to an agreement.'

Living in Wales full time wasn't working for her. She'd tried it, and that was enough. But Jack understood what she needed — and she hoped she did now, too.

It might not be the most conventional marriage — they probably wouldn't be the average retired couple, not least because neither of them was really all that interested in retiring altogether. They might live together most of the year, but not all of it. They could travel together, but also separately. And sometimes she'd solve murders with her best friends.

Conventional was overrated, anyway.

'I might need to buy another flat in London, though,' she said, thinking. Hotels really weren't the most convenient for longer stays.

'You can always stay here with us,' Annie offered.

Caro caught her eye and Rosalind winced.

'You know, the area around me really *is* up and coming these days,' Posy put in. 'We could go flat hunting together!'

Maybe hotels weren't all that bad.

Fortunately, at that moment the oven timer went off, and Annie hurried them all over to the table while she pulled out the last bits from the oven. Caro opened the wine, and poured, before fetching Posy a brightly coloured mocktail from the fridge. The doors to the garden were wide open, letting in the summer air, and the scent of rosemary from the garden echoed the lamb Annie was serving.

Rosalind sat back at the head of the table, and relaxed. Yes, she'd marry Jack, because she loved him. And she'd visit London often, because she loved these women, too. And she'd solve crimes with them, and laugh and cry with them, because they were all family, every bit as much as her husband-to-be.

Family, after all, was the people you chose to let in, just as much as the one you were born into.

But for now, she'd just enjoy a perfect summer evening as one of the three Dahlias.

Two Months Later

Posy

Rosalind's new flat was bright, airy, large – and in an area of London that had already up and come some decades ago and remained excruciatingly expensive.

'Welcome to the palace,' Jack joked when he opened the door. 'Apparently I'm marrying into even more money than I'd thought.'

Money had clearly smoothed the house-buying process, too, since it had taken Rosalind only a fraction of the time to purchase her flat than it had taken Posy.

'Enjoying being a kept man, then?' Posy asked.

'Kept man in London, handyman and cook back in Wales,' Jack replied. 'Could be worse. Take a seat and I'll fetch you a coffee.'

Of course, they'd kept the cottage on the river in north Wales too, but Posy definitely liked the idea that Rosalind could split her time between the mountains and the city. Even now, she felt better knowing that her fellow Dahlias were close by, if she needed them.

It had been a long few months, Posy reflected, as she sank into the pristine white sofa she was sure Jack had nothing to do with choosing. Rosalind and Caro were nattering in the kitchen, and Posy wondered if she should join them, but it was so nice to just . . . sit for a while.

She let her gaze wander out of the large picture window looking out over one of London's many parks, and gave her thoughts permission to drift.

Kit had returned from filming a week after Amber's arrest, and dug Posy out of the hermit cave she'd turned her flat into while the newspapers and online media rehashed every possible angle of the case over and over, usually including that awful photo of her covered in blood by the stage door.

She'd thought that once the case was solved, it would all be over. But there were still trials and appeals and new exposés from Luke's PI, and many of his ex-girlfriends. And it wasn't just the murder trial, of course. Shannon and her husband had also been hauled over the coals by the media when stories of their parties got out, and it looked like charges might actually stick against them at last, after so many years of rumours. Of course, Posy's connection to Shannon *and* Luke was being exploited for as many stories as possible.

It seemed like the media circus might never end. Kit had taken one look at her and pulled out his phone, and the next thing she knew they were on a plane to some island where even the mocktails came in coconuts and their private cabana was completely secluded.

It was exactly what she'd needed.

By the time they returned a month later, things had finally quietened down – or, at least, Posy felt like she had the emotional strength to deal with them again. Kit had put a lot of effort into reminding her how loved, strong and amazing she was. He was a man of many talents.

He was off filming again now, while Posy had – after discussion with her agent – granted herself a bit of a break. She wasn't ready to get back on stage at the Arcadia after all that had happened, and besides, *Lights Out*'s run had already finished. The next Dahlia Lively film was scheduled to start filming in the new year, but for now . . . Posy thought she'd earned a little time off. From acting, from murder, and definitely from the media.

Jack returned with her coffee, followed closely by Rosalind and Caro, who both perched on the edge of the sofa opposite Posy, on the other side of the coffee table.

Oh, that didn't look good.

Posy took a sip of her coffee then placed it on the nearest coaster. 'Okay, what's all this about a letter, then?' It was why they'd asked her to come over, after all.

The other two Dahlias exchanged a look. The sort of look that meant they'd already had extensive conversations about whatever was in this letter, and only just now decided to bring it to her.

Really not good.

'You might as well just show it to her, Rosa.' Jack leaned against the archway to the large, open-plan kitchen-diner. 'It's addressed to her too.'

Posy raised an eyebrow at that. Rosalind and Caro returned the look with matching ones of their own.

Rosalind produced a creamy envelope from between two oversized coffee-table books on art or architecture or something. She passed it across to Posy, who studied it carefully.

Just as Jack had said, it was addressed to *The Three Dahlias*, care of Rosalind's agent. Inside was nestled an equally luxurious and thick piece of paper, which Posy fished out carefully and started to read.

Dear Mses King, Hooper and Starling,

I am writing on behalf of my employer, Mr Percival Pendleton, to enquire as to your availability to act as consultants in a case of expected murder.

'What on earth is an "expected murder"?' Posy asked.
'Keep reading,' Caro told her.

To explain, my client anticipates being killed by one of his associates this autumn, and would like you to solve the case – ideally before his death, if at all possible.

Posy snorted. 'Well, yes, that would be the ideal, I suppose.'

He requests to meet with you to discuss on the afternoon of Friday 13 September, in Monte Carlo. Should the meeting go well, you will be expected to board his yacht, the Silver Lining, *that evening. Dress code: maritime formal.*

Payment will be discussed prior to boarding.

Yours faithfully,
Barnaby Yarrow

Posy had no idea what 'maritime formal' comprised of, but Rosalind would know, for sure. And Monte Carlo in the autumn didn't sound half bad. And payment? Well, that was a new one for the cases they tended to get involved in.

Then she saw the postscript, and both her eyebrows flew up this time.

P.S. Pack for a two-week voyage.

'Two weeks on a luxury yacht in the Med trying to stop a murder?' Posy refolded the letter and placed it back inside its envelope. 'That's what you were afraid to talk to me about?'

'To be fair, it was more the murder aspect than the Mediterranean part,' Rosalind said. 'We weren't sure if you maybe . . . wanted a bit of a break from all the death for a while.'

All the death. That was one way of putting it, Posy supposed.

'Of course, if we do the job we're being hired for, the idea is that nobody dies at all,' Caro pointed out. 'And those of us who didn't just spend a month in the Maldives can have a nice holiday.'

'But we're leaving it up to you.' Rosalind shot a stern look in Caro's direction. 'If you don't want to take the job, we'll send a nice "thanks but no thanks" note to this Barnaby fellow to pass on to his boss.'

Posy stared down at the envelope in her hands, thinking hard.

On the one hand, wilfully putting themselves in another situation where a murder might occur – was *expected* even – seemed . . . foolhardy, at best. On the other . . . the opportunity to *stop* a murder for a change, rather than just trying to solve it after the fact, was appealing. She knew that none of the other murders they'd been involved in had been directly her fault, but all the same . . . it seemed a little of the guilt she felt over the events around Luke and especially Darcy's deaths still lingered. If she'd spoken up about who Luke really was sooner, maybe . . .

No. She wasn't responsible for Luke's abuse, any more than she was responsible for the choices that Shannon had made, or Amber. She knew that.

Even if she didn't always feel it.

Rosalind and Caro were still waiting for her answer. The envelope crinkled a little between her fingers as she looked up at them.

'We should . . . we need to look into this guy, Percival Pendleton. And his assistant, and his boat. Make sure this is all legit – or, well, as legit as it can be.'

'I can get Ashok to help us with that,' Caro said eagerly. 'But if everything checks out?'

'Then we should do it.' Posy took a breath, then smiled. 'Let's go stop a murder.'

Acknowledgements

My love of the theatre pre-dates even my love for murder mysteries. It grew from watching my cousins, Emma and Helen, in Clwyd Youth Theatre productions all the way to seeing Emma's own plays performed on West End stages. I was even lucky enough to work as a lowly production assistant on one of her shows, and the thrill of walking through the stage door at a genuine Theatreland playhouse never, ever grew old.

I've also been fortunate enough to sit in the audience of some incredible shows, in the West End and beyond, and to introduce my kids to the wonder of live theatre, too. There's nothing quite like the hush of a theatre, right in that moment before the applause starts.

So it was a no-brainer for me to take the Dahlias back to the London stage for this, their fifth adventure. But as always, I needed a lot of help to shepherd this book from first idea to first night . . . I mean, publication.

First, as always, thank you to super-agent, Gemma Cooper, for all the encouragement, ideas, and for always saying, 'Okay, this needs some work,' even if I hate to hear it in the moment. My books are always a hundred times better for you telling me everything that sucks, then helping me figure out how to fix it. Congratulations, too, on starting your own agency! I'm so proud of you, and proud to be represented by Gemma Cooper Literary. And I'm excited to see where we go next together on this fabulous bookish journey we've been sharing now for over a decade.

Huge thanks also to the wonderful team at Constable. Most especially to the Dahlias' first editor, Krystyna Green, who has championed them right from the first adventure, and who will be missed greatly now she's moved on to new adventures of her own. Fortunately, the very capable Hannah Wann has stepped in, and has already had a huge impact. Thank you both for the edits that made this book the best it could be.

Thank-yous are also due to:

Amanda Keats for shepherding the Dahlias' theatre adventure towards publication.

Howard Watson for being the best copy-editor in the business. (Still don't know how I ended up with two chapter eighteens. Sorry.)

Daniel Long for another incredible cover illustration – I think this one might actually be my favourite yet.

Beth Wright, Ellen Turner and Brionee Fenlon for all their PR and marketing support.

And to everyone else at Little, Brown who keep the pages turning.

For theatre expertise, I have to thank Callum Runciman, Emma Reeves and Mark Bentley. Mark also gets extra thanks for hiring me as a production assistant all those years ago, paying me more than I deserved *and* letting me write novels on company time.

Thank you to the team at the Theatre Royal, Drury Lane for a fascinating backstage tour. And if you were inspired by the Theatreland audio walking tour that Rosalind takes in the book, I highly recommend the free VoiceMap Theatreland Tour, narrated by the incomparable Ian McKellen.

But beyond the helpful tips and theatre information, Emma deserves a fuller mention. Emma, as my older cousin and birthday twin, you've been a huge influence on my life, and I don't think I'd have ever had such a love for the theatre without you. Even better is watching you instil that same love in my daughter. The fact that she has grown up watching incredible theatre – often while sitting in the audience with the actual writer – is amazing. We're so lucky to have you – and not just for all the generous theatre trips you sponsor!

Thank you to my parents for taking me to the theatre often as a child (even if I did sometimes ask what I could do *while* we were watching a show), paying for and sometimes chaperoning school trips to musicals (even if Mum did cry all the way home from Manchester after seeing *Les Mis*) and watching me in my own school and college productions (well done for making it through me being walled up alive in *Antigone*).

One of my most memorable family holidays is the summer we went to London when I was sixteen or so, and we explored the West End, and my brother Kip and I got to see *Miss Saigon*, just the two of us, at Drury Lane. I knew then that no city in the world could be better than London.

Thank you to my brother Mike, who seems to have borne the brunt of my moaning about this book! I very much appreciate your listening, and thank you for putting me in touch with Callum. I can't wait to come see *your* next show, whatever that turns out to be. And to take the birthday theatre trips we have planned . . .

Thank you to my husband Simon and son Sam, for patiently putting up with how theatre seems to have taken over our lives over the past few years. And thank you, most of all, to my daughter Holly. Watching you fall in love with the theatre has been a joy, and sharing that love with you is a delight. What shall we go and see next?

As the final curtain falls on this Theatreland mystery, I really want to say my biggest thank you to all the readers, librarians and booksellers who continue to turn out and support our three Dahlias. So many of you have made contact over recent months to tell me your own stories about your love of theatre, and how excited you were to see Rosalind, Caro and Posy tackle a murder in the West End. I hope it lived up to expectations!